IT TAKES A SPY

AN ATTICUS WOLFE NOVEL

DAVE SINCLAIR

ALSO BY DAVE SINCLAIR

Atticus Wolfe Novels

Out of Time

It Takes a Spy

The Coldest War

Charles Bishop Novels

Kiss My Assassin

Agent Provocateur

Venetian Blonde

Eva Destruction Novels

The Barista's Guide to Espionage

The Rookie's Guide to Espionage (novella)

The Amnesiac's Guide to Espionage

The Dead Spy's Guide to Espionage

For Quinn.
Thank you for your support, patience and laughs.
Love you more than pizza.

CHAPTER
ONE

There was a terrorist in Atticus's lounge room.

Instinctively, he wanted to reach for a gun he knew wasn't there. The next best thing was to throttle the man. It took every ounce of self-control to keep the impulse at bay. The terrorist had broken into his Covent Garden flat and now sat casually in one of Atticus's green cocktail armchairs, sipping tea as if he didn't have a care in the world.

Gritting his teeth, Atticus forced out words to fill the chasm of silence. "You're old."

It was true. The man was old, decades older than the last time Atticus had seen him. Which, by his reckoning, was only a couple of weeks ago – but also sixty years into the future. Closing his eyes, Atticus rubbed his left temple, realising he lacked the required lexicon to discuss time travel in any meaningful way.

Hell, who wouldn't?

For Atticus, it had only been a short time since he'd been working for MI6, on the trail of the mysterious Omar Ganim. After an unsuccessful raid on Ganim's townhouse,

Atticus had chased him down a small laneway where the newly crowned terrorist had exploded a bomb. Except it wasn't a bomb. The green flash had sent Atticus from 2024 all the way back to 1963. But Ganim's weathered face indicated he'd been sent back even further.

Omar Ganim snorted. "Of course I'm bloody old." He shook his head. "Been here since 1914, I have. Arrived right in the middle of the night, during a blizzard, no less. Almost died." The old man shrugged. "But I didn't, because I'm a survivor. Always have been."

Atticus folded his arms. "Am I meant to applaud?"

Ganim sneered. His outwardly casual veneer started to tarnish. "You popped up on my radar a week ago. To be perfectly honest, it had been years since I'd even given you a thought. In the end I figured I'd been the only one sent back, though there was always a part of me that suspected you'd pop up somewhere along the timeline. You got the better part of the deal, let me tell you. The early twenties were no walk in the park for someone with my dusky complexion."

In the short time since he'd arrived in the sixties, Atticus had already had plenty of run-ins with people who thought the tone of his skin made him a lesser being, but he chose not to mention it. He didn't wish to get into a pissing contest over who'd had the easier time of it.

"Although," Ganim's eyes took on a wistful air, "the late twenties were a riot. Ended up in the Weimar Republic. Anything went in those days, let me tell you. I got caught up in—"

"Can I get home?" Atticus cut him off.

"Ah," Ganim grinned. "Done with the pleasantries, are we?"

Atticus unfolded his arms, then, in fear of what he

might do, folded them again. "I wasn't aware there were pleasantries."

Ganim squinted. "Quite." He took a sip of tea and quietly placed the cup to the side, prolonging the moment. He stared off into the distance, gaze unfocused. "Like I said, I went back over a hundred years." He turned to Atticus, his face etched in genuine despondency. "I couldn't stop it. None of it. The Sykes–Picot Agreement still happened. Iraq was still ruined for a hundred years by the sadistic Churchill. The lands of the Middle East were still carved up by indifferent imperial bastards, serving up betrayal, hatred and revenge." He leaned forward, elbows on his knees. "Nothing changed." He shook his head dolefully.

There was so much to unpack in that one statement, Atticus didn't know where to start. For a moment he forgot about his own plight. "How… what did you do?"

Ganim gazed inattentively at Atticus for a moment, as if he'd forgotten he was even there. "I tried, in my arrogance, to change things, to save the Middle East. I spent years rallying against imperial conceit. I did everything I could." He sighed heavily. "It wasn't enough."

Atticus knew the history well. Following the First World War, the Ottoman Empire was sliced up like cake and proffered to the victors, mainly England and France, to the detriment of Arab nations who'd been promised much in return for supporting the Allies. Instead, they were betrayed. The partitioning of the Middle East was done without regard for ethnic or sectarian characteristics, and resulted in endless conflict still felt in their own time, over a century later.

"So, despite decades of you trying to rewrite the world, nothing changed. Does that mean those of us hopping around time can't change history? It's fixed?"

It would be a relief if it were true. In Atticus's short stint in this time period, he'd already left a big footprint. Knowing he couldn't change future events would help him sleep at night.

"Not exactly." Ganim smiled. It was a cheeky, knowing smile.

Who needs sleep anyway? Atticus thought to himself.

Ganim went on. "The man responsible for the Sykes–Picot Agreement, the esteemed Colonel Sir Tatton Benvenuto Mark Sykes, surprisingly died of acute arsenic trioxide poisoning in 1916."

"Why was that surprising?"

"He was meant to have died from the Spanish flu in 1919."

"I wonder how that happened."

Ganim shrugged enigmatically. "A mystery for the ages." His expression became less self-satisfied. "The bastard survived long enough to broker the deal, unfortunately." He straightened his back. "We can change the future we know; it's possible. I've had many years to look back at it with the wisdom of hindsight, as only old farts can. My plans were too unrealistic, I think. I should have been more careful, more practical." He stared Atticus in the eyes. "But I was rushed. You chasing me halfway across the globe forced me to accelerate too quickly. I lost focus. I wasn't prepared." Ganim's gaze slid off, as if he were contemplating events that never were. He laughed humourlessly. "If only I'd had time."

Atticus wasn't concerned with Ganim's shortcomings. "I'll ask again. Can I get home?"

"I tried, oh how I tried. For me, no."

The implication of the statement sank in. Atticus

slumped into his chair. "Oh. So it's all over, we're stuck here?"

"I said I *couldn't* go home." Ganim left a theatrical pause. "Past tense." He hefted the keypad he'd discovered in Atticus's flat. "Until now. Without this, all I had was theory and bitterness, and neither of those things are conducive to time travel." He smiled. "But now, at least there's a chance—a theoretical one I'll admit, but still a chance."

"Why are you telling me this?" Atticus didn't trust the man. He was sure the feeling was mutual. "You could have stolen it and done it all yourself, but you waited for me. Why?"

Ganim shrugged, conceding the point. "I just want to get home. I miss wi-fi. I miss googling things." He sighed an old man's sigh. "It's been decades. Oh, I hated you at first, of course, but that feeling faded away years ago. Now I just want to get back to my own time, and rest. But I can't do this alone, Mr Wolfe. As clichéd as it sounds, you're the only one who understands. The only one who wants this as much as I do. The only one I trust."

Actively working to avoid laughing in the man's face, Atticus did his best to appear neutral. The statement was pure fluff, rhetoric of the highest order. Ganim should have known better than to make such a trite attempt to garner his favour so early in their discussions. It screamed of desperation. Trust had to be earned. Atticus was a million miles and a hundred years away from trusting the terrorist before him.

But really, what choice did he have? There weren't many alternatives. If Atticus really wanted to get home, the only option was sitting right in front of him.

"Fine. What happens now?"

"I..." For the first time there was hesitancy in Ganim's demeanour. "I have to do some calculations."

"I'll wait."

Ganim chuckled. "I'm afraid this will take some time. I will come back when I'm done." On seeing Atticus's sour expression, he went on. "I need to figure out a way to reverse my theories. You see, I only ever envisaged going backwards in time, not forwards. I need to source computer equipment and the like." He examined Atticus expectantly. "Unless you happen to have brought a smartphone with you?"

Atticus didn't want to get into that conversation just yet. It would only complicate matters further.

"I... I don't have a smartphone, no." Atticus held his breath at the mostly true statement.

"Shame. Would have made life easier."

"I have a smart watch, though."

Tilting his head, Ganim frowned. "Not exactly a super-computer, but it might help." Ganim ribbed his chin. There was something in his eyes that, if pressed, Atticus would categorise as shifty. "If I could have that and the keypad, I might just be able to get back to our time. Theoretically. The previous base unit I used, the one in the backpack, I could try and replicate with today's hardware, but it could end up being the size of a house. The keypad holds the brains. This," he rattled it for effect, "gives me hope—gives us hope, I mean. I've spent a lifetime trying to find it; there was no point gathering the components without the lynch-pin. That's the keypad. We may have a way back home now; I just need to work out how, exactly. Hence the calculations."

The statement should have filled Atticus with joy. *A way back home.* But it didn't. Was it because he didn't trust

6

Ganim? That was a given. Or was there more to it, perhaps?

Before he'd walked through the door and seen Ganim in his flat, Atticus had been getting used to the idea of living in the past. It wasn't all bad. In fact, he was beginning to like a lot of it—some parts more than others. When he'd first been thrown back to this time, he'd been disorientated, anxious and alone. But he'd started to make a life here, found reasons to want to stay. One reason in particular was always on his mind.

Unaware of Atticus's doubts, Ganim stood. "I'll do the necessary work, find components if I can." He held out his hand. "Partners?"

Atticus hesitated. Had the man he'd hunted for months become an ally in a matter of minutes? It didn't sit well with him. Sure, he was older, seemed far less manic than the last time they'd met, several days ago—as far as Atticus was concerned. But it still didn't feel right.

Although Ganim had killed, he'd generally gone out of his way to avoid harming others. He hadn't always succeeded, but the fact that he'd tried meant Omar Ganim was more complex than the title "terrorist" suggested. However, it didn't mean Atticus trusted the man.

Avoiding Ganim's proffered hand, Atticus picked up the keypad and slipped it into his pocket.

Now it was time for Ganim to hesitate. He hadn't been expecting that. "I'll... I'll need that, and the watch."

"I know. And they'll be right here when you've done those calculations of yours. As *partners* there's trust on all sides, right? I trust you won't try and get home without me." He tapped his pocket. "But trust goes both ways, Ganim. And what better way to cement the partnership by entrusting me with this?"

The other man screwed his mouth to one side. "It'll be more difficult."

"I imagine it will be." Atticus let the ensuing silence play out.

The other man's eye twitched, and then, apparently in spite of himself, he extended his hand. "Deal."

Seemingly acting of its own volition, Atticus's hand shook Ganim's.

"Deal."

As Ganim made his way out the door, he seemed to notice Atticus's slight hobble for the first time. He pointed. "What's with the limp?"

"Someone shot me."

Ganim snorted. "You haven't been here long enough to piss people off."

"If only that were true."

Apparently aware he'd get nothing further on the subject, Ganim gave Atticus a faint wave and left. As he closed the door and stood alone in his flat, Atticus couldn't help thinking he'd made a deal with the devil.

NEEDING to clear his head after his unexpected confrontation, Atticus walked. And walked. After he'd been shot in the leg, the doctors had recommended exercise, although perhaps not quite as soon, and definitely not as far. But Atticus wasn't one to be cooped up. After days in hospital, he had no desire to stare at four walls.

He gingerly made his way down Piccadilly. Thankfully the bullet had only passed through muscle tissue, missing arteries and anything else Atticus valued, but he was still hurting. The cool crisp air was bracing, providing a welcome distraction from the odd ache and twinge.

Piccadilly Circus was as hectic as it was in his day; the crowds, the chaos, people darting between cars. It was nice to see a recognisable scene, even if the billboards and stores weren't as familiar.

He passed Swan & Edgar, a seemingly high-end department store. It was huge, but Atticus had never heard of it. Most of the advertising signs adorning the Circus were familiar enough: BP, Guinness, Gordon's Gin and Coca-Cola shone bright. But he was sure Fremlin's beers and Dixons hadn't survived to his day. Likewise, advertisements portraying 'Smoke Players' and Wrigley's Gum as being 'Healthful' would never fly in 2024.

He forged on, thankful that the scenery served as a fascinating distraction. Passing the well-known sights of Buckingham Palace and Hyde Park Corner he almost felt at home, a twinge of nostalgia nibbling at his soul. As he passed Old Park Lane he had to admit he wasn't disappointed at the absence of the gaudy Hard Rock Café.

The walk seemed to have ironed out the kinks of his injury, although the memory of how he'd received it was almost as painful as the injury itself.

There was one part of his recent history Atticus had kept from Ganim. It wasn't exactly in keeping with their newly forged "trust", but it was more a lie of omission. It was something Atticus would need to take care of before he could get back to his own time. Far easier said than done.

The first person to know Atticus's truth when he arrived in 1963 was Oliver. Oliver had brought Atticus into the fold of 1960s MI6, set him up with a place to live and put him on the path to creating a real life in this decade. He'd been a confidant and a friend.

Pity it was all a lie.

At first, Atticus had assumed Oliver's eagerness to cosy up to a man from the future was out of a desire to get the inside scoop on future events—an undeniably alluring prospect for any spy—but Oliver's intentions were far more sinister. He'd betrayed, robbed and shot Atticus in quick succession. It was almost like you couldn't even trust a Soviet double agent these days.

Heading down Brompton Road, Atticus rubbed the spot where he'd been shot, vowing to return the favour. And soon. That would be his task on returning to MI6: hunt down Oliver and undo any damage he'd already wrought. Atticus was going to bring the fight to Oliver.

The tenuous partnership forged with Ganim would surely shatter the instant he found out that Oliver not only knew when Atticus was from, but also knew the outcome of the Cold War. And worse, he possessed Atticus's time-apocryphal phone, which held in its password-protected innards history books outlining the next half century in great detail. Atticus had to hope it remained unlocked, and that the Soviets wouldn't invent a charger anytime soon.

But history would not be saved with hope.

The more Atticus thought about it, the more he was convinced not telling Ganim about Oliver was the right thing to do. In part because it would confuse things unnecessarily, but mainly due to the shame he felt, knowing his actions had caused the problem in the first place. He couldn't have Ganim thinking he'd recklessly messed up the timeline.

Only when he'd dealt with Oliver could Atticus return home. He had to right the wrongs he'd committed in this timeline, and prevent Oliver from inflicting further harm—if he could.

Atticus shook his head. He should be focusing on more positive things, like his destination. The very thought put a spring in his step, and suddenly his leg didn't hurt quite as much.

He slowed to join the smattering of people gawping through the windows of Harrods. Glancing at his watch, Atticus decided he could spare a couple of minutes to do some window shopping. After all, it wasn't every day a twenty-first century man could peruse the displays of the world's most famous department store in its heyday.

A grey-haired man in a Harrod's green coat doffed his bowler hat at shoppers as he opened the door for them. It was a quaint piece of old-world charm—antiquated in Atticus's time, but delightful in this older setting.

The afternoon was veering into evening, the briskness of the day giving way to a genuine chill. Flipping up the collar of his coat, Atticus scanned the window displays. The mannequins were dressed in long skirts made from heavy fabric. Far more conservative than he'd anticipated. It wasn't exactly Swinging Sixties. The fashions were quaint in their conservatism. He knew that would all change soon enough. Cultural revolutions don't hit everywhere at the same time. Some parts need to be dragged along, kicking and screaming.

Atticus was aware of the danger before he even knew what the threat was. A man in a long leather coat and dark fedora stood casually next to him, appearing to hold no malice. He simply sidled up and glanced indifferently at the window display. But his manner put Atticus on edge. Automatically searching the reflection in the window for anyone else in case he was boxed in, for the second time in an hour Atticus wished he were armed.

"Pah. Typical capitalist bourgeoisie overindulgence."

The other man shook his head. "*This* is what your house-wives should strive for? Maybe is better you keep them in kitchen, da?"

Unmistakably Russian. The man didn't even try to water down his thick accent. In this time, it wasn't exactly common for anyone from behind the Iron Curtain to walk around so brazenly. That meant he was either overconfi-dent or knew something Atticus didn't. Either way, it didn't bode well.

Without turning, Atticus asked, "Do I know you?"

"Nyet." The reflection in the mirror gave Atticus a crooked-toothed smile. "But we have mutual friend."

"Is that right?"

"Da, it is," he tilted his head menacingly, "Future Man."

If it were possible to physically manifest an alarm, Atti-cus's would be ringing so loud they could hear it in Liverpool.

A rigid body was no good in a fight. Atticus forced his tension to ease, knowing what was coming. "This friend you speak of, he wouldn't be anywhere nearby, would he? I have a favour to return."

That Atticus had just been thinking of Oliver could be considered a coincidence, if not for the fact that he'd spent a considerable amount of time thinking about the man. More specifically, about what he'd do when the two finally met again.

The Russian rubbed his chin and shook his head with a knowing smirk. His facial expression said, *he's not stupid enough to be here*.

Pity.

"Then how did you know it was me?"

Atticus thought it a fair question. It wasn't like anyone from this time had pictures of him. They couldn't exactly look him up on Facebook. Or worse, check out the pictures from his clubbing days that were somehow still on MySpace.

"Our mutual friend said to find an arrogant black man, and here we are."

Atticus suspected this was more than just a convenient insult. What did it mean? Was it a warning?

Atticus turned to the man for the first time. He didn't flinch. "You know me. So I seem to be at a disadvantage. Do you have a name?"

"I do." The Russian bowed, but never took his eyes off Atticus. "Quite a few, in fact."

"Care to share any of them with me?"

"You may call me Mikhail."

"And what is it you wish to say to me, Mikhail?"

"Just that you should know your time is over." He paused thoughtfully. "That was vague, was it not? Linguistically imprecise interpretation of the gradable predicates, yes?"

The length of the words suggested he was well educated. Atticus had no idea what the man had just said, but it *sounded* smart.

Mikhail went on. "Let me be more precise. Your corrupt imperialist society is soon to end. The phrasing our mutual friend used was: the future you knew is no more. *We* are writing history now."

"Is this a warning? That's why you're talking to me?"

"Who said anything about talking?"

Faster than Atticus would have thought possible, Mikhail reached into his pocket and extracted a hunting knife, the blade glinting in the light of the shop window. It hung between them menacingly. Mikhail gazed down at the weapon seemingly with as much surprise as Atticus, as if he hadn't been expecting to pull the knife himself.

"You will come with me." Mikhail's voice was a growl.

"My grandmother always warned me about situations like this." Unarmed and without backup, Atticus had only two choices: run or fight.

Mikhail seemed bemused that Atticus wasn't more panicked. "What did she tell you?"

Atticus chose the latter option. He lowered his gaze. "Don't get in cars with strangers and if anyone pulls a knife on you..." he backed away, putting distance between them, "make sure you kill the son of a bitch."

Atticus waited for the attack. He didn't have to wait long. Mikhail telegraphed his lunge and Atticus was ready. Using both hands, he grabbed his attacker's arm as it drove forward and used Mikhail's momentum to throw him off balance. Thrusting out his hip, he forced his opponent to lose his footing. With his arm twisted at a right angle, Mikhail winced in pain as Atticus relieved him of his weapon and he fell to his knees.

It wasn't Atticus's most elegant move, but it did the job. Laying his thick hand on the scruff of Mikhail's neck, Atticus hoisted him gracelessly upright. Making sure his foe was aware of the hunting knife to his belly, Atticus did his best to shield it from onlookers, concealed by the flaps of his coat.

Instead of alarm that his attack had been so abruptly subverted, Mikhail seemed positively amused. Chuckling, he frowned in admiration. "Very good, very good. He said you were a man of hidden talents, but is nice to have these things confirmed, da?"

"I have a message for our mutual friend." Atticus's eyes darted around, in case Mikhail had more comrades. The street seemed free of henchmen, but one could never be sure. "Tell him—"

Atticus didn't finish the sentence. His movements a blur, Mikhail lunged forward, using the blade of his palm to chop down on Atticus's knife hand, forcing it down and away from the Russian's belly. Mikhail used his hands to push and hold Atticus's arm back so the knife stayed away from him, and then in a final move, he slammed his knee into Atticus's arm and twisted the knife from his hand.

In a blink of an eye Mikhail stood in front of Atticus, knife in hand. The tables had been turned again, and he didn't like the arrangement.

The son of a bitch had deliberately overplayed his first attack to gauge Atticus's reaction. *Smart.* Atticus wouldn't underestimate him again.

Just as Atticus had, Mikhail kept the knife hidden to avoid alarming passers-by. Both men tried their best to hide their heaving breaths, each casting death stares at their counterpart. Their battle was both intimate and covert.

Over Mikhail's shoulder, the top-hatted doorman turned in their direction. "We're about to close up, sirs." Oblivious to the knife fight taking place mere feet away from him, the aging gent beamed genially. "Twenty minutes if you boys want to pop in and grab a little treat for the wife."

Evenly matched, the two could engage in a perpetual conflict until one of them made a mistake, or members of the public became involved. Stalemate was unlikely. Each awaited the other's next move.

Atticus decided it was his to make. He shoved Mikhail's shoulders back and followed up with a swift side kick, sending the man reeling backwards onto the roadway. He landed with an "oof" as the knife skated across the asphalt. As Mikhail lay sprawled on the road in a daze, a black cab skidded to a halt, missing his head by inches.

Realising his predicament, Mikhail clambered towards the knife, but the blade lay steadfastly lodged under the front wheel of the cab. The Russian's furious heaving failed to extricate it. Simultaneously, the tubby cloth-capped cab driver and Atticus advanced on the prone man. Both were angry, though for differing reasons.

"What the ruddy hell do you think you're up to, mate?" The cab driver wiped his sweaty brow. "I coulda bleedin' well killed ya."

As the two men closed in on him, Mikhail frantically yanked at the knife. With an almighty heave, the handle came free—unfortunately for Mikhail, without the blade attached.

"Ah." Mikhail stared at the fractured handle in his hands and shook his head despairingly. "This would have never happened with Soviet knife."

Before Atticus could attack, Mikhail shoved the cab driver between them and sprinted towards Harrods. Ignoring the furious cabbie, Atticus gave chase.

Sprinting through the entrance, he came to a halt, searching for any sign of the Russian. He couldn't see any, nor could he hear anyone screaming that a madman was running through a high-end department store. If Atticus were in Mikhail's position, he'd want to put as much distance between him and his attacker as possible. He wouldn't find his opponent by standing still. Atticus ran.

If he had to hazard a guess, he'd say Mikhail was KGB. The man was highly trained, in a foreign country and had no problem handling himself. *Great.* KGB. Just what he needed.

The late afternoon meant the narrow, winding walkways were bereft of much foot traffic. Atticus sped heedlessly and unarmed past racks of gaudy women's clothes, and soon found himself charging through department after department in the staid, old-fashioned store.

He wondered what he'd do when he caught up with Mikhail. They seemed evenly matched, but he knew the deadlock couldn't last.

In no time he entered the food department, passing the baker, deli and confectioner. The fromagerie was no good to him unless they sold a particularly sharp cheddar.

The fishmongers and wine department flashed by. Attendants gawped at the sprinting black man, but seemed too bemused to ask him to stop.

Having found no trace of his prey, Atticus slowed his pace and took in his surroundings, aware he was placing undue stress on his injured leg. He stopped near the florist, with its heady scents and vibrant bouquets. Could Mikhail have gone into hiding, intending to stay after closing? Atticus eyed a particularly large arrangement of flowers, but he doubted he'd find a communist in the chrysanthemums.

He briefly considered contacting MI6 for backup, but dismissed the idea. By the time they arrived Mikhail would be long gone. It was the second time that day Atticus had been caught flatfooted and unarmed. Tomorrow he'd requisition a gun from Mrs Abernathy at the first opportunity.

As Atticus assessed his options, a grey-haired gentleman approached in a Harrods-green three-piece suit. "May I help you, sir?"

Still sucking in lungfuls of air, Atticus stepped towards him. "There was a man running through the store, he attacked me just outside. Long leather coat, black hat. He would have been holding a knife handle."

Atticus expected to hear, "Well, I shall call the police immediately!" or "Are you alright?" Something. Anything. Instead, the attendant maintained the same indifferent demeanour. "Very good. Silverware, third floor, sir."

"I... did you hear what I said?"

"Indeed, sir. Silverware. Third floor. Escalator to your left." He motioned with his hand to elucidate the point.

Too stunned to argue, Atticus simply nodded and turned in the direction the attendant had indicated. Either the man only heard the word *knife* and gone into autopilot or he was so completely unflappable he knew exactly what a man in a one-sided knife fight required. Either way, Atticus gave a wave of thanks and kept moving.

He spied a door along a brown wood-panelled wall. In gold lettering it declared "Harrods Staff Only", and was wide open. Certain that the staff of this particular establishment would be disinclined to leave such access available to the general public, Atticus decided this seemed like a better option than the silverware department. Ensuring no one was looking, he slipped through the door and out of sight.

Doing his best to dispense with any thoughts as to why he'd been attacked in the first place, Atticus concentrated on the one aspect he could control: finding the bastard. A captive strapped to a chair would supply far more answers than retreating empty-handed and ruminating about it later on.

A flight of rickety wooden stairs descended ahead of Atticus, illuminated by a single bulb. The subterranean world at the base of the stairs was the exact opposite of the elegant old-world charm above. The scuffed whitewashed brick walls were scratched and chipped from years of use. A cacophony of workmen's shouts fused with clanking machinery echoed off the walls.

Beneath Harrods was a series of underground concourses, cold-storage rooms and various machines performing unknown functions. Overhead, pneumatic tubes *whooshed*, no doubt sending messages and cash from one side of the store to the next.

Picking up a clipboard hanging on a nail, Atticus adopted a resolute expression and walked briskly. Nobody ever stopped a determined man with a clipboard.

The sound of the street grew louder as he neared the loading dock. He examined every face he came across, but none were the quarry he sought. When one brown-coated gent glanced in his direction, Atticus scowled and tapped the clipboard. Quick smart, the brown-coat doubled down on his loading efforts.

In the pale remains of daylight at the end of the loading dock, a leather-coated man was doing his best to slip past some men loading a Harrods lorry. Atticus approached cautiously. He couldn't spook his prey. He had to be smart. Stealthy. Be a silent apparition, shadowing his target until he was within striking distance. He planned his approach meticulously.

"Oi, where do you think you're going, Sunshine?"

Atticus spun around to see a foreman with slicked-back hair pointing at Mikhail at the far end of the dock. It seemed Atticus's clipboard had done the job. He'd blended in perfectly, but the other man wasn't as invisible.

Startled, Mikhail turned and saw the approaching Atticus some thirty feet behind him. The two foes locked eyes, and the clipboard clattered to the floor. Both men ran.

Mikhail hit the street first, well ahead of his pursuer. He

was fast. Jacket flapping behind his pumping legs, he tore around the corner and out of sight. Atticus exploded onto the street, ready to do battle. Except there was no one to battle. The street was clear of any sign of Mikhail. Atticus sprinted, limbs thrusting him forward. Reaching the next corner, all three options were equally empty of his quarry.

"Who is this guy, Batman?" Wheezing, Atticus bent over with his hands on his knees and inhaled sharply.

Atticus spent precious minutes searching between cars, driveways, anywhere Mikhail could possibly be. He came up short. Leaning against a pub wall, he tried to work out what the hell had just happened.

He'd evaded an attempted kidnapping, or whatever it was Mikhail had wanted. But *why*? Why confront him on the street so brazenly, only to abandon him just as quickly? Why only send one man to do the job? In retrospect, it seemed slapdash and amateurish, although admittedly, when he'd been staring down the business end of a hunting knife it hadn't been the first thought to pop into his mind.

Atticus realised his previous assessment had been all wrong. He thought he'd be taking the fight to Oliver.

But it seemed Oliver had other ideas.

The fight was coming to Atticus.

CHAPTER
TWO

S till reeling from the daylight attack and what it meant, Atticus rang the doorbell. The innumerable conflicting thoughts swirling around his cerebral cortex all evaporated the moment he saw her face.

"I... I thought we had a date tomorrow night?" The confusion on Maggie's face was adorable.

"We did." Atticus shrugged. "I just didn't want to wait that long." He thumbed in the direction behind him. "I can go if..."

Glee washing over her face, Maggie grabbed him by the lapels and dragged him into her flat. Their lips entwined before the door even slammed shut.

Eventually coming up for air, Atticus said, "Hi."

Giggling, Maggie replied, "Hi." She slowly unbuttoned his coat, taking her time, enjoying the process. "This is a nice surprise." She ran her delicate hand along his stubbled cheek, then followed it with a soft kiss. "This is nice too."

She hung up his coat behind the door and went to her tiny kitchenette. Atticus called it a kitchenette; it was too small to be classified as a kitchen. In fact, the whole place could be called a flatette. Off the small lounge, three doors led to what he assumed were the bathroom, Maggie's room and a spare room. The door to the latter was closed.

The lounge was decorated with mismatched furniture, odd little knick-knacks, crates of records beside a well-used Dansette turntable and multiple pot plants of various sizes. Half the plants were half dead, while the other half were half alive. It was cosy and chaotic, but somehow it all worked to give a warm, inviting feel. It was a welcoming place, much like the hostess.

Maggie handed him a vintage gold leaf glass. "I'd offer you a tour," she waved her own glass around, "but you've seen it all." Maggie nodded to the closed door. "My friend Mary. The nutter pulled an all-nighter because she's got a fashion show next week and the poor thing's freaking out. She crashes at mine rather than fall asleep on the way home." Maggie wrinkled her nose. "She'll be out of it until tomorrow, if that's what you're worried about."

Atticus hefted an eyebrow. "Presumptuous."

She sniggered and guided him to the couch. He took a sip, doing his best not to wince. Dry sherry. For him, it was an old person's drink. In retrospect, it was a drink preferred by someone born when Maggie was. Admiring her figure-hugging knee length pinafore, Atticus just couldn't think of her as old. He took another sip. He was sure he could get used to it.

Sheepishly peering over her sherry glass, Maggie whimsically shook her head. "I'm sure I'm going to get a talking to from my landlady for letting a gentleman into my apartment past sundown." She grinned to let him know she didn't care. "Have they done away with nosy landladies in the future?"

"We have, but only because instead of old ladies

peering through a crack in the door, we air our dirty laundry on social media instead."

Maggie smiled as if she knew what that meant. "Sometimes I think you just make up stuff to confuse me."

"You'll find the internet is so weird there's no need to make anything up. Not when you've got planking, cinnamon challenges and the Harlem Shake to look forward to."

Maggie laughed and shook her head. Her little chuckle said, *there's no comeback to that.* "I apologise, I don't have much to eat."

Atticus shrugged with a roguish smile. "I'm not hungry."

Finishing her drink in one gulp, Maggie placed it on a wooden crate which served as a coffee table. Ever so slightly, her lips parted. "Me either." Her finger traced the back of the couch. "Sorry the flat is in such a state. Wasn't expecting company. Everything's a mess." She motioned around the flat. "I mean, the only thing I've managed to tidy up today is my bed."

"Shame it's out of sync with the rest of the flat."

"You mean we should clean my flat?"

Atticus put the sherry down and hoisted a mischievous eyebrow. "No."

Maggie leaned forward, stopping just before their lips met. "That's the right answer."

They kissed and the world fell away.

THE SUNSHINE WOKE HIM. Maggie's head rested in his arm like it had always been there. So many things from last night felt familiar. It was odd, he had no reason for it, but being with Maggie felt safe, it felt right. It felt like home. There was no denying it, he was hooked.

Almost on cue, Maggie blinked her eyes open. Her brilliant toothy grin outshone the sun itself.

"You're right, he is very pretty."

Both Maggie and Atticus turned to see a dark-haired woman with a bob seated at the end of the metal bed. She took a sip of tea as she held another in her left hand.

She handed the cup to an uncomfortable Maggie and tilted her head towards Atticus. "Sorry, I would have made you one, but I wasn't expecting gentleman callers."

Taking the tea with a knowing chortle, Maggie replied, "Neither was I, Mary." Turning to Atticus she beamed again. "But I'm glad he came."

"Oh, I know you are." Mary stood, amusement plain on her face. "You have thin walls."

Eager to move on, Maggie made the introductions. "Atticus Wolfe, Mary Quant."

It took a moment, but Atticus realised he'd heard the name before. Once, on a night out in Brixton, Maggie had called it, but he realised he'd heard it before then, too.

"You're the inventor of the mini."

Mary frowned. "I'm pretty sure that's already been invented. There's one in my garage at home."

"I meant the mini skirt..."

Atticus closed his eyes and wished the bed would swallow him whole. He had to learn to keep his mouth shut.

"The mini... skirt?" It was plain Mary's mind was already ticking.

Seemingly keen to move on before Atticus invented Tickle Me Elmo thirty years too soon, Maggie spoke up. "What time do you have to be back in the studio, Mary?"

Completely ignoring the question, Mary's head swivelled to Atticus. "How long have you lived in London, Atticus?"

Fully aware he was being interrogated, Atticus grinned pleasantly. "All my life."

"Yet," Mary blew steam from her tea, "Maggie says you don't have any friends or family here." She squinted in Maggie's direction. "Isn't that odd?" She waggled her head from side to side. "It's almost like those two pieces don't fit."

It was mostly true. Besides the woman in the bed next to him, Atticus had no friends in this time period. He thought he'd had one other, but as he'd ended up shooting Atticus in the leg, it seemed safe to exclude him from the final tally.

Family was another matter entirely. Atticus's history with his own family was... complicated. When he was a child it had taken Atticus a few years to realise just how powerful his family was, then a few more to understand how feared they were. Atticus's grandfather, Joe, was known as "The King of Brixton". On their home turf of Brixton, the crime lord was venerated as the Black Robin Hood; when they weren't calling him "Sledgehammer Joe". The local reverence did not extend to his son, Atticus's father. The notorious "Prince" was as feared as his father, but certainly didn't live up to the Black Robin Hood moniker. An angry man from an angry neighbourhood, Thomas Wolfe lashed out at every living soul within striking distance, including Atticus and his mother (who didn't hang around past his ninth birthday). Atticus's beloved grandmother, Eliza, raised him and instilled in him a clear sense of right and wrong. She was the greatest influence in his life.

Each of those people were alive in 1964. More than once, his wandering thoughts had contemplated seeking them out in the lonely pre-dawn hours. Eliza Wolfe had passed away many years ago in Atticus's time, and there wasn't a day he didn't think of her laughter or wisdom. He'd fought the urge to seek her out her fierce presence in this time, knowing that if he did find her, he wouldn't be able to resist wrapping his arms around the woman who'd made him the man he was. His bitter father would be in his teens, far younger than Atticus was now. He wondered what kind of man he would be.

No, to say Atticus was without family was incorrect. But he had to pretend he was.

"As a child I moved from school to school; my father was a not-very-successful salesman in the plastics industry. We moved every few months, no real time to make lifelong friends. I was an only child, my parents died early on. Then I was in the Navy for many years."

For an on-the-spot lie, it wasn't too bad, but scepticism coloured Mary's features.

She puckered her brow. "No old Navy buddies?"

"They died."

"All of them?"

"Yes."

"That's a really sad tale."

"It is, isn't it?"

Sitting up, Maggie pointed at the alarm clock. "Oh, would you look at the time? I have to get ready, Atticus I'm sure you do too, and Mary you said you had to get back to the studio so I don't want you to be late, oh my I really must dash this has been fun let's do dinner sometime bye Mary talk later."

Standing, Mary nodded, getting the hint. It didn't

26

prevent her from giving Atticus the evil eye as she closed the door behind her.

"She seems nice."

Maggie rolled her eyes. "Oh, she's just giving you the third degree because she cares. She'll thaw out. Eventually. Probably." Her mouth skewed to one side in amusement. "Mini skirt?"

With a sigh, Atticus shrugged. "I think I may have accidentally invented one of the most iconic fashion items of the twentieth century."

"Look, when I said you were inventive in bed, that wasn't what I meant."

"Funny." Atticus looked at his watch on the bedside table. "We should get up."

Maggie didn't react with any movement. It seemed she had something else on her mind.

"Before Mary appeared, I was going to ask you something." She sighed, as if summoning courage. "I've been thinking..."

"In my experience conversations that start that way never turn out well." Atticus smiled to let her know he still wanted to hear what she had to say.

"Shh, lady talking. I originally joined MI6 to find out the truth about what happened to my mother." Neither of them needed to mention just how she'd finally obtained that information. She went on. "Since I achieved that, I've been thinking about my role in MI6. I have a renewed commitment to the job." She playfully gave him a little kick under the covers. "You helped, but there's more to it. Now that I don't have that weighing on my shoulders, I can forge my own path."

"And what path would that be?"

"A field agent."

"A field…"

She frowned, doubt darkening her features. "You don't think I'm cut out for it?"

Atticus screwed his face up. "If there's anyone on this planet with more faith in you than me, I'd like to meet them."

"Is it because I'm a woman?"

Mischievously, Atticus looked under the sheet. "Oh my god, you're right, you are!" He dropped the sarcastic tone. "I think you'll find that the man from the future is more in favour of women agents than anyone."

"Then what?" Her mood had buoyed somewhat, but traces of doubt remained.

"There's a lot of death." Atticus lowered his gaze, blank eyes from his past staring back at him. "It changes you."

"I know that."

She did. On a mission to Berlin last year Maggie had been forced to take a life. He'd helped her through it, and even though there'd been all the justification in the world for her actions, the memory still haunted her. There had been a darker aura around her since. That one moment had changed her forever, hardened her. As much as Atticus wanted to support her, he knew that death altered a person, and never for the better.

"You don't think I should?"

"I didn't say that." Atticus did his best to be encouraging. "I just want you informed, that's all."

"Then I'm informed. Will you help me?"

"Of course. Believe me, you'll be the most heavily trained applicant they've ever had."

Conscious not to project his own prejudices, Atticus was determined to help Maggie in any way he could.

Although he feared for her safety, he knew the better prepared she was, the better her chances of survival.

Above all things, Atticus wanted Maggie to survive. This was obviously something she'd spent a long time debating and had come to a firm conclusion. One thing he'd grown to appreciate in a short amount of time was that when Maggie made her mind up, that was it. He watched her slip out of bed and ready herself for the day, quietly humming. Atticus sighed contentedly. He knew it all too well, but soon the world would too: there was no stopping Maggie Dunbar.

Twenty minutes later Maggie, Mary and Atticus stood in the small kitchenette consuming their second strong tea of the day. Maggie was about to leap into the shower, and Atticus had to make his way home to get ready for work.

Maggie bid them adieu with a promise of a late supper and a nightclub in their near futures, then disappeared into the bathroom.

Bidding Mary farewell, Atticus pivoted towards the door when a hand clasped his sleeve.

"She's one of a kind."

Atticus snickered. "She is at that."

"You might be a big bugger, but know this, Atticus Wolfe: if you hurt that sweet innocent child, I will hunt you down, kill you, and turn your skin into a suit. You know that, right?"

"I do now."

"Good. As long as we have an understanding." She uncrossed her arms, pleased her point had been received.

"She's thoroughly smitten with you. I want to make sure you take the right care of her."

"Believe me, the feeling is mutual."

"Well, good. Just as long as I get to design the wedding outfits." With that, she gave a dismissive wave of her hand. It said *You may go*, but was delivered with humour, making Atticus feel he'd been invited into the friendship circle. That was good. Counting Maggie, he currently had a grand total of one friend in this time period.

As the sound of the shower told him Maggie was getting ready for work, Atticus had to rush home to do the same. It would be his first day back after being shot by the only other person he'd thought was a friend. How wrong he'd been.

THE UNASSUMING BUILDING at 54 Broadway was not what the brass plaque outside claimed. Housed inside was not the "Minimax Fire Extinguisher Company", but instead, the Cold War factory of MI6.

In the reception area sat a rigidly upright middle-aged woman in glasses behind a hardwood desk, her prim demeanour as prickly as always.

Atticus held her gaze. "Mrs Abernathy."

"Mr Wolfe."

Atticus was lucky no one was about. Their interaction was scandalously familiar.

"Back to save the world, are we?" she asked without a crack in her deportment.

If you only knew. "Something like that, Mrs Abernathy."

"Good to have you back."

The lack of emotion in the delivery had Atticus doubt

her sincerity. That was the thing about Mrs Abernathy, you never quite knew where you stood with her. Outwardly, she appeared a staid, conservative middle-aged maiden. You'd never know she'd once strangled three SS officers in one night. Atticus was careful to keep on her good side.

She pressed a button under her desk to allow him past the low mahogany gate to the right. The rickety old elevator arrived and as soon as the doors opened, Atticus was instantly filled with dread. That elevator held bad memories. He did his best to block them out.

He arrived in Rathdowne's office at exactly nine o'clock. His boss waved him in without fanfare.

"You're welcome," the small man with the laughable comb-over sneered.

Atticus blinked in confusion. "I'm sorry?"

"You're welcome." Rathdowne made his way behind his battered desk with its teetering piles of folders and sat heavily. "The toffs out there wanted to give you a big welcome back celebration. Some idiot even mentioned confetti. All hail the conquering hero and all that bollocks." He scratched his thick moustache. "I told 'em all to shove it. You got shot, it happens. You're here to work, not to be paraded about. Am I right?"

"Absolutely, sir. I'm keen to get back to work."

"Bloody right."

Taking in the office while Rathdowne settled himself, Atticus noticed the room seemed more cluttered than usual.

"What's with the boxes?"

Rathdowne scanned the cardboard boxes stacked high beneath the tiny window on the far wall. "We're moving the Service again, to a tower block on Westminster Bridge

Road. Century House, it's called. Here's hoping they have bloody heating that works this time."

Century House was the location in between SIS moving to the locale Atticus knew well, Vauxhall Cross. He didn't know much about it, other than that old members of MI6 had been glad to get out of there into modern amenities when the time finally came in the nineties.

Lighting a cigarette, Rathdowne inhaled deeply. Atticus noted that he hadn't asked him to take a seat. The two hadn't particularly seen eye to eye. It hadn't helped that Atticus had falsely accused Rathdowne of being a mole, knowing full well it was Oliver. Speaking of...

"It seems we can add one to the total population of the USSR."

Rathdowne slid a black and white photograph across the desk. Atticus took in the photo, which had apparently been taken with a telephoto lens. It wasn't crisp, but the subject of the photograph was clear enough.

"Where was this taken?"

"The Kremlin. Three days ago."

Atticus leaned forward, taking in every detail he could. A bespectacled man in his early thirties was rugged up against the cold. He didn't appear under duress—mildly bemused, sure, but Oliver Preston seemed completely at home behind the Iron Curtain. He was flanked by two men who could have been poster children for Soviet frowning.

"The one on the left we identified as Alaksiej Barinov, also known as the Red Scorpion. A nasty piece of work. He's only young, but he has a death toll that would make Stalin blush. The one on the right is a known KGB agent, but we don't know his name."

With a sigh, Atticus scratched the back of his neck. "I do."

Rathdowne's brow furrowed and he shook his head in bewilderment. The meaning was clear. *How the hell do you know that?*

Atticus shrugged. "His name is apparently Mikhail. I'm sorry, I don't have a last name, but he was last seen at Harrods at about half past four yesterday afternoon."

Like a character from a Warner Bros cartoon, Rathdowne's jaw dropped open. "I'm afraid you're going to have to elaborate on that somewhat."

Atticus outlined his recent encounter, tactfully leaving out the portion where Mikhail had referred to him as Future Man. He explained how the knife fight had gone undetected, the most noteworthy aspect for the general public being a black man running through a high-end department store.

Taking a long while to process the information, Rathdowne leaned back in his chair. "And when did you plan on telling me any of this?"

"Right about now, as it turns out."

Rathdowne took a long pull on his cigarette and blew the smoke skyward. "What the ruddy hell was he doing in London?"

"Attempting to kidnap me. And running. A bit of stabbing. Kidnapping, stabbing and running mainly."

"Should we be putting you under guard?"

Atticus shrugged. "I've been thinking about the incident. It was ham-fisted at best. Like he never intended to confront me and changed his mind at the last minute. If it were a true KGB operation it would have been far smoother, but this was pure amateur hour stuff. For a start, he had a knife, there was no backup, he had no vehicle nearby. It's like he confronted me on a whim."

Scrutinising the black and white photo, Rathdowne

tapped Oliver's image and glanced up. "Seems you have your next assignment."

"Seems that way."

"What do you need?"

Atticus planted his fists on the table. "Every piece of information the Moscow bureau can give us on these three. I'll need an office, access to a vat of industrial strength coffee and permission to conduct an operation on Soviet soil."

"You know you'll never get clearance to get him. He's in the USSR now, he's gone."

Atticus looked his superior dead in the eye. "He's a traitor who murdered members of your department. We can't let that go unpunished."

There was far more to it than Atticus could tell the man before him. Oliver had in his possession a phone that didn't belong in this century. Contained within its futuristic innards were Atticus's Cold War history books. If Oliver somehow unlocked the phone, he would have access to an account of how the next fifty years were to unfold. If he managed that *and* gained the ear of the Soviet leadership, Oliver could alter the course of history.

Rathdowne thought Atticus wanted to stop Oliver because of revenge. But that wasn't what drove him. Well, mostly it wasn't. If the nightmare scenario he'd conjured up came to fruition, Oliver would become one of the most powerful individuals of the twentieth century, possibly even *the* most powerful. He could manipulate history, twist events to his own end. Hell, he could even make the USSR win the Cold War.

"You alright, Wolfe? You look like you've just seen a ruddy ghost."

Swallowing hard, Atticus realised his mind had stumbled down a dark path. He refocused on the present. "We have to go get him."

Unaware of Atticus's darker scenario, Rathdowne appeared unmoved. "While he's in the bosom of the Union of Soviet Socialist Republics that's exactly where he will remain."

Mind already six steps ahead, Atticus spoke before his thoughts had even fully formed. "And what if he was somehow enticed away from their protection?"

"What do you have in mind?"

"I'm not entirely sure." Atticus rubbed the back of his bald skull. "Whatever it is, I'm sure you won't like it."

"Oh, that's absolutely guaranteed."

Rathdowne exhaled deeply. The two of them had never clicked, but there was a grudging mutual respect, though the admiration only went so far. In their limited interaction they hadn't had time to create an unquestioning trust in each other. They may never reach that point, especially if the plan forming in Atticus's mind came to fruition.

"This has to be handled delicately. The press hasn't gotten wind of Preston's defection yet, thank Christ. We can't afford to cock this up. This operation has to be executed with delicacy and tact. That's what you have in mind, isn't it?"

Giving a salute, Atticus pivoted and walked towards the door. "Oh, you know me."

"I do..." Rathdowne raised his voice as Atticus passed the threshold and strode out of his office. "What... what are you going to do? You're not going to do anything stupid are you? Wolfe? Wolfe!"

Atticus laughed all the way to the elevator.

CHAPTER

THREE

Atticus didn't do anything stupid. Though it wasn't for lack of trying.

Weeks turned into months. In early May 1964 Atticus and Maggie sat alone in their cramped office on the third floor of the soon to be abandoned MI6 headquarters at 54 Broadway.

Despite what the movies would have you believe, espionage investigations don't often happen quickly, or indeed in a linear way. Witnesses could misremember information and intelligence could be tampered with. Months could be spent chasing down leads that go nowhere. Worse, disappearing ink never revealed key information. Still, they persevered.

The photograph of Oliver had been taken by an MI6 agent operating out of the Moscow station. As far as the USSR were concerned, the photographer was a low-ranking secretary to the cultural attaché in the British embassy. In reality, she was a highly experienced spy who'd been operating for years supplying crucial intelligence under the noses of the Soviets. But even her expertise had failed to find a trace of Oliver after that initial photograph.

No intercepted communications mentioned the former double agent by name. No State dinners hosted him as a guest. He wasn't seen at operas or the ballet. None of their clandestine resources could find any mention of his existence. He hadn't been seen again at the Kremlin.

Additionally, there was no press conference, no Soviet gloating. In fact, there was nothing but silence from the red side of the map regarding the man who had so thoroughly humiliated the British Empire. That alone was highly suspicious. Kim Philby was publicly hailed as hero of the Soviet Union, even while he was virtually under house arrest. The lack of crowing about Oliver's defection was obviously a tactical decision, but just what that tactic was remained to be seen. Not knowing something always made Atticus wary. That was the nature of spy work. It only made him work harder.

There had also been no further information on the elusive Mikhail, if that was indeed his name. For a man so keen to confront Atticus, he'd disappeared as quickly as he'd appeared, although Atticus was sure it wasn't the last he'd see of him.

Atticus did his best to concentrate on the job. He worked tirelessly to find the man who'd spied on his homeland and jeopardised its very future as well. But after months of vigorous effort, he had yet to find Oliver. He wouldn't stop. He couldn't stop.

His work wasn't a wasted effort, though. In the past weeks he'd learned the ropes of his archaic organisation. Spy craft in the sixties certainly wasn't spy craft as he knew it. While the principles were essentially the same, the practical application was like the Wright Brothers trying to land on the moon. Atticus had to work with what he had.

Or, more accurately, what he didn't have. He had no data farms, no computer programs set up with alerts should a subject pop their electronic head up anywhere in the world. The GCHQ existed, but was nothing like it was in Atticus's time. It was positively prehistoric by comparison. In the twenty-first century, GCHQ monitored all online and telephone signals intelligence to pinpoint a target anywhere on the globe. What computers there were on the planet in this time wouldn't even be networked for decades. It was all coded communications and seemingly endless mountains of paper. So much paper. The work was laborious, tedious and frustrating.

Atticus had almost forgotten about Ganim. Almost. The fellow Future Man had thoroughly failed to make contact. Perhaps he was traversing the world, sourcing the materials he needed to get them home. Maybe he was committing acts of terrorism to further his old agenda. Maybe he was dead. Atticus didn't know, but as time drew on, he found he cared less and less.

There was a possible reason for his diluted interest in returning home. She sat across from him in a knee-length dark blue box-pleated skirt and light blue cardigan.

Sitting in their cramped office, Maggie and Atticus partook in one of their morning rituals, coffee for Atticus (or the nearest approximation this decade could supply) and tea for Maggie. Every morning at eight they'd run through the overnights from the Soviet Bloc and plan out their day.

Maggie's field services training was going from strength to strength. He'd even heard passing conversations in the corridors mentioning how a *woman*—they always emphasised that word—had blitzed the training.

Atticus helped where he could, but mostly Maggie shone on her own, excelling at the rigours of becoming a field agent. She passed whatever they threw at her with flying colours. He'd done far less than he'd anticipated. Maggie took to field service training like a natural. She seemed to surprise even herself with how quickly she'd adapted. It was as if a new augmented Maggie was forming before his very eyes. He hadn't thought it possible, but Atticus cared for this Maggie even more.

The two sat trawling through countless messages from Teufelsberg, the listening station in Berlin that intercepted, listened to and jammed radio signals from the Eastern Bloc. Like the Nazis before them, the Soviets used a complex indecipherable code to communicate across the Soviet world. The encrypted messages could be intercepted, but were impossible to understand. The Soviets used Fialka, built on the bones of Enigma. Like the Enigma, it was an electromechanical wheel-based cipher machine. It was never cracked, only declassified in the twenty-first century. To anyone without the encryption code, it was impossible to find any rhyme or reason to the messages. Well, almost impossible.

Maggie pointed at a piece of paper she'd been poring over for the better part of an hour. "Would you classify that as queer, Atty?"

"I certainly would not." Atticus smirked. "For one thing, the word queer has quite a different meaning in my time."

Returning his smirk, Maggie tilted her head. "Is that right?"

Atticus nodded. "Also, Atty? When did this become a thing?"

"It's new, I'm trying it out." Maggie shrugged. "What do you think?"

"It's better than Wolfy."

"I never thought of that!" Voice dripping with derision, she added, "That's way better!"

"We're not going with Wolfy."

"Such a Wolfy thing to say."

"Stop it."

"Yes... Wolfy. Anyway, look at this." Maggie turned the paper around so Atticus could see it.

He shrugged. "Oh wow, a set of meaningless letters and numbers. I wish I'd seen stuff like this for the last, oh, I don't know, two months."

"Sarcasm. Helpful." Maggie didn't try to hide her amusement. "Now if you could stash it for just a minute, I'll explain myself." She settled into the uncomfortable wooden seat. "I've gotten my head around the communication styles out of Teufelsberg. Even though they're encrypted, they have a certain pattern to them. There are different styles at certain times of day. In the morning they're crisp and short, businesslike, yeah? In the late afternoon they're similarly styled for the most part, then almost every day after the three o'clock communication another message follows, and it's always much longer."

Atticus shrugged. *And?* He bobbed his head in encouragement, wanting the full story.

"The usual three o'clock message is pretty standard. The same length as the 9 am one. I assume it's something like yay, how cool is communism?"

Atticus stifled a laugh. "How cool is communism?"

"I don't know." She shrugged. "I had a nice bit of gruel last night?"

"How sweet are tractors? Vladimir Lenin is way better

than John Lennon. I'm sure this is exactly what the Russians talk about."

"Soviets."

Atticus occasionally used terminology unsuitable for an MI6 employee of this time period. He dipped his head in acquiescence. "Soviets."

Maggie gave him a wink, getting back to the topic at hand. "Anyway, the messages are all about the same length, then roughly five minutes after the three o'clock message, a different type of message is sent, I assume from West Berlin. Then it turns into a bit of back and forth, all varying lengths."

"And you're thinking..."

"This is a conversation. A personal one. The back and forth sometimes overlap one another."

"Like when you're both on Facebook Messenger and you see the little dots because the other person is typing as you're typing."

"The what?"

Atticus waved his hand, as if to say *ignore that bit*. "I see what you're saying. It's like, hey the bosses are out, how are you, what's up? Miss you and the like."

Maggie fidgeted in her chair, glad Atticus had the gist of what she was saying. "So, if these are personal then it's a matter of cryptoanalysis. Search for common lovers' language. Darling, miss you, that sort of thing. Break the code down to the basic elements. It narrows the parameters a little. In theory it should make cracking the Soviets' code a little easier. Or find out who's sending the love notes, on either side, see if they can be compromised and turned."

"That's fucking brilliant." Atticus leaned back in his chair, impressed. "I could kiss you."

A wide grin broke across her beautiful face. She cast her

eyes towards the door. "Oh, I know you *can*." She wrinkled her nose. "Tonight, my love."

They dove into the evidence Maggie had gathered so she could take it to her department head in Signals. Atticus loved the energy she had when her mind was set to a task. She was certainly a woman of passion.

Their romance was known only to them and a select circle of friends, which, much to Atticus's surprise, included Mary Quant. After their initial frosty introduction, the two had become formidable friends. Certainly no one at MI6 knew Maggie and Atticus were a couple. Fraternisation amongst the ranks was strictly forbidden. The fact that they actually used the word fraternisation was archaic in itself. Except for the occasional grope in the coat closet, Atticus and Maggie managed to keep their interactions professional and above reproach.

"You'll earn some brownie points with Vincent with this discovery." Atticus made a teasing face. "They might even invite you onto their floor."

It was the height of sexism that Maggie had graduated from the typing pool through sheer tenacity and talent yet had been prevented from joining the boys club due to her gender. The hollow excuses ranged from her being a distracting influence to concern that they would offend Maggie with their bawdy language, which for anyone who knew Maggie was the most laughable of them all.

Now she was well on her way to field agent, she was surpassing them all. There was a sexual revolution occurring in the halls of MI6, even if they didn't know it yet.

There was a knock at the door. A short, weedy teen by the name of Anthony wheeled in his squeaky cart. After all this time, Atticus was still amused at the sight of a mail cart. External mail and internal memos were continually passed between floors. There wasn't a day that went by that he didn't lament the lack of email.

Plopping a small bundle of envelopes and folders on the table, Anthony gave the pair an apathetic wave and left, closing the door behind him. Maggie picked up the pile. There were internal memos, a manila folder with what seemed like photographs inside, and regular mail. Indifferently flipping through the pile, Maggie halted when she reached a crisp white envelope. It was her excited squeal that alerted Atticus to the fact there was something of note.

"A letter from a Nigerian prince offering a million pounds? Wait, that's probably not a thing yet, is it?"

"What?" Maggie didn't take her eyes off the envelope. "It's here."

"What's here?" Atticus sat up. "Oh, shit. As in *it* it? The acceptance letter?"

"Or rejection." Maggie's voice was filled with anticipation.

"Let's think positive, shall we?"

"Like it's going to make a difference now."

"Shhh, open it."

Hands fumbling, Maggie did just that. It took her several seconds to read the letter before her hand darted to her mouth. Composing herself, she read, "Dear Miss Dunbar, we are pleased to inform you that you have passed the requisite requirements to progress to full field agent status. Please present yourself to blah blah blah." Maggie threw the paper in the air and did a little jig, followed by a shimmy. "I bloody well passed!"

Atticus swept her into his arms. "I knew you could do it. Well done. Never doubted it for a minute." He kissed her passionately.

Breaking the embrace, she leaned back and held her

hand to his chest. "You never did, did you? Thank you, for helping me."

"This was all you."

"We should celebrate." There was a mischievous twinkle in her eyes.

"Let's go out tonight. We can see what Mary and Alexander are up to. Maybe..."

Maggie slowly shook her head. She walked over to the door and locked it. Resting her back against the closed door, she raised one foot and tilted her head seductively.

"We might get caught." Atticus's protest was half-hearted.

Unbuttoning the top of her cardigan, Maggie raised an alluring eyebrow. Throatily, she said, "Then we'll get caught."

Atticus knew better than to argue. His hand swept across the table, clearing it of the cumbersome piles of papers. They fluttered to the floor in a cascade of forgotten importance. He had other priorities now.

AN HOUR LATER, both parties were dressed and were mostly respectable, if somewhat flushed. Straightening his tie, Atticus idly scanned the pile of documents strewn across the floor, including those that had just been delivered by Anthony. Interspersed amongst the mounds of white paper and manila folders were a smattering of black and white photographs. Out of sheer curiosity, he picked a folder at random.

Tucking her shirt into the waist of her skirt, Maggie glanced over. "What you got there?"

Opening the folder, Atticus indolently flipped through the photographs. "It's marked 'holiday'..."

He stopped dead and his eyes went wide. Head snapping up, he said, "We need to speak to the head of the Latvian bureau. Is there even a Latvian bureau?"

"There is—well, Northern Europe. From memory it's Estonia, Latvia, Lithuania, Denmark, Finland, Iceland, Norway and Sweden."

Atticus smirked. "From memory?"

Ignoring the jibe, Maggie went on. "The head is an old friend who's just rotated back into headquarters, he was stationed in Stockholm for the last couple of years. It'll be good for you to meet."

"Well, let's go then."

"Can I put my heels on first?"

He laughed. "Sure."

Five minutes later they stood in a cramped office with a suitably hunched individual. Dressed in a heavy taupe wool suit with elbow patches, he sported a waxed moustache more suited to a hunting lodge than MI6.

Maggie strode in casually and exclaimed fondly, "Giggy!"

Douglas Laughton's toff exterior evaporated the moment he saw Maggie. "I say, Dunbar, you look positively radiant! What the devil have you been up to?"

Maggie cast a wide-eyed glare at Atticus, concealing her amusement.

Laughton shook his head and poked his smoking pipe in her direction. "I tell you, if I weren't a married man I'd ravish you before lunch, what!"

Atticus had decked men for less.

But instead of calling down the might of HR on his head, Maggie chuckled. "Oh, Giggy."

She slapped him lightly on the shoulder. Atticus deemed the action far too light and about a foot off target. He steadfastly refused to adjust to the institutionalised sexism of the sixties.

Swivelling her hands to Atticus, Maggie said, "This is—"

"Oh, no need to introduce this gentleman." He placed his pipe on the table and extended his hand. "The famous Atticus Wolfe. A pleasure, a genuine pleasure, sir." He shook Atticus's hand so vigorously it almost came off. "I must say I've been looking forward to this. I heard what you did with Preston. Top show, really, top show."

"What we both did. Maggie was instrumental in the investigation as well."

"Oh, no doubt, no doubt. I always said a mind like hers was wasted in the typing pool."

"If you'd only said it a little louder, I could have been out of there a year or two earlier."

Atticus gave her a knowing smirk. It was good to see Maggie wasn't averse to calling out the entrenched chauvinism.

The statement seemed to have gone over Laughton's head. Slightly perplexed, he said, "Er, quite."

Atticus found it curious that Maggie wasn't inclined to advise her "friend" she'd passed the field agent tests. Was it because she wanted to come to terms with the news herself, or was it that she doubted he would share her enthusiasm?

Letting her friend off the hook, Maggie moved on. "How was your tour?"

"Marvellous, simply marvellous. You'd love the bars in Stockholm. They have this brännvin which literally translates to 'burn-wine'."

Atticus thought an MI6 agent would have been more concerned with geopolitical machinations than alcoholic beverages. Then again, the priorities of this time period were often polar opposites to his own.

"What was it you were working on over there?" Atticus thought he'd better at least pretend to be interested in exchanging pleasantries with the man.

Laughton waved his hand vaguely. "Oh, so many things, my good man."

"Can you name one?" Atticus was beginning to actively dislike him.

As if annoyed at having to discuss work, Laughton huffed. "We're trying to agitate the residents of the Abrenes apriņķis to reverse the annexing to the USSR and put it back into Lithuanian hands."

"You mean Latvian?"

"Yes, that's what I said." Shifting in his seat, Laughton asked, "What can I do for you two?"

The two explained the photograph they'd come across, although not the nature of its discovery.

Laughton nodded in understanding, if not enthusiasm. "I recall them coming though yesterday in a diplomatic pouch. Taken by someone in the Leningrad consulate while they were on holiday in Latvia. Jeremy something... I'm terrible with names. Maybe it was Brian. Ryan? Some name. Anyway, he thought we'd be interested how the Soviets spend their holidays. There were an awful lot, I must say—too many to go through, obviously. I hope he doesn't want us to reimburse him for the film. I gave a couple of photographs a scan, but there was nothing of importance, I'm afraid."

Atticus thought it bizarre that the head of the Northern Europe bureau wouldn't have the time to review intelligence in his patch. He hadn't even delegated the task.

"Respectfully, I beg to differ." Atticus tilted his head. "Especially in light of you just mentioning Oliver Preston."

"Terribly sorry, old man, I don't follow."

Atticus placed a black and white photograph on the table and waited.

Laughton's eyes lit up. "Oh, I say... I say!"

"I'm glad we're on the same page... finally." Atticus cracked his knuckles. "Now, I'm going to need a few things."

AN HOUR later they stood opposite Rathdowne's desk. Their boss seemed irascible as always, though there appeared to be no particular reason for his cantankerous disposition other than that was the way he lived.

"Well done on passing the exams, Dunbar. Thomson said you did bloody well."

"Thank you, sir."

Jiggling the folder in his hand, Atticus addressed Rath-downe. "I've got some holiday snaps to show you."

"Wolfe, I'm not particularly keen on the idea of seeing you in swimming trunks. No offence."

Ignoring the sarcastic tone, Atticus went on. "They're of Jūrmala, near Riga."

Rathdowne shrugged, apparently not seeing the point of the discussion. "Latvia isn't really on my list of go-to holiday destinations."

Pulling out the same photograph they'd shown Laughton, Atticus laid it on the table. It was of a seaside crowd; the main focus of the picture was the beach and foreshore. On the right-hand side, three men strode along the boulevard, apparently oblivious to the cameraman. At the centre of the group was Oliver, walking cheerfully beside Alaksiej Barinov and the infamous Mikhail.

"It's only days old. We've got him." Atticus tapped the picture. "It's pure dumb luck we even saw this at all, but we have the son of a bitch."

Rathdowne glowered at the photograph of Oliver, the man who had humiliated him and the entire organisation he held so dear.

Atticus saw an opportunity to stoke his boss's interest. "My guess is Oliver is trying to ingratiate himself into the local elite. After all, that's what he's good at. Being close to power, using his outward persona to fool those around him into thinking they're the smartest in the room, all the while manipulating and building his own empire. The Communist Party is the perfect place for Oliver Preston, wouldn't you say?"

What Atticus didn't say was that if Oliver truly was toadying up to Soviet leadership, the world was in more danger than it realised. If he managed to achieve a position of influence in the superpower with knowledge of what was to come, he could very well become the most influential man on the planet.

Picking up the photo to inspect it more closely, Rathdowne asked, "How did you come across this?"

Maggie coughed and covered her grinning mouth with her fist.

Atticus moved on quickly. "The photo wasn't meant for us. It was in a pile of photos that, ah, became dislodged." He cast a sideways glance in Maggie's direction. "Sometimes things just slip into place."

Coughing loudly, Maggie rushed out of the office, shaking her head.

Doing his best not to smile, Atticus gestured towards his exiting partner. "Bad Chinese for lunch, I think."

Rathdowne frowned as though he understood. He squinted at the photograph intently, as if hoping he could reveal more by sheer will.

"I've spoken to Laughton, the head of the Northern Europe bureau. He's spoken to the Leningrad consulate. They'll keep their man in Jūrmala to see if they can come across Oliver again. Apparently Leningrad weren't too pleased, as their man was set to return tomorrow, but I stressed the urgency."

Folding his arms, Rathdowne harrumphed. "That's taking a bloody liberty. You should have run it by me first."

"That's what I'm doing now. Keeping you informed. You know within an hour of us knowing." Atticus rocked on his heels, waiting as long as he could before asking the next question, trying not to rush it. "When do I go?"

"Go where?" Rathdowne shook his head, confused. "Latvia?"

"I need to go and extract him." He paused. "We, obviously. MI6."

Carefully, Rathdowne placed the photograph on his desk and leaned back. "You won't half stand out in a Baltic resort town."

Doing his best to strip all emotion from his tenor, Atticus said, "I need to go get him."

"I know this is personal for you. It is for all of us. But he's well behind the Iron Curtain. We can't exactly stage a smash and grab."

That was exactly what Atticus had in mind. It went far beyond capturing the man Atticus had thought was a friend, who had not only betrayed his trust, but had utterly fooled him. There was another reason, one Atticus couldn't share with the man before him. Oliver potentially had the power to bend the course of history to his will. The thought kept Atticus awake at night. Now, for the first time, he had a chance to sleep well, knowing he'd found the madman who could alter the course of the Cold War.

"Can I go?" Atticus tried not to appear too eager. He suspected he had failed. "I can help coordinate the search, give them an insight into the man that could help narrow down the—"

"No." Rathdowne clasped his hands in front of him. "I'm not starting World War Three because of your thirst for vengeance."

"Then why assign me to finding him in the first place?"

Rathdowne held up the photo. "Because I knew you'd get results."

The statement grated on Atticus for two reasons. One, they'd found the man not through good espionage work, but pure dumb luck. Two, it seemed the hard work he'd actually put in had been for nothing. What was the point of finding Oliver if they would do nothing with the information?

Waggling a finger in his direction, Rathdowne scowled. "I'm not saying we're never going to get the traitorous bellend, but I need to give a solid justification to the suits upstairs. Vengeance isn't on their list of approval reasons. Give me a location and a credible threat to Queen and Country and I'll give you your retribution. I want him as much as you do, believe me. But I need more than happy snaps. You hear me?"

Atticus nodded. He heard. Now they knew where Oliver was, he had to find a solid reason for Rathdowne to send him on a mission to extract their former colleague. And he'd make damn sure he found one, so he could go and sort this mess out once and for all. If setting the timeline right again required the sacrifice of a former friend, Atticus wouldn't hesitate to kill the bastard.

CHAPTER

FOUR

A tticus and Maggie alighted the double decker bus and stepped into another world. As usual, the streets of Brixton were packed with people of all ages darting from one place to the next. Be it a store one couldn't find anywhere else in London, or one of the multi-coloured restaurants or welcoming bars, Brixton was a world unto itself. With the shouts, the colours, the jostling humanity, the place was *alive* in a way the rest of the city couldn't equal.

Although most of the stores no longer existed in Atticus's time, it still felt right; familiar. This was his town, the streets of his youth. It felt like home. It *was* home.

The two strode together down Atlantic Road, past where the underground station would be one day built. Hence their need to endure the meandering bus route to get there. Atticus was gradually lessening his judgement on how things compared to his day. It was a long road, but he was getting better at it.

He also was slowly getting used to the culinary

"delights" of the time. Slabs of beef were the norm, not exactly in line with his previous meat-free diet. Oddly, pizza was almost impossible to find, and when you could it was only cheese and tomato—and even that was considered exotic.

One thing Atticus refused to get used to, however, was the preoccupation with food on sticks. Every dinner party Maggie had taken him to, the hostess (not one male had ever hosted) served up platter after platter of skewered fare. Cheese and pineapple on sticks. Cheese and olives on sticks. Cheese and walnuts on sticks. Cocktail sausages... on sticks. Hell, he'd gone to a dinner hosted by Maggie's best mate Mary, and her husband Alexander had served oysters on sticks. It was a weird obsession that bordered on mania.

There would be no food on sticks tonight, though. The locals here didn't go for on-trend fancy dinner party cuisine. Tonight, it was to be down and dirty Afro-Caribbean fare. Even though decades separated his visits to Brixton, the smells were gratefully similar. It was a welcome break from tireless espionage work.

It had taken weeks, but they'd finally found Oliver again. He'd passed a couple of operatives in Laughton's team on a beachfront street on his way to the market. He was being escorted by Mikhail. Apparently neither man was aware they were being followed. The report stated that Oliver didn't seem harangued or coerced—in fact, he appeared to be having the time of his life in the seaside town.

The operative had lost them in the crowd. So far they hadn't managed to find where Oliver was staying, but the confirmation that he was still in town meant they were close.

The town was apparently full of Soviet-era sanatoriums for the Party elite. There was a concert hall built in the thirties, museums, nearby forests, and rivers. There were worse places to be a traitorous defector.

The orders had been to keep an eye out for him and if they could do so discreetly, to find where he lived. It wasn't the same as hauling him into Scotland Yard, but it would have to do for now.

Atticus shook his head to dismiss the notion. He focused on one aspect of his recent drifting thoughts: Ganim.

In retrospect it had been an oversight to leave communications solely in the hands of the man himself. A phone number would have been helpful, or at least a mutual intermediary to pass messages between the two. Instead, Atticus had to wait for the now-old-man to emerge. The powerlessness of the situation had long ago descended into apathy. Now apathy had given way to indifference. The further Atticus got from the odd conversation in his flat months ago, the less eager he was to believe he could ever return home.

The other reason for his waning desire to return held his hand as they strode down the Brixton street on an oddly warm May night. There were a few odd fleeting looks cast at the black man and white woman with hands intertwined, but the sight was far less scandalous here than it would have been in other parts of the city. For the few bigoted glances, there were more genuine smiles of delight at seeing two young people who clearly adored one another.

Adored was right. Atticus and Maggie had spent a blissful few months together. It was perhaps the happiest time he had ever known. It was also the reason for their visit.

"Now we've arrived, are you going to tell me what we're doing here?" Maggie tugged on his arm mischievously. "If you're aiming to unveil the delights of Brixton, I hate to burst your bubble, but I've been here before."

"I know."

"How do you...?"

Moving on quickly, Atticus steered her around a corner. "I'm not here to show, I'm here to introduce."

Maggie's forehead crinkled in confusion. "But you don't know anybody here."

He tilted his head, acknowledging the point. "I know them. But they don't know me..." he sighed, knowing the gravity of what he was about to say, "... yet."

The confused creases on Maggie's forehead doubled down into concern. "Isn't this dangerous? Like if we meet someone from your future we'll disrupt the timeline? Accidently invent the Daleks or something?"

"You've been watching too much Doctor Who."

"They're terrifying! Exterminate, exterminate!"

Maggie thrust her arm out in impersonation, totally devoid of inhibition on the busy street. Another reason he adored her. Still laughing at her antics, he stopped in front of Kingston's Kitchen & Grill.

Confusion returned to her features. "Who are we meeting *exactly*?"

"My grandmother. Well, a much younger version, I guess. This is where she worked—I mean works." Atticus leaned down to kiss her forehead in an attempt to relieve Maggie's disquiet. "I'm just letting the most important woman in my past meet the most important woman of my future."

Her jaw dropped slightly, but there was no hiding Maggie's perplexed delight. She nudged him with her elbow. "That line is so hot I'm pretty sure my underpants are melting." Her beaming smile died away. "Are you *sure* we're not disrupting timelines and whatnot?"

"We're just having some dinner in my family's restaurant, like thousands of other people have. Nobody is disrupting anything. We're going to have some fungee and pepperpot, la bandera, maybe some jerk chicken. All we're doing is eating fantastic food, paying and leaving, just like everyone else."

"You sure?"

"Absolutely. My grandmother's la bandera is legendary."

That earned him a good-natured punch in the arm. "This is important to you, isn't it?"

"It is." He gently placed a finger under her chin and tilted her head up. "You are."

"Aaand there go the underpants." She tucked her arm though Atticus's. "Come on, Mr Smooth, let's get some dinner."

Inside, Kingston's Kitchen & Grill was jam-packed. Far smaller than he recalled, every table was filled with lively patrons laughing, back-slapping and devouring the steaming food served on multi-coloured mismatching plates. The rear wall opened up to the kitchen where pots and pans clanged in a non-stop chaotic symphony. The yelling from the kitchen staff almost drowned out the clientele, and the smells were otherworldly. The mix of spices, the scent of the fresh vegetables and chargrilled meats intertwined to create a joy-inducing aroma Atticus had searched for his entire life but never found anywhere else.

The place was owned by the King of Brixton, Atticus's

grandfather, Joe, but there was never any doubt as to who ran the joint. The redoubtable Eliza managed the place for decades and was the driving force behind its success. When she died, many years from now, the place was never the same. It took a few years, but without its guiding soul, the restaurant began its slow but inevitable decline. Last Atticus heard, the location was now a Burger King.

Doing his best to not appear too obvious, Atticus craned his neck, searching for any sign of his grandmother's formidable presence. "Sledgehammer Joe" rarely stepped inside, knowing full well there was only one captain of the ship and it certainly wasn't him.

In her youth, Eliza had held sway over the entire establishment, greeting newcomers and regulars with equal warmth, dispensing Jamaican wisdom or roughly ejecting any patron who dared break one of her solemn rules of etiquette. But instead of seeing her behind the main desk, a slight and greasy gent in a beanie greeted them with a tiny wave as he handed change to a parting couple. Atticus vaguely remembered the man, whose name was likely Neville. It suddenly occurred to him that his grandmother may not even be working this particular evening, or even at this time in her life.

"I'll be wit' you in a minute, hon'."

A confident woman swooped past, expertly balancing four plates in her arms while swerving around the jumbled tables. It had been the briefest of flashes, but it was enough. She must be in her mid-forties, but seemed a good twenty years younger.

Maggie softly placed her hand on his sleeve. "That's her, isn't it?"

Too choked up to respond, Atticus just grinned.

Moments later Eliza Wolfe approached, wiping her hands on an apron tucked into her jeans. "Two ye?"

They nodded in response. It was clear Maggie was taking Atticus's lead. He appreciated it, even though he couldn't quite verbalise it at that precise moment.

Eliza leaned back and seemed to target a stout man at the rear of the room. "Burgess, you be finished wit' dem crab cakes or we gonna be pulling out a cot for de night?"

"Irie, irie, woman." Burgess stuffed the remainder of the food in his mouth and between chomps added, "We not married, why you gotta bust my bollocks like dat?"

"Because you costin' me money, dat why. Scoot."

And scoot he did. The big man bowed dramatically but good-naturedly and exited towards the front of the restaurant. Eliza scooped up the plates and gave the table a cursory wipe with her apron.

"I'll be back wit' some menus, darlin'," Eliza said, giving Atticus a wink.

The two sat. For Atticus it was surreal. The place he knew so well from his youth was alive once more. He remembered growing up in the corners of this restaurant, quietly observing the goings on, taking in the mannerisms and the dramas of the hub of Brixton life. It was a fascinating and eye-opening way to grow up.

"Now I know where you get those good looks of yours from." Maggie kept her voice low. "She's a striking woman."

Atticus kissed her on the cheek. A million thoughts fought for attention in his brain.

Despite his bravado, it *was* dangerous to be here. He didn't intend on making a habit of it. All the more reason to bring Maggie along; make it a once-off. It hadn't been a line, him telling her how important it was for him to bring her here. It wasn't a decision he'd taken lightly. As he watched the woman flit from table to table, he was reminded exactly why he'd been drawn here. With no mother and his father and grandfather more frequently in than out of jail, Eliza Wolfe was the bedrock that laid the foundation for the man he would become. He had to see her at least once. If he didn't, her presence would continue to be a black hole that threatened to wrench him from his own orbit. He only hoped this one fix would be enough.

"Can I get you started wit' anything?"

It was a shock for her to be so close, yet he couldn't embrace her. Atticus did his best to assume the demeanour of a regular customer. "Fried plantains, the Jamaican fried dumplings, the veggie patties and a side of slaw, please."

"Ooee, they be some of my favourites. Top shelf choices, 'dem." Eliza tapped her pencil on her small pad. "You been here before, handsome?"

"Yes, er, no." Atticus's words were stuck in mud. "I don't think so."

"Dat a'ight." She patted his arm, her hand lingering longer than it needed to. "You so pretty, yo don' have to be smart." Her million-watt smile lit up the room. "I be getting' you dem quicksmart."

She disappeared and hollered orders into the kitchen while picking up steaming plates from under the warmers. She seemed to control every aspect of the hectic operation.

"Atticus..." Maggie pursed her lips, doing her best not to laugh.

"I know."

She lowered her gaze. "Your grandmother is flirting with you."

"I know, I know. It's..."

"Weird and creepy."

"Yes, it is."

"And fucking funny."

"No, it isn't."

Unable to hold in her laughter, Maggie shook her head. "Oh, I assure you it most certainly is."

Minutes later the table was overflowing with food, and it stayed that way until their bellies were well and truly full. Maggie said she'd never tasted food like it and the meal was likely the best she'd ever had. Whether she was being polite or not, a sense of pride enveloped Atticus, giving him an even warmer feeling than the food.

Atticus rubbed his belly and put on his best impersonation of his forebears. "Betta belly buss dan good food waste."

Eliza appeared from behind him. Picking up plates, she grinned. "Ay, I say dat all de time!" She gave him a slap on the shoulder.

Atticus translated for Maggie. "It is better to overeat than to waste great food."

She flashed a toothy smile in return. Her face lit up every time Eliza came near.

"I love your restaurant."

"Oh, thank you child." Eliza started to clear the plates. Her gaze switched between the two. "You boyfriend and girlfriend?"

Atticus's response was firm. "We are."

In an instant fear gripped him. He hadn't thought the topic would come up, but now that it had he was overcome with dread that his grandmother could somehow disapprove of their union. It was, after all, uncommon for the time.

"You two make a damn handsome pair." Eliza tilted her head at Maggie. "She's a wildcat this one." She elbowed Atticus and lowered her voice. "I can's always spot them wildcats. Takes one to know one. You keep her happy, y'hear?"

Until that moment Atticus didn't know it was possible to blush and beam at the same time, but that's exactly what Maggie did. The delight on her face was priceless. It was if the Queen herself had slapped a sword on both shoulders and given her a castle.

"Oh, I will." Atticus doffed his head towards Maggie, eyes shining.

"Good. Now, y'all want some rum cake or bread pudding?"

As they went to reluctantly call for the bill and make their leave, fierce yelling emanated from the centre of the restaurant. Three young black men launched themselves from the table, chairs ejecting behind them, plates clattering to the floor. Whatever the problem was, they were wound up with fire in their eyes. In fact, that fire was better described as murder. The details of the dispute weren't apparent amongst the incoherent jumble of accusations and derogatory insults. But although the cause may have been uncertain, the outcome wasn't; bloodshed was coming, and soon.

"Oh Jesus." Eliza spun and headed towards the kitchen, shouting, "Jacob, we got a problem."

It seemed the fracas was two against one. The one with his back to Atticus seemed capable of handling himself, muscled and standing looser than the other two. He hadn't tensed up, his feet were defensibly set, ready to repel an attack when it came. His stance, his demeanour, his attitude screamed brawler, but the other two just didn't hear it.

The two men paced in front of each other, winding each other up. Patrons backed up where they could, giving the fighters room in the cramped space. The two grew increasingly incensed while the brawler with his back to Atticus remained outwardly calm, ready for whatever they had in store for him.

One of the two stepped forward with a wild haymaker, but a short sharp jab to the jaw sent him reeling backwards onto his arse. The other was more cautious, but no less determined. He strode in like a boxer, ducking and weaving. It was a better approach, but ultimately as futile as his compatriot. A lightning-fast cross sent him staggering backwards and into a table of startled white teenagers.

The calm man cracked his neck. "That it?" His voice was dark and menacing.

The last one to be hit wiped blood from his mouth. He pushed himself up from the table, seemingly ready for round two.

But before he could act, his opponent stepped forward, his large shadow falling on the man before him. "What was that, Teddy? Losin' your fucken' teeth make it difficult to speak?"

The first man on the ground was behind Atticus. He reached into his coat and extracted a large flick knife. When he stood, the knife flashed in the light. He pulled his right arm back, about to shiv the brawler from behind.

Instinctively Atticus leapt forward, punching down the attacker's knife hand. Grasping his left wrist, Atticus twisted violently and brought his forearm down heavily on the other man's elbow joint. The crack was followed by the piercing scream of a man who'd just had his arm broken. As his body crumpled, Atticus stomped on his ankle, hampering the man's mobility and taking him out of the equation.

The brawler spun, fists raised. When he spied Atticus he crouched, expecting another fighter to have entered the fray. When he saw the knife tumble from his foe's hand and realised Atticus wasn't an attacker, he gave a wide grin of thanks. The pleasant disposition disappeared the instant he turned to his attacker.

"You stabbin' me in the back Ned?" He shook his heavy head. "Really? You're a fucken' dog."

Clomping footfalls caused Atticus to turn. A man sprinted from the kitchen—the aforementioned Jacob, Atticus assumed. His meaty hands held massive cleavers in each fist. Jacob certainly gave the impression of someone not to be fucked with. The tattooed hardman screeched to a halt, seeing there was no need for his cleaver-wielding services.

Eliza approached Atticus, more upset than he'd ever seen his unshakable grandmother.

"Thank you, thank you." She patted Atticus's arm as she stepped forward, and did the same to the young man standing victorious. She turned to Atticus. "You have no idea... Thank you for saving my son."

Son.

Son.

She was right. He really had no idea. The man's face was familiar. In retrospect, so similar he *should* have realised. The brawler's face was nowhere near as hard and scarred as the one his father possessed in his memories. The years between now and when Atticus met him would be harsh, and would morph that pleasant teen face into the cruel façade of an angry and vengeful gangster.

Maggie's eyes were wide. It was plain what she was thinking. *You done gone and fucked up, dickhead.*

Atticus was in no position to argue the point.

WITHIN MINUTES the restaurant had returned to some semblance of normality. If only Atticus could have joined them. The staff had done a skilled job of settling the scene. Three of the burliest had quietly removed the two aggressors without fuss. The remainder scurried about righting furniture and placating the panicked patrons.

Seated across him at the table, Maggie plastered on a hopeful expression. "Maybe it was good. You saved him, right? Maybe you were always meant to do it? Save your dad?"

He shook his head. "No. No, I don't think so." In a hushed tone to avoid prying ears Atticus gravely went on. "I... I think I royally, *royally* fucked up." He inhaled deeply. "My father was always quick to tell the story of when he was a teenager and a friend stabbed him in the back."

"Oh... shit."

"He perversely wore it as a badge of honour, used it as an excuse to never trust anyone, to lash out at those closest to him, including my mother and I—anyone. The speech I heard a million times growing up was, 'Never turn your back on anyone, you hear me, Atticus? Cunts'll stab you in the back every chance they get.' If I had a pound for every time I ever heard that I'd be a damn rich man. The incident *defined* him, it twisted him into the bastard I remember." Atticus rubbed his hands over his bald head. "What have I done?"

"Maybe that wasn't the moment? Maybe..." Maggie

gawped at Atticus, and on seeing his dubiousness bowed her head. "Yeah, okay. This is bad."

The teenage Thomas Wolfe strode towards them, positively dripping with arrogance. Atticus found it mind-bending that he was probably a good fifteen years older than his father.

Thomas extended a hand. "They call me the Prince, but you can call me Tom, mate. Thanks for taking out that dog back there. You handle yourself well. You local?"

Shaking his father's hand for the first time in decades, Atticus stuttered a response. "Local-ish, I guess you could say."

Blinking, not quite understanding the response, he turned to Maggie. "Hello, darlin'." The leer was more predatory than friendly. "Alright?"

"Fine. Thank you." The warmth Maggie had shown to Atticus's grandmother wasn't extended to his father.

At the front desk Neville hung up the heavy black Bakelite phone and arched his back. "Excuse me, ladies and gentlemen. I'm sorry for the disturbance this evening. In recompense, we offer you tonight's meals on the house." He waited a beat to let the jubilation subside. "But I also must regretfully ask you to leave this fine establishment to allow us to clean up. We hope to see you all again soon, but I must politely request that you depart," the genial smile dropped like a music hall curtain, "right now."

The sudden change in their amiable host was enough to propel the clientele to grab their belongings and leave. There were no complaints. This wasn't an establishment where one backtalked the owners.

The Prince placed his meaty hand on Atticus's wrist. "Not you." He swivelled his head and flashed the harsh features Atticus recalled all too well from his youth. "You stay."

In less than a minute every customer had left, the doors were locked and only staff remained. Neville, the now cleaverless Jacob, Eliza and Thomas Wolfe milled near the rear of the restaurant. None seemed happy; in fact, Atticus sensed palpable tension in the air. Something was up, he just didn't know what.

"Care to tell me what's going on... Tom?" Even facing this far younger version of his father, Atticus found it difficult to address the man in such a way. There was a time—a very long time—where such familiarity would have earned him a backhander.

Folding his arms so emotionlessly it would make the Sphinx proud, Thomas Wolfe shook his head. *No.* The added implication was, *and don't ask again.*

Atticus found it strange that the fear that had dominated his formative years was actively fighting the training he'd received since. Truth be told, the fear was winning. It was hard to reconcile the man who had intimidated him so thoroughly for so many years with the teen who sat before him now.

The back door opened and closed with a groan. The bearing of every staff member tilted, as if their unease had ratcheted up in an instant. A solitary figure casually strode towards the group. Neville and Jacob seemed on the verge of bowing. That's how much respect the man commanded. Even Maggie sat up straight, as if royalty had entered the room.

It had. The King of Brixton had arrived.

No matter which side of the law enforcement fence one was on, Joe Wolfe was treated with respect, either due to his efforts to minimise the involvement of innocents or out

DAVE SINCLAIR

of outright fear. While the police were relentless in trying to bring him down, even they accorded him a semblance of deference, though it only extended so far. The man hadn't earned the moniker "Sledgehammer Joe" by handing out lollipops.

He would eventually die in prison, his once proud kingdom diluted and tarnished by the actions of his—by then equally incarcerated—son. In the end, he was given a send-off worthy of a king, but his empire had long before fallen into ruin.

"Sledgehammer Joe" Wolfe kissed Eliza on the cheek. The exchange was more perfunctory than emotional. She jerked her head towards the table where Atticus and Maggie sat. *This is them.* Her previous friendliness was muted by the presence of her husband.

This wasn't the same grandfather Atticus dimly remembered from his youth. This man was vital, alive. There was a spring in his step, his beaming face free of the wrinkles and hardness of running a criminal empire.

His menacing presence broke the moment he smiled. He extended his hand to Atticus, palm down, in the classic dominant handshake used by aggressive politicians and real estate agents the world over. And gangsters, apparently. He gave Maggie only a cursory bob of his head. When the two men shook, he clasped Atticus's hand in his other, encasing it in a far friendlier gesture.

"I wanted to thank the man who saved my boy. I'm meant to be out of circulation, you see." He gave a conspiratorial wink. "The rozzers and I have a slight misunderstanding at the moment. The local bobbies are under the misapprehension the money I nicked from a raid on Jimmy the Finger's bookie operation—highly illegal, I'll add—was theirs and not mine. The fucken' cheek, right? So to avoid

68

confrontations I'm erring on the side of stayin' out of their way to avoid any unnecessary work on their behalf putting me away. That's how fucken' considerate I am."

"Understandable." Atticus did his best to maintain an even tenor.

"Glad you understand, lad. Glad you understand. Now," he strode around the two seated at the table as if holding court, "when Neville here told me what you did, I wanted to personally come down, at great personal risk, to thank you face to face."

"I appreciate that, Mr Wolfe." Atticus remembered how to defer to the strong man.

It seemed to do the trick. Joe nodded at the acknowledgement of his authority. "And also make you an offer."

"An offer?"

"That's right. Today you saved my only son. My heir. The way I hear it, he was about to be shivved in the back. Now, where I come from, that's a low act. A fucken low act. You saw it happening and stepped in. That's the action of a man of honour. I wanted you to know it won't be forgotten. Do you know what a solemn vow is?"

"I do."

"In my line of work, well, a man's word is everything. I see these young punks coming in, their word means shit. Not me. You ask anyone, Joe Wolfe's word is like diamonds, they'll say. Unbreakable, you hear me? My offer is this: you need anything, I mean anything, be it next week, a year from now, you look me up. I owe you a debt not easily repaid. You get yourself into trouble, you come see me, I'll sort you out."

"Thank y—"

"I need you to understand I don't make this offer to just any Tom, Dick or Harry, understand?"

"I understand. Thank you."

As quickly as possible Atticus and Maggie made their leave and got the hell out of Kingston's Kitchen & Grill. Hand in sweaty hand, they made their way down Atlantic Road as fast as they could without breaking into a run.

Atticus had no intention of cashing in the offer. He'd disrupted the timeline enough for one lifetime.

CHAPTER

FIVE

"Right, I think I've got it."

Sitting across from one another in their cramped MI6 office, Atticus and Maggie were concocting a list.

There was a knowing smirk on Maggie's face. "Alright, let's hear it."

"Number one, don't fuck up the timeline."

Frowning approvingly, Maggie nodded encouragement. "Good. Keep going."

"Two. Don't fuck up the timeline."

She tilted her head. "It sounds awfully similar to number one."

"Yes, but it's very important so I put it in twice."

"You're an idiot. Fine. Three?"

"No hanging out with future parents."

"That seems super wise. Where was this list yesterday?"

"I know, right? Four, stay hydrated."

"Hydration is important. I'll allow it. Go on."

Atticus tapped his list with a pen. "Anything to do with

me personally, give a wide berth. Anything to keep history on track, that's the focus."

Maggie sighed. "All this is quite interesting—"

"I have another eleven to go..."

"— but all this altering history talk comes down to this: either you can change your past or you can't."

Atticus scratched the back of his head. "Well, yes."

"Well, I have an answer for you, and I didn't even need a list to come up with it." Maggie folded her arms, amusement dancing on her features.

Delight creased the corner of his mouth. "Okay, I'll bite. Can I change the future or not?"

"The answer is yes. To both." She leaned forward, animated. Like Atticus, she'd clearly been thinking about this for some time and seemed eager to discuss her ideas. "You said Ganim couldn't change the chaos that occurred in the Middle East for the last fifty years, right? I'm guessing with all he did to get into the past he would have tried really *really* hard. On the opposite side of the ledger, without even trying you potentially changed the entire course of your father's future."

"This is meant to be an uplifting discussion, is it?"

"I never said that."

"Just as long as I know that going in." Atticus sighed. "Okay. Where does that leave us? Besides with a headache?" Time travel discussions did Atticus's head in. "Ganim's been here for fifty years longer than me and as far as I can tell, nothing's changed."

"Just because he wanted to change the future, doesn't mean he could. How many men over the last few millennia *really* wanted to change the course of events but were powerless to do so?"

Atticus rubbed his temples. "This kind of talk boils my noodle."

"We need to work this out."

"I know. But it's lunchtime and I'm hungry." Atticus grimaced. "And now I feel like noodles."

"Shhh. Think about it. Oliver has the ears of Soviets. Even if he's not trusted yet, when he gets access to the history books in your phone and starts predicting the future he'll be goddamn Nostradamus."

"I have given that scenario some thought."

"Maybe we need to give it some more. If he gets those Cold War books and the right ear, the whole might of the superpower will be forced to listen to him, and then we'll be well and truly screwed."

"You just said Ganim couldn't change the future." Atticus rubbed his left temple.

"I said he wasn't successful, not that he couldn't. You've proven you *can* change the future. Therefore, we have to take this deadly seriously. We have to work harder so Oliver *doesn't* win. You've damaged the future, but you haven't broken it—not yet. But you can. Don't you see? Oliver isn't the one who's going to destroy the future, you are. If you fail."

"That's so very helpful, thank you. I didn't quite have enough pressure on my shoulders."

"Context, it's important." A wicked grin crossed her red lips. "Alternatively, all this is *meant* to happen."

Atticus laid his head on the table. He wondered what he could take for a time-travel talk induced headache. "What?"

"All this might be a self-fulfilling prophecy. Like *Oedipus Rex*. Oedipus becomes king of Thebes and therefore fulfills a prophecy where he kills his father and marries his mother.

Side note, ew. The prophecy was the motivation for all his actions, therefore it was self-fulfilling. Boom. Oliver could be creating events that ensure the timeline you know."

Lifting his head slightly, Atticus said, "So, you're saying all we're doing could have already happened in my day?" Atticus snapped his fingers. "Like the guy who invented transparent aluminium?"

Maggie's face was deadpan. "The what?"

"*Star Trek IV: The Voyage Home.* The crew of the starship *Enterprise* go back in time to grab some whales and they show a guy how to make transparent aluminium. Now, did they break the timeline or was that guy the bloke who invented it all along?"

Maggie let out a frustrated sigh. "How does that help us exactly?"

"It gets us closer to lunch?" He shrugged. "Plus I get to talk about *Star Trek*."

"This is important."

"I know." He turned serious once more. "Believe me. I don't want to be responsible for the end of the world if I can avoid it." His hand slid across the table to touch hers. "My favourite people live here."

She smiled sweetly, but it was plain she wouldn't be distracted. "Or we could be completely wrong on all of this. None of this is preordained and the timeline has already been messed up irreparably and we're headed for nuclear Armageddon."

Atticus lurched off the chair and sprawled out on the wooden floor. With so much pressure on his shoulders, he knew all too well any misstep would result in disaster, not just for him, not even just for his country, but for the entire world. Everyone knew that if the superpowers came to blows, if diplomacy failed, a few terrified men could kill everyone on the planet. It was a time of fear. It was a time of volatility.

While Atticus was thinking global annihilation, it seemed Maggie's attention had turned to a more intimate subject. Tracing her finger across the tabletop, she failed to meet his eyes. "What if we stop Oliver, get the phone back and things return to normal? What if Ganim can get you home? Would you go?" The delivery was a little too hurried to be natural. This had clearly been on Maggie's mind for some time.

Before Atticus could answer there was a knock at the door. Before they could respond, the door opened and a waxed-moustachioed face stuck itself through the door.

"Hello, lovelies."

"Hi Douglas." Maggie's reply was devoid of the usual delight at seeing her friend. "What brings you our way?"

"Boss wants to see the three of us." His face scrunched in confusion. "What are you doing down there, old boy?"

Not lifting his cheek off the floor, Atticus replied, "Waiting for my brains to leak out my ears."

"Right'o." Laughton nodded as if the response made sense. "He said it was rather urgent. He's got his knickers in a twist about something, apparently. No dilly-dallying."

Exchanging curious glances with a thousand unsaid questions, Atticus and Maggie straightened themselves out, grabbed notebooks and readied themselves.

Saved by the bell. Laughton's visit couldn't have been better timed. Atticus watched Maggie's beautiful and dejected face transform into her game face as she prepared herself for the meeting with Rathdowne.

Truth be told, Atticus honestly didn't know if he still wanted to return home. It was exactly that—*home*, familiar. But was that enough? It was truly where all logic said he belonged, but he didn't know if it held what he'd once thought it did.

That was a topic for another time. He had to save the past before he could think about the future.

THE THREE GOT to Rathdowne's office as fast as they could. It was in its usual chaotic state, even more so thanks to the addition of more moving boxes. The scene seemed normal enough, except for the prim wool-suited maiden sitting on a wooden chair in the far corner of the office. It was the first time Atticus had seen Mrs Abernathy outside her usual position at the front desk of MI6. Her presence was no less formidable here. She greeted each of the arrivals with a courtly bow, but there was no doubt her shrewd eyes were sizing them up.

"What's she doing here?" Laughton motioned to Mrs Abernathy.

Rathdowne dismissed the question with a wave of his hand. "We'll get to that."

He held out his packet of Embassy Filter cigarettes. Maggie and Laughton each took one and accepted a light from their boss. Rathdowne jangled the packet in Atticus's direction half-heartedly, knowing full well what the response would be.

Shaking his head in Atticus's direction, Rathdowne said, "My father always said never trust a man who doesn't smoke."

"My father always said never trust a man who stabs you in the back."

He cast a sideways glance at Maggie to gauge her reaction. While she threw him a knowing grin, the reaction was muted. It was obvious her thoughts were back in their office, the question regarding Atticus's future choices lingering between them.

Mrs Abernathy, who had remained silent in the corner of the room, wasn't offered a cigarette. Her impassive face didn't reveal if that displeased her.

Casting his gaze around the messy room, taking in the desk piled high with files, the moving boxes stacked against the wall, Laughton rocked on his heels. "I say, I hope she's here to clean your office, old boy. If cleanliness is close to godliness—"

"The idle have time to clean. I'm here to work."

The bluntness of the reply left no doubt as to Rathdowne's opinion of Laughton. With a working-class background and attitude, Rathdowne was the thorn amongst MI6's upper-class roses. Laughton's posh accent was one of the many things that usually set Rathdowne off. "Pillar and Woolley and the like have time to tidy their offices before they totter off to polo. I'm here when the lights go off."

"That would make it rather difficult to read, I imagine."

Laughton's unease at Rathdowne's bluntness was evident in his expression. When his attempt at humour failed, he sunk into the closest chair and smoked his cigarette in silence.

Ignoring Laughton's witticism, Rathdowne motioned for Maggie and Atticus to follow suit and take a seat. "I'm not going to beat about the bush," he said, doing exactly that as he slowly took a drag on his cigarette. "The agent who was sending back surveillance on Oliver Preston, your man Edgar Ryan, has disappeared."

Laughton, Maggie and Atticus eyed one another in surprise.

Leaning forward, Laughton placed his elbow on his knee. "Define 'disappeared'."

"As in, hasn't reported in three days."

Laughton smoothed out his waxed moustache. "Why am I hearing this from you? He's my resource, not yours."

"Primarily because his handler sent you a message two days ago and you've neglected to respond, so he reached out to me. I'd say that's primarily why you're hearing it from me. Another way to say it would be 'dereliction of duty'." Rathdowne stabbed out his cigarette. It must have been for effect, as he'd only just lit the thing. "*Your* agent hadn't reported in three days, so *I* called *you* into this meeting to inform *you*."

"This is... this is highly irregular, even for you, Rathdowne." Laughton stood and paced. "This should have come through me."

"It did, twice. Your secretary confirmed it is still sitting in your inbox. You ignored it." Rathdowne pulled out a fresh cigarette.

Laughton pushed out his chest. "As head of the Northern Europe bureau I get dozens of messages every day—"

"That's just the thing," Rathdowne stood and placed his fists on the desk, the unlit cigarette dangling from his lips. "You're not the head of the Northern Europe bureau. Not anymore."

Face slapped with shock, Laughton eyeballed his friend Maggie for support. Wisely, she remained mute, waiting for the drama play out. All she offered was the slightest shake of her head, confirming that she didn't know what was going on either. Atticus was impressed with her restraint. Once she would have leapt up to defend her friend, but now she remained neutral, allowing events to unfold. She'd come leaps and bounds in recent months, her training and his mentorship paying dividends. She was becoming a field agent before his eyes.

There were politics at play here. Atticus despised politics. He didn't know what Mrs Abernathy had to do with all this, but he knew enough to let it alone and reassess later, when he had the facts.

Without any allies coming to his aid, Laughton sucked in air through his teeth, attempting to calm his escalating temper. "Why, may I ask, have I been removed?"

"Incompetence, mainly." Rathdowne lit his cigarette. While he tried to maintain his managerial persona, it was plain he was relishing the moment. "Maybe if you looked after your own turf instead of worrying about cleanliness of offices you would have known when your own people failed to report in. That's your bleeding job, Laughton. It's your *only* job. You should have come to *me* two days ago. Don't sit there under a helmet of Brylcreem and act all surprised. This place needs a complete overhaul and I'm starting with you."

Jaw flapping silently, Laughton's brain seemed to short out. After several attempts at speaking, he jerked his head towards Mrs Abernathy and managed to blurt out, "What's she got to do with all this?"

Rathdowne sneered. "She's the new head of the Northern Europe bureau."

"A *woman*? You're putting a damn woman in charge?" Laughton's arms flailed around. "You've lost your goddamned mind!"

"Giggy!"

Maggie's mouth was open wide in shock. It didn't interrupt Laughton's rant.

"She's a goddamn *receptionist*. Are you mad?" The

contemptuous sneer on his face gave his features a sinister veneer.

Rathdowne stood and rounded the desk, his red face the same hue as Laughton's. "Not as mad as a man who doesn't know where his own people are. Clear out your desk, you're through. Mrs Abernathy's replacement at reception has your severance cheque. Collect it on your way out."

"You've gone too far this time, Rathdowne. Too far! It's bad enough you've got a jigaboo running around, and now you're—"

The right hook surprised Laughton. He wasn't the only one who was shocked.

Rathdowne glared down at the wide-eyed and now terrified former head of the Northern Europe bureau, who lay sprawled on the floor. "You disrespect my people again and you'll have more to worry about than a bloody nose. Do we have an understanding, you snivelling little ferret-faced cretin?"

Standing unsteadily, Laughton puffed out his cheeks in bluster. A brief scan of the room was enough for him to realise he was without allies. Red-faced and full of impotent braggadocio, he stormed out, slamming the door behind him.

It wasn't the first example of ingrained bigotry Atticus had witnessed, but it certainly was the most dramatic. Systematic prejudice was familiar, and not just in the sixties. Even those who professed enlightened leanings often harboured racist and sexist beliefs, whether they admitted it openly or not. Laughton's proclaimed friendship to Maggie was nothing of the sort. Nor was his apparent admiration of Atticus's achievements. All it took was the slightest of nudges for him to tumble out of the bigoted cave he lived in.

But the biggest revelation was Rathdowne. It would be a complete lie for Atticus to call the two of them close. "Grudging acquaintance" was generous. They'd never been on friendly terms, but seeing Rathdowne to strike another man over a racial slur meant Atticus would have to reassess his opinion of the man. He had leapt in to defend Atticus without a second's hesitation. That went beyond loyalty to one's employees. Was it possible Atticus had underestimated the man?

"My, wasn't that lively?" It was the first time Mrs Abernathy had spoken since they'd entered the room. She rose from her corner position and sat at the edge of Rathdowne's desk. "I do hope the remainder of the meeting is more civil."

"Congratulations, Mrs Abernathy." Maggie gave her a little round of applause.

"Thank you, dear."

Atticus couldn't help wondering what the ramifications of this latest ripple would be. If he hadn't uncovered Oliver, MI6 never would have lost an agent in Latvia, and Laughton may never have been found wanting. Would this have further ramifications for history? Had he saved MI6 from a blunder Laughton would make in the future, or had he made it worse? The headache returned.

Bringing himself back to the present, Atticus forced himself to focus. While he supported a woman being promoted to such a prominent position, it was far from being the prime topic of conversation for him. "Will you allow me to head up the team to go get him now?"

"I won't," Rathdowne said, sitting down again.

Atticus balled his fists. "He's murdering our men!"

Rathdowne tilted his head. "You're so quick to anger, aren't you?"

"I'm not the one who just decked someone in his office."

Rathdowne ignored the jibe. "We don't know that he's murdering anyone. Edgar Ryan is *missing*. Those are the facts as we know them right now. No, I'm not sending you to seek your vengeance. That's not my call. You'd best speak to the one who will be running the operation."

Rathdowne turned to Mrs Abernathy. It seemed to amuse him to fluster Atticus. Despite unexpectedly leaping to his defence, it was likely Rathdowne hadn't forgiven Atticus for hauling him through MI6 as a supposed mole. It would take a long time for the sting of that to fade, if it ever would. Perhaps the two weren't as congenial as he thought.

"May I ask who you have in mind to head up the operation?" Atticus asked Mrs Abernathy.

"That would be me, dear." She smiled genially. "I'll be going personally."

"Personally?"

"Yes, that is what I said. This may come as a shock, but it won't be the first time I've been in charge of a mission behind enemy lines." She straightened her jacket. "It will be my ninth, in fact."

Atticus gave her a friendly bow. "I've heard stories about your previous exploits."

"Believe me, dear, whatever you've heard is a watered down version of what truly transpired."

"What I've heard is pretty graphic."

She pursed her lips, amused. "Like I said, watered down."

Atticus gave a slight chuckle. Her understated confidence was a trait he greatly admired. Even if he hadn't heard the stories of strangled SS officers, he wouldn't cross Mrs Abernathy if given the choice.

"I'd like to be considered for the mission."

Mrs Abernathy seemed to be sizing him up once more. "With you, it seems even the simplest of tasks ends in a shootout. If I were to bring you onto my team I would hope you could demonstrate more subtle attributes." She sighed. "Ones that don't result in gun fights, if at all possible."

"Sometimes the other side shoot first."

"If they do, then you've failed. Espionage is an art, not a bunch of Neanderthals clubbing each other with sticks."

"I... I actually agree with you. You're right."

Atticus was impressed. Mrs Abernathy had transformed into her role almost instantaneously. "I'd consider bringing you on, but I'd like to see some subtlety, some, dare I say it, tactical thinking."

Atticus suddenly felt like he was in a job interview. "That was my previous role. Tactical officer."

"Then let's see what you are now. First briefing is at fifteen hundred hours. Don't be late." Mrs Abernathy folded her arms. "Either of you."

"What?" Maggie's forehead creased in confusion. "Me?"

Mrs Abernathy tilted her head and looked Maggie in the eye. "As I hear it, you've passed all your field training with flying colours." She grinned. "In fact, they're some of the highest scores we've ever seen. Man or woman. You've earned your shot, young lady. It's time to test you in the field." She turned Atticus. "You two have worked together before; I assume that won't be an issue?"

They shook their heads. Now was not the time to rock the boat.

"So... we're going to go get him?" Atticus tried not to appear overeager. "We're going to Latvia to extract Oliver?"

"That won't be our primary goal, no." Mrs Abernathy shook her head. "We need to find out what happened to our man; *that's* our focus. Before that, we need to form a team. I have a couple of other names in mind." On seeing the disappointment on Atticus's face, Mrs Abernathy leaned forward. "Having said that, if there is an opportunity to haul the traitorous defector back with us and it presents zero chance of discovery or the potential to trigger World War Three, I will consider it. But let me be elementally clear on this point: our goal is to find our man. That is our only goal. Anything else is inconsequential unless I advise otherwise. Are we clear on this, Mr Wolfe?"

"Crystal."

Satisfied that her point had been received, Mrs Abernathy went on. "It will be risky work, fraught with danger and the likely chance of discovery every minute we're there."

Mind racing ahead to what the mission would look like, Atticus was overcome with concerns. "Oliver knows us on sight. He and Maggie were friends."

"I know. I'm counting on it."

Atticus's apprehension multiplied. "You're going to use her as bait?"

"What I do and don't use Miss Dunbar for is hardly your concern. Might I say, you seem awfully interested in her. Is there anything I should be aware of?"

Oh, she's good. Regardless of his mounting fear regarding Mrs Abernathy's plan, he couldn't help but admire the way she'd pivoted the conversation so expertly. She'd turned a question of safety into a personal attack in an instant, completely negating his query.

"Miss Dunbar knows Oliver better than anyone, and what better way to put her recent training into effect?" Mrs

Abernathy tilted her head, challenging Atticus to fault her logic.

Reading the lack of counterargument as agreement, Rathdowne slapped his hands together. "Right. Better go and pack your bags. You don't want to keep the Soviet Union waiting."

CHAPTER

SIX

Atticus had to yell to be heard over the roar of the Lockheed C-130 Hercules engines. "Where have you gents been stationed before?"

The recipients of his question, Cohen and Doyle, gazed at him blankly. Doyle, the taller and ganglier of the two, pointed to his ears and shook his head with a bemused grin.

Cohen, Doyle, Maggie, Atticus and Mrs Abernathy were strapped in place in the cargo compartment. The belly of the global lift transport would normally hold a hundred troops or a few tanks, but this one held only the five of them. They were the sole cargo of this chartered flight into the darkness of night.

Yelling, Atticus tried again. "Stationed, where?"

Cohen, the more solid of the two, with darker features, laughed amiably and shook his head. *Can't hear a thing.* Atticus gave a friendly defeated wave of his hand.

Doyle and Cohen had boarded the USAF transport about a minute before they took off from RAF base Fairford. There was no time for anything more than a cursory greeting before they were strapped into the rumble seats and were wheels-up.

They were headed to Ramstein Air Base in Stuttgart, then to Kolsås leir, a NATO air base in Norway. From there they would take a ferry to Estonia and cross the border into Latvia. The trip was to take them three days. That would give Atticus ample time to get to know the two new men.

Mrs Abernathy must have been reading his mind. She tapped him on the shoulder and handed him two manila folders. Inside were their MI6 personnel files. Atticus flipped them open and began to read.

Cohen was a highly decorated agent. Most notably, the lead MI6 operative on Operation Boot, which in 1953 orchestrated a coup d'état in Iran. When UK and US commercial interests were threatened, they sought to overthrow the democratically elected Iranian government. Like so many times throughout the century, it all came down to oil; more specifically, the West's fetish for controlling it. Cohen's mission was a success, but came at a cost that no one in this time comprehended.

Cohen's success set up the Shah to unpopularly rule for another twenty-five years before being toppled by the Ayatollah Khomeini. Maybe Ganim had a point after all. The West had continually ruined the Middle East for their own selfish reasons, time and time again. It wasn't Cohen's fault, of course, not directly. The orders came from on high. He'd just been the trigger man, and he did his job superbly well.

Atticus swapped folders. Doyle was no slouch either. He'd been the principal agent who'd recruited Colonel Oleg Penkovsky of the Soviet military intelligence, or GRU. Penkovsky had provided thousands of documents, including Red Army rocketry manuals, that allowed the

Allies to recognise the deployment of Soviet MRBMs and IRBMs in Cuba in October 1962. Without that occurring, the US could have had fully functional nuclear weapons on their doorstep and not known until it was too late. Indirectly, Doyle may have saved the world from nuclear annihilation.

On meeting the man, Atticus thought there was something familiar about Doyle but just couldn't put his finger on why. Not having been in the time period for long, Atticus hadn't met that many people. Yet, he was sure he'd met Doyle somewhere, but he just couldn't place where. It would come to him eventually.

These two men were heavy hitters in the espionage game. They had credibility and an extremely solid track record. Mrs Abernathy had chosen exceedingly well. Given her limited MI6 field experience, excluding her war record, combined with Maggie's inexperience, the two veterans augmented the team, balancing it out nicely. Atticus doubted he could have chosen a better team. He was liking the way Mrs Abernathy worked more and more.

With an approving thumbs up, he handed back the files. She accepted his acknowledgement with a good-natured dip of her head. It said, *I know what I'm doing.* Atticus wasn't about to argue.

He glanced over at Maggie to see how she was. She gave him a confident nod, but it was her eyes that put him at ease. She was a master at presenting outward calm, and over the last few months Atticus had become adept at reading deeper. Even when she tried to put on a brave face, he could always tell if she was troubled. Now, while there was the usual trepidation any field agent felt upon leaving for a new assignment, she was genuinely composed. The woman was far more formidable than anyone at headquarters realised.

Waiting until no one was looking their way, he gave her a sneaky wink. She caught it and screwed her mouth to one side to keep from smiling in return. It was plain she wanted to.

Taking his cue from years of experience, Atticus did his best to block out the ceaseless whine of the engines and closed his eyes. He'd need the rest.

JŪRMALA WAS FAR PRETTIER than Atticus imagined. Twenty-five kilometres west of the capital Riga, the resort town on the Baltic coast was studded with romantic Art Nouveau wooden houses, huge Soviet-era sanatoriums and long sandy beaches. There were concert halls dating back to the 1930s, lush parks and museums. Couples and families sauntered along the Lielupe River eating ice-cream and laughing, taking advantage of the unusually warm May day.

Only a small minority of the Soviet population could afford to leave their own country, and Baltic states like Latvia had become a sort of symbol of "holidaying abroad" in Europe. In Russia they had invented a word, *zagranitsa*, combining *za* and *granitsey* ("beyond" and "border"). Towns like Jūrmala were places where Soviet tourists could sample the wondrous and unfamiliar architectural styles, walk the alien sun-drenched streets, a world away from their dull grey existence. That was, of course, if they were granted permission to do so.

Jūrmala, in particular, was a favourite holiday resort for high-level Communist Party officials, including Brezhnev and Khrushchev. Atticus was reminded of the quote from *Animal Farm*: *all animals are equal, but some are more equal than others.* The town seemed to manifest the sentiment perfectly. It was a place for the elite, favoured by the most senior in the Soviet regime to holiday and relax. It was also a place to hang out if you happened to have betrayed your own country and committed treason.

Mrs Abernathy and Atticus rode in the back of a locally made GAZ Volga driven by Doyle. It was late afternoon, and the suitably red setting sun shone through the Spring trees on the quiet street. Atticus had never heard of the car manufacturer GAZ, but he figured the angular front grille was likely the reason this particular model was called the "The Shark". As they rattled around in the back of the heavy car, which had terrible suspension, being flung against the bare metal doors and with no seatbelts, Atticus thought a more suitable name would be The GAZ Deathtrap. Maggie and Cohen followed in their own Deathtrap, fifty metres behind.

Over the past few days Atticus had gotten to know the two new men. They were seasoned professionals who seemed perfectly happy reporting to a woman. The tall Doyle had a bone-dry sense of humour; he was easily mistaken for a tedious bore, but could be exceptionally amusing if one paid attention. Cohen, on the other hand, was more your run-of-the-mill boisterous beer drinking bloke. But as soon as they set foot on foreign soil it was clear that the two were consummate spies, fully aware of their surroundings. Atticus would enjoy working with them.

Mrs Abernathy was equally skilled. She'd run briefings and tactical updates like she was born to it. Her strategic planning was well crafted and thoughtful, but she was equally open to feedback and suggestions. The sign of a good leader was knowing when to accept feedback and when to insist that orders be followed without question. So far, she was well-balanced—in short, what all good field ops leaders should aspire to be.

The team had their assigned roles. Atticus was the tactician, second to Abernathy. Cohen was the group's scrounger, tasked with finding whatever they needed at short notice. Doyle was munitions and explosives. Maggie was in training, and Mrs Abernathy had tasked her to be across everyone else, ready to step in at any minute if needed.

Mrs Abernathy had even assigned their codenames for the mission. Maggie was Cricket. Doyle's codename was Post because, as Mrs Abernathy explained it, he resembled a lamp post. It was a suitably dry name for the man. Cohen was Snatch, due to his misspent youth as a pickpocket. Atticus was to be known as Shadow. Unsure if the name was racially motivated or a complimentary espionage moniker, he took it. Mrs Abernathy was to be known as Boston. It took the group a while to figure out that one, until Maggie mentioned the Boston Strangler.

The group's first task was to visit Edgar Ryan's apartment and determine if there were any clues as to whether he was still alive and his possible location. It would be their first test together. They were on the wrong side of the Iron Curtain with five million trigger happy Red Army troops eager to defend the motherland. They had to be ready.

~

IT DIDN'T TAKE LONG to check the place out. In fact, it took less than five minutes.

Atticus returned to the car and sat in the driver's seat. The entire team had piled into the one car and the atmosphere was getting a little ripe. The sun had set and there was a distinct chill in the air. Doyle was in the passenger seat; Maggie, Mrs Abernathy and Cohen in the back. All had broken out the warmer clothing.

"And?"

Atticus had cased Ryan's apartment to determine if it was safe to enter. He assumed his crestfallen expression had already conveyed the answer.

"The place is absolutely being watched." Atticus turned to the back seat. "Two by two teams front and back."

"You're sure? They weren't just a lip-flapping leaner or something?" Everyone in the car turned to Maggie. With a smirk, she elaborated. "A person who's not up to much at all."

With or without the Mod-speak, Atticus appreciated Maggie's scepticism, especially in a group dynamic, so they didn't all just agree with everything the others said. He shook his head.

"The way they did their best to appear casual but never took their eyes off the apartment for more than a second or two, there's no way they were just hanging out. They're good, too. Their positioning was right out of the espionage textbook. Separate positions, so if one view was obstructed the other had a clear line of sight. They're professionals." He rubbed his hands together to get some warmth. "And not that I want to racially profile anyone, but the watchers were definitely not local. Pointy chin, flat cheeks, protruding face and thick eyebrows. The only thing that would make them more Russian would be a fur hat and a tractor tucked under each arm. As soon as we open a door we'll have Soviets on us like winter on invading Nazis."

Cohen scratched the back of his neck. "What's racially profiling?"

Maggie stepped in quickly, so the question didn't hang in the air. "So that's it? We can't get in?"

Atticus gave a slanted grin. "Doors aren't the only way into buildings."

∾

LANDING LIKE A PANTHER on the tar roof, Atticus made sure his movements were as silent as possible. Securing the impromptu zipline system, he trod carefully across the rooftop of Ryan's apartment.

Atticus hadn't asked where Cohen had sourced the harpoon and steel cable so late at night, nor did he need to. He'd built a zipline across two buildings in record time. Their scrounger had done his job well.

Standing to confirm he hadn't injured himself on landing, Atticus turned and gave Cohen the thumbs up from the opposite rooftop above a boarded-up restaurant. In return, Cohen held up a black and white scorecard, giving Atticus's landing a nine out of ten. The zipline wasn't the only item he'd managed to appropriate. The scorecard was accompanied by a wide, cheeky grin. The man was not only an excellent scrounger but had an off-kilter sense of humour too. Atticus liked it.

It was freezing; the biting wind off the Gulf of Riga cut through his thin overcoat like knives of ice. What he wouldn't give for a North Face puffer jacket. The sooner Atticus made it inside, the better. In his day he would have sent up a few drones, used facial recognition to identify the surveillance team, and hacked into the local power grid to cause a power outage. Now he had no such luxuries. All he had was an untested team and a walkie talkie the size of a first-generation mobile phone that weighed more than a statue of Stalin.

He headed towards the roof hatch and pressed the talk button on the weighty comms equipment. "Heading in."

"Acknowledged." Cohen's voice seemed distant, even though he was only one rooftop over. "Nice landing, Slick."

"Thanks. One day you'll need to tell me where the hell you got the scorecard." Atticus opened the hatch and said in a low voice, "Start timer, mark."

He had five minutes to report back. The clock was ticking. Hypervigilant for any surveillance, he trod carefully. It was historically too early for pinhole cameras or motion detectors, but he proceeded like they existed anyway. The hatch wasn't locked. *Bless those trusting Soviets.* It took Atticus a minute to find Ryan's apartment. Using his own lockpicks, he made his way into the apartment stealthily, but there was no need for stealth. It was empty. Apparently, the opposition thought their outside surveillance was sufficient.

Stepping into the apartment, Atticus corrected himself. It wasn't complacency that kept the stakeout team outside. It was the stench.

Walking into the apartment proper, Atticus hit transmit on his sizeable walkie-talkie. "Shadow to Boston, over."

"Boston here, report."

"I have to report Edgar Ryan had appalling taste in home décor. It's all tartan and taxidermy. One is a bad enough, the two together is just a crime."

On the other end on the line, Mrs Abernathy sighed. "Need I remind you we have a missing agent to find?"

It wasn't heartlessness that spurred Atticus's attempt at a joke, it was purely a reflex mechanism. Like millions of soldiers before him, Atticus used gallows humour to cope with the horrors of war. He knew the awful scene he was about to face.

Atticus stepped into the bathroom. "I'm sorry to correct you, but he's not missing."

"I hate to correct *you*, my good sir, but the whole purpose of this endeavour is to—"

"I'm looking right at him."

"Is he alright?"

"He's just kicking back, having a bath." Atticus pinched his nose and breathed through his mouth. "Now, I don't know how they do things over here, but does one normally have a bath with a toaster?"

"Is he..."

"Looking like he's spent a week decomposing in a bathtub? Yes, he is." Atticus stepped backwards out of the lime green bathroom. "Smells like it, too."

The scene was horrific. The skin of the bloated corpse had turned black, and the water, now mixed with the death juices of a decomposing body, was just as dark. MI6 photographs showed a ruggedly handsome man with mischievous eyes, but that image had been replaced with a grotesquely distended and contorted corpse. The blackened blotchy skin still allowed identification of red and weeping scarring around the victim's neck. He'd been strangled soon after the electrocution, or vice versa. Either way, his killer or killers had been thorough.

With nothing to offer the dead man besides a few consolatory words, Atticus set about searching the apartment. There were minimal furnishings, a tiny kitchen, a two-seater table, two armchairs and a magazine rack.

Atticus attacked every crevice, every floorboard, every

ceiling tile. Eventually he found a secret tray hidden under the cutlery drawer. It contained a bound notebook.

Atticus flicked through it. It contained detailed notes of Ryan's mission. There were several entries Atticus had already seen back at MI6. The notebook must have been what Ryan had used to get his reports ready for transmission. It was sloppy spy work. Any transmitted material should have been immediately destroyed, not left around for the enemy to discover. Laughton hadn't trained his team well. No surprise there. Flicking to the last entry, Atticus saw it was dated the day Ryan had sent his last message. For some reason he couldn't quite put his finger on, Atticus smelled a rat. And for that to override the stench of rotting corpse, it must have been a particularly ripe rat.

Twenty minutes later Atticus had traversed the rooftops and made his way back to the GAZ Deathtrap where the rest of the team awaited him, four blocks away. After briefly describing the scene, leaving out the most gruesome details, he took a sip from the canteen Doyle handed him. It didn't wash away the bad taste in his mouth.

"How do we get him out?" Cohen voiced the thought they'd all had.

"We don't." Mrs Abernathy's tone was even. "The moment we do, we're blown. As far as the other side is concerned, no one has discovered Ryan. We need to keep it that way."

She was right, but that didn't make it any easier to accept they would be leaving a fellow operative to literally rot on enemy soil. Atticus didn't know Ryan, but every spy understood the brutal truth. It was an unglamorous profession. An ugly and untimely end could happen at any moment. Spies never received glory, recognition or ticker-tape parades. If you were lucky you went home at the end of the mission. If you weren't, you were left to decompose in a bathtub on the wrong side of the Iron Curtain.

To distract the spiralling mood, Mrs Abernathy asked to take a look through Ryan's diary. The atmosphere improved as they shifted their focus to their work. They agreed that the diary must be genuine, as the entries matched the reports they'd all seen. The only part none of them had seen was the last two pages, dated the last day he'd been heard from. The entry detailed how he'd finally managed to track Oliver to his house, a task he'd previously been unable to do.

"That's why he was killed, then," Doyle said from the front seat. "He'd found Preston and the blighters killed him for it."

Atticus said nothing, but watched Maggie's face as she examined the final entries of the diary. She tilted the pages to vary the angle of light, then drew the diary to her nose and away again. Forehead crinkled in concentration, she slowly shook her head.

"Oh, these buggers are good. I mean, very good." Her gaze didn't waver from the diary as she ran a finger over the ink. "They used the same pen, replicating the handwriting —it's almost spot on, but there's..." She drew the notebook level with her eye. "See here," she held it out to Mrs Abernathy, "the dots on the 'i's aren't exactly in the same place. The margins are slightly off, but the clincher is the pressure of the ink on these last pages isn't uniform with the rest of it. The last page is competent, but far from an expert forgery."

Cohen let out an extended sigh and scratched the back of his neck. "So, if this is a forgery..."

Doyle took up the thread, "... then the last entry giving up his address is..."

"... bogus." Mrs Abernathy completed the thought. "The blighters are setting us up."

The prime mission complete, Atticus was aware Mrs Abernathy could pull the pin. But her resolute disposition told him she had no intention of doing so. At least, not yet.

"It's a trap, obviously." Mrs Abernathy folded her arms. "The question is, what do we do about it?"

In the dark of the front seat, Atticus smiled. "Set our own trap instead."

CHAPTER
SEVEN

On the way to their safe house Atticus got to planning his trap, but he didn't get far before the pull of bed was too great. After exhaustive travel and a late-night clandestine operation, he needed sleep to function. The next day he'd be refreshed and able to concentrate for more than five seconds before his eyelids felt like lead.

As they weaved through deserted streets their sparse chatter fell away. They were all running on fumes. They collected the other GAZ Deathtrap and the mini convoy drove to the safe house on the outskirts of town. After the mandatory security checks, they unloaded the cars in silence. The house was nothing special: a solidly built holiday house in the forest overlooking the city. Secluded and defendable, it served their purposes.

As Atticus carried the last of the bags inside with Mrs Abernathy, she halted by the front door and dropped her bags, forcing him to stop as well.

"Can you two try and work it out?" Her impassive

expression made it difficult to get a read. It may have been her fatigue.

Atticus stared at her blankly. "Me and Oliver? Why would I need to—"

"No, you dunce." She gave a tired sigh. "You and Dunbar. I don't know what sort of disagreement you've had with that young girl but sort it out, will you? You're the older one, mend the bridge or fence or extend the olive branch or whatever cliche you want to clutch straws at, but make nice, alright?" She gave him a friendly poke in the chest. "You two have been avoiding each other like the plague since you boarded the plane in London. I'm not prepared to have this mission fail because two of my people had a tiff. Am I making myself clear?"

It seemed his and Maggie's efforts to appear less familiar had been taken the wrong way. They'd need to find a way to return their fraternisation to near-normal without revealing the true nature of their relationship.

"Yes ma'am. Crystal clear."

As if on cue, Maggie walked out the front door. "Anything left to unpack?"

"Funny you should say that." Mrs Abernathy motioned to Atticus. The gesture said, *you're on*. She disappeared into the safe house and closed the door behind her.

Turning curiously to Atticus, Maggie asked, "What was that about?"

"Apparently we need to get closer."

She took a step closer, a wry, vulpine smile on her lips. "That right?"

"Uh huh." He lowered his head. "Meet me in my room in twenty minutes and we'll see how close we can get."

"Sounds fun. Deal."

UNSURPRISINGLY, Atticus slept well. When he finally made his way downstairs, the rest of the team were eating breakfast. At the stovetop, Doyle had a tea towel slung over his shoulder and was tackling seemingly noncompliant scrambled eggs. Throwing them on some toast, he handed the plate to Atticus, cigarette dangling from his lips.

"Good timing, otherwise Cohen was getting thirds."

Cohen slapped his belly. "Oi, I'm a growing lad."

The team laughed as Atticus sat at the table. He did his best to avoid lingering too long on Maggie's shining face, lest Mrs Abernathy think the two had taken her encouraging words too far.

Seemingly unconcerned, Mrs Abernathy poured him a cup of coffee, black as night. It was the spy's default. Luxuries like sugar or milk could never be relied on. In the field, anything other than black coffee for breakfast was an anathema.

Absentmindedly taking a sip, Atticus took a double take at the beverage and had to drink more to be sure.

"It's good, isn't it?" Mrs Abernathy noticed his reaction. "Imported from Vietnam."

She wasn't wrong. It was better than he'd been able to find in England, and easily the best coffee he'd had in this timeline. He'd have to see if he could smuggle a few bags out with him.

"How goes the planning?" Mrs Abernathy didn't believe in wasting any time. "You're our tactician. I'm hoping for some tactical options."

"It's going." Apart from sleep and the pleasant distraction with Maggie, Atticus had thought of nothing else.

"You'll have a tactical options paper on your desk by twelve hundred."

That seemed to appease Mrs Abernathy. She pushed the local paper towards him to read as he consumed his eggs and surprisingly good coffee. He absentmindedly read the local propaganda rag, the Russian language *Sovetskaya Latviya*. It was a novelty reading an actual newspaper. He couldn't remember the last time he'd physically held one before arriving in the sixties.

Atticus glanced though various articles with varying levels of interest. There was one regarding increased agricultural yields. *Fascinating*. Another told in flowery prose of how a state official had graced a local factory with their esteemed presence. *Riveting*. The main article described how Khrushchev had pressed a button to set off an explosion to divert the Nile as part of the Soviet-financed Aswan Dam project. At least that was actually interesting. After spotting the final article on the front page Atticus stopped eating, fork hovering in mid-air.

He had it. Maybe. *That could work.* He reread the article, his mind racing, then pushed the eggs aside.

"Oi." Doyle looked downcast. "They're not that bad, are they?"

Atticus ignored him. "The First Secretary of the Communist Party of Latvia has died."

"That's very sad," Cohen said without peering up from his plate. "Should we do a whip around for some flowers?"

"No, I'm sure he'll get enough of those," Atticus's idea was still coalescing, "but don't you think a funeral is an ideal place for an opportunist who's trying to make a name for himself to do some networking?"

"Some what?"

Shaking his head, Atticus corrected his phrasing. "Socialising. Mingling. Social climbing."

Mrs Abernathy put her mug down and tilted her head. "What are you thinking?"

Warming to his idea, Atticus sat up. "Every holidaying Soviet official, every toadying sycophant sucking the dick of anyone in power will be there."

Cohen sat up, alarmed. He pointed at Maggie. "There's a lady present!"

"Like fuck there is." Maggie waved a dismissive hand. "You're thinking Oliver's going to poke his head up for the funeral?"

Cohen poked an egg-coated knife into the conversation. "All of a sudden I'm not liking where this chat is headed."

Maggie tapped the table, lost in her thoughts. "For all of Oliver's outward disdain for elite inner circles, he really longed to be part of one." She smirked, understanding Atticus's angle. "Narcissists are particularly prone to aggressive reactions towards love objects, not least when issues of self-identity are involved. In Oliver's case, his hatred of the very existence of an inner circle he wasn't part of may be the only emotion the sociopath ever felt." Maggie paused when she noticed everyone had stopped what they were doing to listen. She went on. "Research suggests love–hate relationships may be the result of poor self-esteem, and in Oliver's case, I'd say that's confirmed. He wants, no, *needs* to be accepted, even though he'd be loath to admit it. Stuck here, he'd want to ingratiate himself with the party lackeys or some Central Committee hacks. It'd be the best way to get ahead. What better opportunity than a funeral?"

Mrs Abernathy gave a pursed smile. "I see you've done some research on the subject."

"I'm not here for my go-go dancing." Maggie's

eyebrows danced. "I've been studying psychology. Amongst all the field training."

"Evidently." Mrs Abernathy steepled her fingers contemplatively. "Now, while I appreciate your enthusiasm, my dear, I'm afraid the Oliver you knew, or should I say, thought you knew—and please note that's not a poke, as he fooled us all—was a façade. The man we all saw didn't exist. How do you know the *real* Oliver wants the same thing?"

"Because there are some things you just can't hide." Maggie leaned forward, emphasising her point. "For all his professed hatred of the elite, Oliver was attracted to power. He craved it. Over here, without support, without friends, he'd be drawn to power like a moth to a flame."

Mrs Abernathy's usual staid exterior showed signs of buckling. She gave Maggie a sage bow of her head. "You make a compelling argument. I commend your well-considered opinion. Keep it up." Folding her hands, her back straightened. "What is it you have in mind, Mr Wolfe?"

Atticus stood and explained the broad brushstrokes of his plan.

After an elongated stunned silence, Cohen was the first to speak. "You, mate, are either the cleverest son of a bitch that's ever graced god's green earth or the most certifiable lunatic I've ever met."

Atticus tilted his head. "Can't I be both?"

"So, what you're proposing..." Mrs Abernathy sounded far from convinced, "is to not only find the man, but abduct him at the same time?"

Atticus clasped his hands behind his back. He remained mute, not wanting to overplay his hand.

"I'll give you one thing, it's efficient." Doyle wiped his hands on a tea towel.

"Thank you."

"I didn't say it was smart." There was a hint of humour in his eyes. It fell away just as quickly as it had arrived. "Are you sure about this?"

Cohen threw his cutlery aggressively onto his plate. "This is mad."

Atticus wasn't about to disagree. "Yes, it is."

"Where did you get this idea?"

"I guess I've watched too many *Fast and Furious* movies."

"*Fast and Furious?*" Doyle's forehead creased in confusion. "I'm not familiar with those, and I'm somewhat of a movie buff."

"Very arthouse. Very niche."

Maggie shot him an amused sideways glance, knowing it was one of his in-jokes she didn't understand.

Not wishing to get into an in-depth discussion regarding the cinematic merits of the *Fast and Furious* franchise, Atticus turned to Mrs Abernathy. "You wanted me to be a tactician. This is me tacticing."

She folded her arms. "That's not a word."

"I'm bloody in." Cohen rolled up his sleeves. "If for nothing else, in fifty years' time my name'll appear in some history book because of this. Or whatever they replace books with in the future. It'll either be a glorious victory or one hell of a spectacular failure."

"It means we're out of the country that much quicker, a two-in-one deal." Maggie bounced in her chair, energised by the discussion. "Tag him and bag him then we're out of here faster than a flashkicker on a Vespa on a blue Benny bender."

Maggie's comment was greeted with confusion from all present.

"Uh, a Mod on a scooter on amphetamines. Fast." Keen to get the conversation back on track, she placed her delicate hands on the table. "Atticus's plan is solid." She turned in his direction without making eye contact. "Mental, but solid. It has my vote."

Mrs Abernathy frowned. "This isn't a democracy, and nobody is voting."

Doyle stood, hand on hips. "What's the call, boss?"

Inhaling deeply, Mrs Abernathy's eyes swept across them. "You'd all better find something black to wear. We're going to a funeral."

ATTICUS GOT TO PLANNING. For the remainder of the day he worked furiously, subsisting on coffee and vengeance, designing the intricacies of his audacious plan. He put the others to work, researching, assisting, scrounging. Lots of scrounging.

When he gave Cohen his list of materials and equipment, the man's jaw dropped before he read it several more times. After the fourth read he tilted his head up, eyes wide.

"You *are* mad, you know that?"

Not about to disagree, Atticus left with Doyle to do some late afternoon reconnoitring. The venue of the funeral was briskly named Jūrmala's Bulduru Evangeliski luteriska draudze. The gothic revival building sat within a forested park area not too far from Jūrmala's town centre. They parked on the opposite side of the street and took in the building.

Doyle turned off the engine. "It seems a bit churchy."

"That's because it's a church."

"That'd be it then." The tall man scratched the back of his neck. "I would have thought given the Soviets' distaste for places of worship and all, this place would have been given a big fat nyet."

Atticus shrugged. He'd thought the exact same thing. "My guess is, in a resort town there aren't a lot of options to have a state funeral for a party leader. It was probably either here or a beach volleyball court."

Doyle nodded as if it made sense. The two sat in silence for a few minutes, bathed in late afternoon light. They watched several workers scurrying about, trimming hedges, attaching a flag bearing the hammer and sickle above the front doors and tidying the gravel path in anticipation of the State occasion the following day.

"How have you been, Lancelot?"

For a long time Doyle didn't respond, only staring ahead with a mute veneer of panic. To save the man from further anxiety Atticus went on.

"It took me a while, but I finally remembered where I knew you from. The Coven. The underground club Oliver took me to once. You were there under the name of Lancelot. I racked my brain for hours trying to place you."

Doyle gulped, his eyes rigidly focussed forward. "Is this a shakedown?"

Atticus understood the question. The group of underground homosexuals Doyle belonged to would be illegal in this time period. He could face jail time, certainly expulsion from MI6 and likely worse.

"Oh god no. Nothing of the sort. I just wanted to mention it in case you thought exactly that. You have absolutely nothing to fear from me. We'll never mention it again if you want. I just wanted to let you know that I remembered you, that's all. We're good here, believe me. Where I'm from homosexuality is quite common. Many of my friends are gay and no one bats an eyelid, as they bloody shouldn't."

Jaw dropping slightly, Doyle asked, "My god, where are you from? I want to live there."

"Maybe I'll tell you one day."

Doyle gave him a curious look but didn't press the matter. He inhaled deeply as if a weight had been lifted. They grew silent once more, though this time it was comfortable.

After several minutes, Doyle stretched. "For the record, I'd like to echo Cohen's thoughts on the matter. This plan is crazy."

In spite of the gruffness of his words, Doyle seemed oddly amused by their mission. Atticus was glad they'd moved on from their previous conversation.

"There is no record, and duly noted."

A wry smile crossed Doyle's lips. "Cohen thinks it's mad but still thinks it'll work."

"And you?"

The tall man shrugged. "Fifty fifty, I reckon. But I'll be in the getaway car blocks away, so it won't be my neck on the line."

"I appreciate your unwavering support."

"The plan needs more explosions, by the way."

"Spoken like a true demolitions expert." Atticus chuckled. "We do have some almost explosions. You'll be busy."

They watched the goings on at the not-church for a while. In the intervening quiet, Atticus's mind wandered. It had been weeks since he'd thought of Omar Ganim, and months since the man had suddenly appeared in Atticus's flat. He'd promised to be in touch, but since then there had been no contact whatsoever. It was possible the man was dead.

If not, Atticus would need to answer the question he'd been actively avoiding. Did he want to go home? He'd been unable to answer the question at the time, and since then he and Maggie and grown even closer. The more time that passed since the meeting with Ganim, the more theoretical the question seemed. It no longer interrupted him during the dead of night.

Doyle disrupted his thoughts. "How long you an' Maggie been together?"

It took all of his training to not react. *Are you a mind reader?* "Why on earth would you ask that?"

"I'm not daft, man." The normally dour expression carried a warmth Doyle rarely displayed. "I've seen you two trying oh so very hard not to intermingle. It's quite adorable. Mrs Abernathy thinks either Maggie's racist or you're sexist." He chuckled. "I didn't have the heart to tell her you're likely shagging when the rest of us go for a kip. She's a top bird, smart. You've done well there."

Atticus didn't respond, but instead studied the not-church for some time. A bombastic general arrived bellowing orders, chest full of big medals and head adorned with an even bigger hat. The two studied the goings on from afar.

"We're not Latvian." Doyle hadn't taken his eyes off the scene before them.

Atticus tilted his head in agreement. "No, we are not."

"Nor are we members of the local Communist Party."

"Another undeniable fact."

"Then, how exactly do you intend on getting us into a Latvian Communist Party funeral?"

"That's where Cohen comes in. If he gets us those

uniforms, we'll be fine." Atticus almost convinced himself.

Bobbing his head, Doyle's usual cheerless demeanour was back in place. "May I say something?"

"Always."

"I don't want to appear like some kind of bigot..."

"Now there's a great way to start a sentence."

"... but wouldn't you say you'll stand out ever so slightly? I mean, the only time I've seen a black Russian was in a cocktail bar." He rubbed his unshaven stubble. "I hope that wasn't offensive."

"Not only was it not offensive, it was funny. So, bonus points." Atticus motioned to the increasingly frenzied scene outside the not-church. "I think there will be so much pomp, a couple of well-dressed individuals will go unnoticed amongst the solemn pageantry."

"I hope you're right."

Atticus watched the overbearing general castigating a lowly private. "I do too."

The belligerent general moved inside, much to the relief of the castigated private, so Atticus and Doyle felt comfortable enough to exit the car. They took a leisurely stroll around the grounds and checked that the nearby streets adhered to the maps they had.

When they finally made their way back to the car, Atticus said, "We best get back. We've got a lot to do tonight. Hopefully Cohen's got all we need."

"I wouldn't worry. He always comes through."

As Doyle reached for the ignition, Atticus placed his hand on his companion's, halting him. He flicked his thumb towards the two figures exiting the building.

"Change of plan. We've got an errand to run first."

Doyle was right. Cohen had indeed come through. And then some.

In a matter of hours the scrounger had somehow managed to obtain every item on Atticus's extensive list and still had enough time left over to add a few of his own frills. Overnight they'd slept little, preparing, enhancing and rehearsing. They were ready.

Stepping into the bright sunshine, Atticus adjusted his Russian Navy Ushanka winter fur hat. In his dark blue dress uniform, he melded with the other officials converging on the not-church. There was a fine balance between not having too high a rank, which would draw too much attention, but ranking high enough to be admitted entry without question. Cohen had managed to source a uniform—he was cagey about exactly *how*—with the Naval rank of капитáн 2-го ранга or Captain, second rank. Atticus found it amusing that his fake Soviet persona matched his fake 'real life' persona of having come from the Navy. Thankfully he still hadn't been asked about yardarms.

Solemn mourners formed a respectful line shuffling into the not-church, and Atticus joined the throng. Ten metres ahead he spotted Maggie, positively resplendent in her green Russian Army military uniform. Her tight-fitting jacket with shoulder boards, skirt and a garrison cap called a pilotka seemed made just for her. The USSR belt buckle was a nice touch. Watching her shuffle forward in her uniform, there was no denying she was fine with five 'i's. It was enough to make a man defect.

He forced himself to get his head back in the game; Atticus had to stick to the plan. So far there was no sign of Oliver, but that could change at any moment. He cast his eyes east to where Cohen was sitting on a park bench feeding pigeons. He gave Atticus a scratch on his left ear.

The go signal. They were on—no identifiable threats. Ironic really, given that he was entering a building with several hundred legitimate enemies who would love nothing more than to execute an MI6 spy in their midst.

Minutes later he was inside. A young uniformed Private who served as usher, although Atticus was sure he wouldn't be called such, checked the rank on Atticus's collar and pointed him to the centre of the vast space. His eyes flared when he looked up and saw the colour of Atticus's skin, but he wisely remained mute. If there's one thing you can count on from a Soviet soldier, it's for them to follow orders without question. Firing squads really put a crimp in one's day.

There were several more sideways glances as Atticus made his way through the slow-moving throng. It was as he'd hoped: collectively, the mourners assumed he belonged. After all, what sort of idiot would draw attention to himself as the only black man for a thousand miles at the state funeral of the First Secretary of the Communist Party of Latvia?

Doing his best to appear smaller than he was, Atticus made his way towards the spot the Private had indicated. That was, until there was a sharp tug on his sleeve. Turning, Atticus was confronted with a sweaty, red-cheeked blob of a man who looked one vodka shy of a heart attack.

"Who the hell are you?" His tone was as angry as his face.

"If you value it, I recommend you remove your hand, sir." Atticus's Russian was perfect. "Before you lose it."

Momentarily put off by the other man's impertinence, the blob of a man, who wore the rank of an Army Colonel, faltered. "You... what are you doing here?"

"This is a funeral. I'm here to pay my respects."

"But you're..." The blob looked directly at Atticus's face or, more specifically, at his skin, "... from the Navy."

"I didn't know one had to be from a specific branch of our military to pay one's respects to an exalted comrade. Are we not all in the same anti-imperialism fight in defence of the international proletariat, combating the evils of capitalism to see the ultimate victory of the great and glorious communism cause?"

The man's sweaty eyes narrowed, seemingly unimpressed with Atticus's commitment to Soviet ideals. "I don't know you."

"Nor I you."

Atticus left the statement hanging. They had chosen a Naval uniform precisely because they'd assumed there would be hardly any other Naval officers present. That meant Atticus would be less likely to encounter questions as to where he was stationed and the like. They hadn't counted on the sweaty belligerent man before Atticus.

Even though a Naval Captain by no means outranked an Army Colonel, there was always more to one's station than just rank.

"But I do know Komandarm Sidorov *very* well." Atticus's words were slow and deliberate. "And I'm sure he would be interested in one of his men accosting a close personal friend of his at a State function for no good reason."

Commander Sidorov was the Army's supreme commanding officer of the region, reporting straight through to the Kremlin. Atticus's team had done their research. Sidorov was on manoeuvres and wouldn't be attending the funeral. The mere mention of his name caused the pugnacious Colonel to step back, the red hue to his skin turning distinctly white. Excessive intelligence gathering was rarely a wasted effort.

"I'm sorry for interrupting you, good comrade," the big man spluttered. "Please give my warmest regards to the Komandarm when you next see him. Good day."

Atticus gave the man a dismissive wave and continued on his way. It had been a close call, but he'd sent the nosy man packing. He hoped that would be the end of it.

Atticus kept a watchful eye on the backslapping, glad-handing and grovelling, but there was still no sign of their prey. It seemed many were jostling for a seat further forward, closer to—literally—the seats of power. The mahogany coffin was closed and surrounded by wreaths and enlarged black and white photos of a wrinkled, humourless man with bushy white eyebrows. The dearly departed.

The crowd grew thicker by the second, making it difficult to see anyone other than those directly in front. Several loud coughs from the front of the not-church told the crowd proceedings would be starting soon and they should take their seats. The jostling resumed in earnest.

An encroaching sense of despondency descended on Atticus. They still had no target. For a moment, he thought his plan had failed. They'd come all this way, put their lives at risk, for nothing.

Then he wasn't so despondent anymore.

Atticus made his way through the crush, doing his best to go undetected. Smiling politely, he used his best Moscow accent to thank people for letting him past. When he finally took his seat, he sat still for a moment before turning to the man to his right.

"Hello Oliver."

EIGHT

There was only one word for the look on Oliver's face: shock.

It was as if he hadn't expected the man from the future who he'd fooled into believing was his friend and then shot in the leg to sit next to him in a not-church in Latvia. If he was so inclined, Atticus could have tossed M&M's into Oliver's open mouth. He wasn't so inclined. Plus, he didn't think M&M's were a thing yet.

"Perhaps we should converse in Russian," Atticus said in flawless Russian.

"That would be wise," Oliver glanced around sheepishly, "given present company." Nervously, he peered over both shoulders, as if looking for someone.

"Speaking of company, if you're after Alaksiej Barinov or your messenger Mikhail, it's unfortunate but their car is strangely having mechanical issues."

The two figures Doyle and Atticus had spotted exiting the not-church the day before were Barinov and Mikhail. They'd followed, but the two hadn't led them to Oliver. Instead, they had driven to a small hotel on the outskirts of town. The small room they occupied was barely big enough for one person, let alone two or three. If they had found Oliver, the whole plan would have changed. Instead, they augmented it.

Doyle had returned overnight and disabled the fuel system of their car. Given the simplicity of the Latvian built GAZ, Doyle advised it had been a simple procedure. He'd insisted it would appear as wear and tear, and would not arouse suspicion.

"You are certainly..." Oliver pushed his glasses back. "I shouldn't be surprised, should I?"

"No, you really shouldn't."

His shocked demeanour was steadily turning nonchalant. "I could yell to attract the attention of the KGB?"

"You could." Maggie turned. She'd sat on the pew next to Oliver when Atticus had made his introductions and hadn't noticed her. "But you'd bring them down on me too." She shrugged.

Oliver's nonchalant attitude was wiped away in an instant. Maggie raised an eyebrow and grinned. She seemed to be enjoying her new role as a field agent.

When Mrs Abernathy had first formed her team, she had intended to use Maggie as bait. Atticus could see the logic, but didn't support it. She'd been Oliver's only friend. They bought each other birthday presents, cared for one another when they were ill. Even after his mask had fallen and the traitor had been revealed, he'd given Maggie her mother's top-secret file, the one she had been searching for her whole life. That wasn't the act of a traitor, it was the final act of a friend. Oliver cared about Maggie. He wouldn't expose her now. She wasn't bait, she was their strength.

Trying to wrestle control of the conversation, Oliver

said, "Wouldn't it have been easier to follow me after the funeral?"

"Perhaps," Atticus shrugged, "but given the number of people, you could easily be lost in the crowd and we'd go back to square one. I hate square one. Hate it. I just want to punch square one in the dick."

Their former confidante bobbed his head, conceding the point. His mannerisms seemed more self-assured, or at least, more self-assured than the Oliver they'd known. Atticus remembered what Mrs Abernathy had said the day before. The man they had known was a lie, a counterfeit personality designed to hide in plain sight. In fact, if it wasn't for Atticus, Oliver would have remained an undiscovered mole, a veiled infiltrator causing unknown havoc throughout the Cold War.

They spoke in hushed tones, seemingly unnoticed by the rest of the congregation, who were equally engaged in conversations at this important schmoozing event. Despite being at a funeral, no one seemed particularly upset— outwardly glum, certainly, but there wasn't a wet eye in the house.

"I have one question, Oliver." Maggie's voice was devoid of emotion. She was handling her first overseas deployment far better than Atticus had. "Why? What made you do it? We were friends, I thought I knew you. You betrayed everything. You..." Her voice broke, but she recovered quickly. "You sold out your country. I want to know why. I deserve to know why."

Oliver shook his head mockingly. "If you're asking, then you'll never understand. I thought I'd make a difference at," he eyed those around them, "at my previous organisation. Help forge a bright future. Instead, I found the privileged class who were hellbent on preserving their past, their station in life. Don't you dare have the audacity to tell me the leaders of your country have their subject's best interests at heart. They're in power so they can retain that power, not share it." He shook his head. "The Soviet Union is far more enlightened than you've been led to believe. The role of women for one." He pointed at Maggie. "Here they're equal—well, more equal than in the so-called enlightened West. Here you never would have been left to languish in a typing pool. They would have recognised your brilliance for what it was. They still can."

"I'm fine where I am, thank you." Maggie folded her arms. Oliver had tried to tempt her behind the Iron Curtain before. He'd been rebuffed both times.

Shrugging as if he'd expected the response, Oliver went on. "Everything is better here, more equal. Citizens don't starve on the streets while the elite dine on venison in their country estates. All people are welcome here, the Soviet embraces all lifestyles."

Atticus assumed Oliver was referring to his homosexuality. If so, he had some bad news. Russia's future certainly wouldn't be the all-embracing utopia he seemed to expect.

Oliver looked Atticus up and down. "I suppose this is about your telephone?"

Atticus was amused that Oliver had used the word Телефон, telephone, the most accurate word the Russian language had at the time for a mobile phone device.

"It had crossed my mind. It must be quite the interesting paperweight, given that you won't be able to charge it for another fifty years."

Unsettlingly, Oliver gave Atticus a knowing smile. "You didn't tell me I didn't need a, what was it you called it, charging wire?"

"Cable."

"Yes, that." He smiled once more, growing more self-satisfied by the second. "But our scientists—"

"It's already *our*, is it?" Maggie sneered.

"— determined that the telephone only needed to be *near* a power source to charge, am I correct?" Oliver waved a dismissive hand. "Oh, I forgot, I don't need your validation. It is true, and your phone is one hundred per cent charged."

But you haven't unlocked it yet or you would have been gloating about that instead. Thank you, Oliver. It should have been a relief, but it wasn't. Now the Soviets had a charged phone it was more likely they'd be able gain access to the secrets within. Then the game would well and truly be over.

"It is asking for a fingerprint. I don't suppose you'd like to provide it, would you?" Even though he spoke in jest, there was anticipation in Oliver's eyes.

"Afraid not."

"Pity." Oliver shrugged. "I suppose I don't need you alive for your fingerprint though, now do I?"

"No, but you need my biorhythmic field data if you're going to unlock the phone." On seeing Oliver's blank face, Atticus added, "On the fingerprint scanner, it needs an identifiable heartbeat consistent with biorhythmic data the phone has collected previously. That is, I need to be alive to unlock my phone or what you have there really is a high-tech paperweight."

It was, of course, complete bollocks. There was no such thing as biorhythmic field data, although it definitely sounded like there should be. The hesitancy in Oliver's manner suggested he'd bought Atticus's on-the-spot bullshit.

If Oliver and the Soviets somehow unlocked the device, the implications were incalculable. Besides the technology itself, the Cold War history books inside meant they could manipulate developments in a period of radical global transformation to their own ends. The implications of a superpower with strategic foreknowledge, as well as a nuclear arsenal, was a truly horrendous scenario. The Soviets could right every wrong before their mistake had even been made. They would roll over the rest of the world as a big red steamroller, all-knowing and unstoppable.

As for the technology itself, if the Soviets could somehow replicate the microprocessors years before anyone else, the world would be irrevocably altered for the worse. Atticus's device had more processing power than all the computers on the planet combined. With computing power a billion times better than anything in this time, the USSR could very well land on the moon first. They'd leapfrog the likes of Japan in technology developments and be a powerhouse unrivalled anywhere else in the world.

The only people on Earth who understood the threat sat in a huddle in an overcrowded not-church. For a moment Atticus thought it may have been easier to strangle the man then and there. Sure, he'd be executed, but he'd take them both out. The neatness did have a certain symmetry to it.

"You won't win." Oliver stared at the whitewashed ceiling.

"That right?"

Shaking his head condescendingly, Oliver patted Atticus's knee. "That's always been your failing. You think in terms of good and evil. Black and white."

Atticus raised an eyebrow.

Oliver went on. "Humanity is neither of those things. The..." he switched to English in a hushed voice, "Soviet regime is excessive, yes." He switched back to Russian. "But with the right hand, the right advice, it can be the answer for the ills of the world, for *all* of the world."

Was that it? Was that what Oliver was truly after? This went far beyond escaping a firing squad in his home country. He wanted to shape the world as he saw fit. He wanted to ensure a global Soviet victory and mould its very nature.

It was possible Atticus had greatly underestimated Oliver's ambition. He wanted to reshape the world. The weight on Atticus's shoulders grew heavier by the second.

"What is it you wish to achieve here?" Oliver gestured vaguely to the room. "Gallivanting aggressively about an enemy's country is hardly the wisest course of action."

"You might want to tell your lapdog Mikhail."

"Ah, the incident at Harrod's." Oliver sighed. "He was tasked with observing you only. He, uh, became a tad enthusiastic. I must have told him too much about you. He was too curious for his own good. He wanted to see what kind of man you were. He was reprimanded."

"I'm all choked up about that."

"I come back to my question. What do you want? It's not like you can drag me out of here."

Atticus checked his watch. "Oh, we're just about to leave."

Oliver shook his head, more confused than ever. "But I—"

He didn't finish his sentence. From the front pews there were several alarmed calls of "курить". *Smoke.* They pointed beyond the coffin to the not-altar.

Most people stood as they saw white smoke billowing from behind the pulpit. Several people near the aisles were already out of their seats and walking backwards, fear etched on their faces. Women screamed, and distressed murmurs rose to a crescendo.

Extracting his small pistol, Atticus poked it into Oliver's ribs. He shook his head in warning. *Do nothing.*

Atticus was impressed by the smoke charge Doyle had set. It was terrifyingly good. Although it was far bigger than they'd agreed.

Taking her cue, Maggie rose to her feet and pointed towards the smoke-engulfed altar. In a terrified voice, she screamed, "Огонь!" *Fire.*

That was all the assembled masses needed. As one, in a cacophony of screams and panicked yells, they stampeded towards the one exit. Women and men jostled, shoved, pushed one another, propelling themselves outward, the venerated Soviet comradeship forgotten in an instant. Within a minute the space was empty, save Oliver, Maggie and Atticus, sitting alone on their pew.

"Now what?" There was no denying the man was rattled. "You kill me?"

"Funny you should say that."

It took an hour, but once the smoke had cleared, the funeral recommenced without incident. No one seemed to notice there were a few less people in the crowd.

The delayed start allowed enough time for Barinov and Mikhail to resolve their car troubles. They arrived flustered and ultimately confused. Despite their frenzied search, Oliver was nowhere to be seen.

When the funeral recommenced, there were endless elongated speeches about the tireless work comrade First Secretary of the Communist Party of Latvia had made for his country, the Soviet Union and the world. They were as sincere as a gulag firing squad confession.

The only glimpse of human emotion came when the First Secretary's son took the microphone and spoke of love and family. He was soon ushered off in favour of some white-haired bureaucrat speaking of ideology, common ownership of the means of production and socioeconomic order.

The son's brief words reminded Atticus of his own father. He wondered how he was getting on. Was he changed, now that he had no longer been stabbed in the back? Did he think back to the strange, vaguely familiar man he'd met ever so briefly? The fleeting thoughts of family were soon forgotten; Atticus had a mission to complete.

Once the speech givers had finished or the assembled crowd had fallen into comas, the party elite rambled out of the not-church. There would be no burial. No graveside lamentations. In line with other Soviet leaders, the good First Secretary would be embalmed and entombed in a crypt worthy of his standing. All mourners were on their way home.

From a distance, Atticus watched Barinov and Mikhail linger at the entrance of the not-church. They appeared increasingly confused by Oliver's absence. It was highly likely he'd pressured them to get him an invite, and then seemingly hadn't showed. Eventually, they too left.

Atticus pulled down his peaked cap and joined Doyle in the front seat of the hearse. He still found it bizarre that there were no seatbelts in cars. It was force of habit to buckle up as soon as he got in.

"All good?"

Doyle bobbed his head. "Can't complain."

The two wore the white coats of the funeral parlour. The heavy casket sat behind them, strapped in the rear of the heavy black undertaker's limousine. Up close, the coffin was more ornate, elaborately decorated with gold trim. So much for collectivist austerity.

The two original designated drivers had been bribed to look the other way for an hour. Doyle had promised them the return of the hearse and the First Secretary unharmed. He'd been so convincing, Atticus had almost believed the promise himself. Their price had been four Picnic chocolate bars and a packet of Smiths crisps. *Who said capitalism wouldn't win?*

Doyle started the hearse, and they took off slowly. The streets had quickly emptied of black-suited bereaved communists. The sun was out and the sky was clear. Uncluttered roads and overhanging green trees would give most people pause to enjoy the scenery. Atticus had no such thoughts. The mission was far from over.

The two men travelled in solemn silence for a few minutes before there was a rustling in the back of the vehicle. It was soon followed by muffled sounds of anguish and several thumps against the interior of the large mahogany coffin.

Doyle sniffed. "Sleeping Beauty's awake."

After a pause the screaming started.

Atticus checked his watch. "Cohen said the drug should have knocked him out for five hours."

"He stole it from a vet, said it was for a horse. I don't think they have human dosages on 'em." Doyle smiled. "Look at it this way, better he woke up now than in the middle of a funeral service."

From inside the coffin, Oliver screamed obscenities in English, Russian and Yiddish.

"Oliver!" Atticus yelled to the box behind him. "Behave or we start digging."

The statement granted them a few seconds peace. "You locked me in here with a fucking corpse!"

"Don't be a baby. He can't harm you." Doyle turned to Atticus, and in a low voice asked, "Communists don't turn into zombies, do they?"

"I'm pretty sure that's not a thing."

Shouting behind him, Doyle addressed the resident in the coffin. "Don't be a big baby. Communist zombies aren't a thing."

Muffled in the mahogany coffin, a confused voice said, "Zombies?"

Reaching backwards, Atticus lifted the lid of the coffin. Inside was a distressed traitor and the strikingly white corpse of the Latvian First Secretary. Oliver's face was beet-root red, his misted-up glasses askew. His hands and legs were bound; he wasn't going anywhere in a hurry.

"Stay quiet and you just might survive this." Atticus aimed a Makarov pistol in his face. "But first you're going to tell me where my phone is. You have three seconds."

The plan was for Oliver to take them to Atticus's phone, then they'd smuggle it and Oliver into Lithuania, and from there onto a fishing ship bound for Scotland.

"What phone?" Doyle took his eyes off the road for a second. "We weren't briefed on a phone."

Ignoring the question, Atticus pulled back the hammer of the pistol and tilted his head at Oliver.

In spite of his panic, the recent citizen of the Soviet Union shook his head. "You won't shoot me. You *need* me. Without me, you'll—"

The gunshot was deafening. Doyle swerved, but quickly corrected. Oliver screamed, gawping at the smoking bullet hole that had appeared in the coffin lid between him and the body of the already quite deceased First Secretary.

"I'm sorry, did I break your concentration?"

Atticus thought it ironic that he was quoting *Pulp Fiction* while aiming a gun in a moving vehicle. He assumed the other passengers didn't mind him mixing scenes.

"Now, I'll ask again. Where's the phone, Oliver?"

All previous arrogance had disappeared. The two bodies in the casket were as white as each other.

Oliver glared at Atticus wide-eyed. There was nothing but fear and hatred there now. Atticus had no doubt what would transpire should the situations be reversed.

Doyle adjusted the rear-view mirror. "I think we have company."

Atticus scanned the road beyond the coffin to see a black town car rapidly gaining on them. He dropped the lid of the coffin. It landed with a thud on Oliver's head, who yelped once more.

"Does this thing have any juice?"

Doyle gave a sly smirk. "My son, this is a GAZ-13 Chaika. One-ninety-five horsepower, V8." He glanced at Atticus's blank face. "It's got juice."

"Hit it."

Doyle floored it. It took a few seconds to kick in, then the behemoth of a vehicle lurched forward, pinning the two men to their seats. Atticus picked up the walkie-talkie.

"Boston, do you copy? We've been made. Repeat, we've been made. Unlikely to make rendezvous point. Over."

"Copy Shadow. ETA two minutes."

Atticus saw how close the encroaching sedan was. "We don't have two minutes. Over."

He dropped the radio. Despite the extra speed, the car was gaining on them. The light reflected off the windscreen made it impossible to see who was at the wheel, but they could certainly drive. Doyle was no slouch, either. He expertly slid the colossus of a car around corners, taking a perfect racing line. For once Atticus was thankful it was the days before traction control. He wouldn't have minded a seatbelt and a few airbags though, just in case.

Atticus wondered what he'd do when the car behind caught up. He needn't have worried. That wasn't the car he should have been concerned about.

Another black sedan roared through the intersection and smashed into the hearse at full speed. The crash was horrific. The heavy metal vehicles crumpled into each other, scraping, careening, grating and colliding in a sickening spectacle. The hearse spun several times. Without seatbelts, Doyle and Atticus were flung about the cabin, becoming part of the chaotic wreckage.

When the crumpled ruin of a car finally thudded to a halt, it lay across the road, completely blocking traffic both ways. Atticus groaned deeply. He was bruised, but his lungs seemed unimpaired. Nothing broken. A minor miracle.

The car, however, was a wreck. The engine had taken the biggest hit, but as the goliath of a car was steel, the damage didn't seem as severe. Not that it mattered; it wouldn't drive again. The coffin still appeared intact, but that wasn't Atticus's priority.

He turned to his teammate, who lay beside him against the bare metal of the door. "Doyle, you with me?"

The tall man grunted, his left side slick with blood. "Think my arm's broken."

"Can you fight?"

He sucked in a lungful of air. "It's not my firing arm. I'm good to go."

"Good lad. I'm going to open the door. You head towards the engine block, it offers the best protection. Got me?"

"Roger."

The two men fell out of the car to a hail of bullets. Thankfully, they were on the opposite side of the car. They returned fire blindly, unsure how many they truly faced. As far as Atticus knew there were only the two cars. That could mean anything from two adversaries to ten. Either way, he didn't like the odds.

They kept firing, hoping to miraculously nail one from the other side. In return, their adversaries pelted the hearse with bullets. If they hit the casket enough times, a large part of Atticus's problem would be solved, but not all. If possible, he wanted the man alive to deliver him the phone. But if his only option was a dead Oliver, he wasn't about to lose sleep over it.

Swapping out clips, Atticus did the same for the one-handed Doyle. He was pale, but the lanky bastard was holding it together. He was a good man to have in a crisis, and this situation certainly qualified as such. They were pinned down, immobile and, given the volley of shots coming their way, outnumbered.

The two returned fire. There was a cry from the other side and the volume of fire decreased. Atticus lifted his head around the hood, aimed and fired. Best he could make out, there were four attackers still active. He was familiar with half of them: Mikhail and the assassin known as the Red Scorpion, Barinov. Not exactly Atticus's ideal adversaries. The firing from the other side petered out.

"Hello again!" Mikhail's thick accent was unmistakable. "It is surprising the people you meet when travelling abroad, da?"

Doyle winced. "You know this joker?"

"We went shopping together once." Atticus shouted to

the other side of the hearse. "Don't suppose we could call it a draw like last time?"

Mikhail chuckled. It was forced. "Nyet. You made mistake coming here, black man. Perhaps you are not as smart as Oliver thought, hmm? Why don't you give yourselves up? Where is it you think you will go?"

"I have a better idea. *You* give yourself up and I'll only shoot you a little bit."

"I see why he likes you." Mikhail's voice took on a harder edge. "Where is Oliver?"

"He's gone the way of your poor First Secretary of the Latvian Communist Party, I'm afraid."

The fact that Oliver hadn't made a noise since the accident could mean the statement was accurate.

"I'll kill you!" Mikhail emptied an entire clip, his shots wild and undisciplined.

The severity and passion with which the statement was delivered made Atticus wonder about the nature of Mikhail and Oliver's relationship. Doyle noticed too, giving Atticus a *what's that guy's problem?* look. Being upset about the demise of the man you were assigned to protect was one thing, but Mikhail's reaction was far more personal. *Interesting.*

From Doyle and Atticus's side of the road, two GAZ cars careened towards their position at what could only be classified as ludicrous speed. The first car skidded and the driver yanked the wheel so it slid to a halt ten metres short of their position. The second screeched to a halt behind it, shielding it from further gunfire. It was a good strategy. Only one car would take the majority of the fire.

Mrs Abernathy was the first to exit the vehicle, cigarette dangling from her lips. She hoisted an AK-47 to her shoulder and fired. She was joined by Maggie, shooting two pistols at once. The suppressing fire sent their adversaries diving for cover. This was their chance.

"Come along, children," Mrs Abernathy waved at them, "time to go!"

Atticus grabbed Doyle by the scruff of the neck and hoisted him onto his feet with a wince. The two crouched low as Mrs Abernathy and Maggie strafed the other side.

"Time to haul arse, people." Mrs Abernathy swapped clips effortlessly.

Doyle slipped from Atticus's grip twice. The tall man was slick with blood and Atticus's rubbery arms were struggling to keep him upright. Sprinting to their position, Cohen took Doyle's weight. He gave Atticus a curt nod. *I've got him from here.*

"You get to the other car. We'll take this one, it's closer." Cohen motioned to the lead vehicle. "Go on. Get a wriggle on."

Not about to argue with the man, Atticus sprinted towards the other two. He addressed Mrs Abernathy. "But Oliver's in there."

She acknowledged the statement and fired a short burst to keep Barinov from raising his head above the hood of his car. "And there he will have to stay." She jutted her chin further up the road. "Look."

Behind the assailants, two more cars raced towards their position. Even if all the immediate threats were neutralised, there wouldn't be enough time to extract Oliver before they arrived.

The hearse blocked any cars from getting across. They could make a clean break for it, but it had to be now. Cohen was already behind the wheel of the other car.

"He was never our prime mission. He stays." Mrs Abernathy's tone left no room for argument. "Get in. Now."

As much as it chafed, Atticus knew that not only was she in charge, but was right. With reinforcements, the battle would grow bloodier and more one-sided. They couldn't win.

This wasn't over, not even close, but in order to correct things, Atticus had to live. If they stayed, he and every member of the team would be dead in minutes.

As the other two continued to dispense suppressing fire through the open windows, Atticus jumped into the driver's seat and slammed the door shut. Cohen's car lurched forward, laying rubber as it did. Atticus did the same, taking the lead. While Maggie and Mrs Abernathy gave a collective sigh of relief, Atticus stuck his head through the side window and watched the scene of the confrontation grow smaller by the second.

Instead of the other GAZ keeping pace, it was far behind, snaking wildly with sparks sprouting violently from the rear of the vehicle. The tyres had been shot out. Cohen and Doyle would never make it out alive.

"Hang on."

Without waiting for a response, Atticus dropped the clutch, pulled the handbrake and yanked the wheel. The heavy vehicle did its best impersonation of a one-eighty-degree turn. He floored it, heading back to the scene of the firefight at an alarming pace.

"Are you mad?" Maggie asked, not realising the plight of the other two.

"Most likely."

"Oh." Maggie and Mrs Abernathy exclaimed simultaneously once they saw the sparks coming from the too-distant GAZ.

In the second they had before they re-entered the fray, both women reloaded. Without having to be asked, they poked their heads out the window and fired to protect their teammates.

Screeching to a halt, Mrs Abernathy flung open her door.

Atticus gave a wave to the two pale men. Cohen half-carried, half-dragged an ashen Doyle with him. They were in the car in seconds.

"Alright, lads? Need a lift?"

Atticus put the car in reverse and hit the accelerator. Their foes were all too close through the front windscreen. Mikhail stood on the roof of the hearse. He gave him a one-finger salute that turned into a finger gun.

When there was enough distance between them, Atticus executed the fastest three-point turn in history and sped away. He zipped through the streets, perpetually scanning for any further surprise attacks.

Cohen wheezed in the back. "Thought we were done for. Thanks mate, we owe you one."

Checking his mirrors, Atticus gripped the steering wheel tight. "I do like a single malt whiskey."

As the distance from the scene grew by the second, Atticus relieved pressure on the accelerator and thought back to Mikhail's gesture. It was less a farewell, more a promise.

CHAPTER

NINE

I f there was a way to do so without making the situation worse, Atticus would have called for an ambulance.

The way Rathdowne reeled about his office, red faced, arms flailing, it was enough to think the man really was in the midst of a cardiac arrest. He wasn't, though. At least not yet.

The three sat on the opposite side of his desk: Mrs Abernathy, Maggie and Atticus. Doyle and Cohen had mercifully been reassigned. Atticus felt like a naughty high schooler being reprimanded by the principal. Given the nature of his youth, it wasn't an unfamiliar sensation.

The office was virtually empty, save for the desk and chairs. The filing cabinets, piles of papers and boxes were all gone. The entire office building was the same. The official move would happen on the weekend. As of Monday, MI6 would have a new home. None of this was front of mind for Atticus, however. The only thing that held his attention was Rathdowne's increasingly red face.

"I sent you to discreetly," he pointed at the three of

them in case it was unclear who he was referring to, "let me say that word again, but slower this time—*discreetly*—find out what happened to our man. If it was prudent to do so, you were to put mild surveillance on Oliver Preston, if doing so would not arouse suspicion. In your defence, I didn't explicitly state that you were not to blow up a state funeral, although I would have thought that was implied."

"We didn't blow it up, as such." Mrs Abernathy was as cool and businesslike as always. "A bit of fake smoke, that's all."

"The CIA claimed it was an out-of-control blaze."

"The CIA also claimed the Bay of Pigs was a splendid idea." On seeing the anger unchanged on Rathdowne's face, Maggie added, "And I am not helping."

"It wasn't a blaze, Oscar." Only Mrs Abernathy used Rathdowne's first name. "It was a controlled smoke bomb." She shifted in her seat. "Look, the report doesn't give you context. Our missing agent was confirmed dead. We deduced that the most likely location to, if you'll excuse the term, smoke Preston out, was the funeral and we were right. I approved the plan to extract him to home soil without the other side finding out."

"While," Rathdowne checked the report in front of him, "kidnapping the First Secretary of the Communist Party of Latvia."

"It was more borrowing than kidnapping."

Rathdowne shot Atticus a withering look. Like Maggie, Atticus concluded he wasn't helping matters.

"Whose plan was it?" Rathdowne's question was for Mrs Abernathy, but he glanced directly at Atticus.

"I approved the plan." Mrs Abernathy's back was rigid. "It isn't a democracy. I was in command. It was completely my call."

Rathdowne sighed, realising that was all he'd get on the question. "You failed to capture him anyway, started a fire-fight in the middle of town and nearly got yourselves killed in the process."

The small group was quiet. They weren't about to argue the facts.

"It was a cock-up." Mrs Abernathy sighed heavily. "I take full responsibility. It was my call, we failed."

Exhaling loudly, Rathdowne stroked his moustache contemplatively. "I'm going to try and smooth this over upstairs. I can't promise there won't be blowback, but I'll see what I can do."

"Thank you, Oscar."

Atticus suspected that if he'd been in charge, the conversation wouldn't have ended there. He turned to Mrs Abernathy. "It was a good plan. A solid plan, given the limited intel we had. Mrs Abernathy conducted a well-oiled operation and should be commended."

He particularly remembered Mrs Abernathy firing an AK-47 with a cigarette hanging from her mouth, eyes ablaze. It wasn't an image one forgets in a hurry.

"Thank you, dear. It seems avoiding shootouts isn't confined exclusively to missions under your command. I believe we'll both need to do better in the future."

"Well," Rathdowne planted his fists on his hips. "While you all congratulate yourselves on a job well done, I have to go justify this to the Minister. Unless any of you want to take my place."

"I would," Atticus partially put up his hand, "but I have a spin class."

Rathdowne huffed and turned his back. Maggie turned and mouthed, *What's a spin class?* Atticus gave her a dismissive, *I'll tell you later* wave of his hand.

"Oh, and Dunbar," Rathdowne turned to Maggie, "the theory you had about the operators at Teufelsberg sending sweet messages to each other? The Berlin Station ran with it."

Rathdowne explained that MI6 agents in Berlin had taken greater notice of the operators entering and exiting the transmission station, giving each an assigned name. They matched the messages to who worked on a particular day, then blackmailed a young woman into revealing what she knew or the details of her secret romance would be handed over to her superiors. She cooperated.

They only managed two meetings with her before she disappeared, likely nabbed by the Stasi. One piece of intelligence confirmed Oliver worked for the KGB and had been recalled to Moscow. The coldhearted way Rathdowne mentioned her fate was another reminder of the deadly game they played.

Atticus saw Maggie's shoulders sag, perhaps realising the ramifications of her theory playing out in the real world. An actual human being had been blackmailed, then likely killed. They'd unpack it later, but it was another lesson for the new field agent. Their actions had consequences; some fatal. It was the harsh reality of their profession. The decisions they made could condemn one individual, or a million.

"Your assumption was right." Rathdowne's voice sounded more positive for the first time. "Oliver was likely attending the funeral to start his climb up the KGB ladder. The little weasel is making a play and we don't know what it is."

The fact Oliver had even joined the KGB was odd. When Kim Philby slipped behind the Iron Curtain he was certain he'd be embraced by the KGB, only to discover they distrusted him and placed him under what was essentially house arrest. Why Oliver garnered special treatment was a mystery to MI6. Atticus held more specific suspicions.

"All of you go home, you look like hell. Don't come in tomorrow. We'll meet up on Monday to see if any of us still have a job."

It was critical Atticus retained his position at MI6. Given how close he'd come to nabbing Oliver and the phone, he needed all the resources he could muster. The newfound knowledge that Oliver was gearing himself up to be some sort of world-shaping Nostradamus *and* a key member of the KGB meant it was more critical than ever. The man wanted to mutate the world, shape it as he saw fit by subverting the course of history.

Atticus was the only person in the world who could stop him.

No one bore the weight of the mission's failure more heavily than Atticus. That was because no one besides Maggie understood what that failure meant. On the long haul home he'd come to an uneasy conclusion: if MI6 gave up on stopping Oliver, it would be up to Atticus to do it himself. If he had to go rogue and infiltrate the USSR, then that was what he'd do. He hoped it wouldn't come to that, but given Rathdowne's irritation it seemed unlikely the man would authorise another mission anytime soon. Atticus vowed to find a way to stop Oliver permanently.

Nobody was about to argue with Rathdowne's order to head home. The last week had exhausted them all. The frantic escape out of Latvia to Scotland and the uncomfortable train ride back to London had done little to relax them. The three hadn't slept properly in days, and had been running on nothing but adrenaline and coffee. They needed sleep.

Minutes later, Atticus and Maggie stood zombie-like in their tiny office.

"I'm so knackered." Maggie rubbed her eyes. "I'm not even sure I'm still awake, I'm that tired."

She yawned with her eyes closed but kept her mouth open, tilting her head back as if she'd fallen asleep standing up. Atticus wasn't sure she was faking it.

"You could always stay at my place."

Maggie's eyes snapped open and she grinned. "Maybe I'm not that tired."

"WHERE THE HELL HAVE YOU BEEN?"

It was not entirely what Atticus had expected when he opened the door to his flat. His expectations mostly entailed he and Maggie ripping one another's clothes off. Instead, he was confronted by a dishevelled old man in his seventies with unkempt hair and a scowl that could curdle milk at a hundred paces. He sat slumped in the same armchair he'd sat on months earlier.

"I could ask you the same thing." Atticus threw his duffel bag on the floor.

Maggie stepped through the threshold and recoiled at the strange man sitting in her boyfriend's flat. She threw her bag down next to Atticus's.

The old man grunted. "Who's this?"

"This is Maggie." Atticus nodded to the other man in the room. "Maggie, this is Omar Ganim."

Maggie strode over and shook the old man's hand. The two men shared no such pleasantries.

"You both smell awful."

Maggie sighed. "He's a charmer, this one."

Eyeing his kitchen, Atticus scowled. "Did you... go through my kitchen?"

Various boxes of food had been removed from the cupboards and not returned. In fact, the whole place seemed to have been searched.

"I was looking for Pop Tarts."

"It's 1964."

Ganim shrugged. "You might have brought some with you."

Atticus shook his head incredulously. He highly doubted Ganim had been searching for sugary treats. It was more likely he was after Atticus's smart watch, and/or the keypad. Both of which were well hidden. Originally stored at Maggie's, they now resided behind fresh brickwork in the caverns beneath Covent Garden.

"Brought some with me? Like, just in case I travel through time today I'd better stuff some Pop Tarts in my pockets. You never know, right?"

Ganim sat up straight, alarmed at the mention of time travel.

Atticus gave him a dismissive wave. "Maggie knows all about me, you," he shrugged, "everything."

"I'm sure she does." Ganim assessed Maggie from head to toe and back again. "I can see why you were unsure if you wished to return home."

Ignoring the comment, Atticus asked, "Where have you been?"

"Like I said, I had to do the necessary work, work through the calculations, find components and such."

Ganim's demeanour put Atticus on alert. He was hiding something. But what?

"That was four months ago."

"Granted, it took longer than anticipated, but—"

"You didn't call. No letter, no postcard, nothing. I thought you were dead."

"I'm touched you were so concerned." Seeing that his snide remark was not met with humour, Ganim's features darkened. "I've been busy."

"Perhaps you could tell me why you've come to us now?" It was plain Maggie saw the escalating tension and wanted to step in to calm the mood. "Because as far as I can tell, all you've given Atticus is some bullshit nebulous promises without offering one concrete piece of scientific proof you can reverse what you've done. My suggestion is for you to either drop the mysterious pretence and talk to us like we possess intelligence above that of a Yorkshire Terrier or Atticus tosses his well-hidden keypad in the Thames. That clear enough for you?"

Then again, maybe she didn't want to calm the mood at all.

"I like her." Ganim pursed his lips. "Fine, sit down and let's talk shop, shall we?"

Atticus pitched Maggie an impressed grin and the two sat.

"Let's start at the beginning, shall we?" Atticus did his best to dispense with any emotional investment and approach Ganim as someone he was interrogating. "How does this all work? The time travel?"

Ganim wobbled his head as if it were a reasonable question. "It all hinges on Einstein's theory of general relativity, and his theory of gravity. According to the *theory*, space and time can bend so much that time wraps back on itself. All you need to do is warp a piece of spacetime. I managed to do just that."

"Uh-huh." Atticus wasn't in the right headspace for such a discussion. He doubted he ever would be.

"Okay, let me back up." Ganim held up a hand. "Are you familiar with the work of Seth Lloyd?"

"Let's just assume I'm not."

"Okay, he did some experiments with quantum teleportation in a laboratory at MIT. The experiments were the moral equivalent of sending a photon, a particle of light, a few billionths of a second backwards in time. He wanted to test out certain paradoxes of time travel; primarily, the grandfather paradox." Ganim leaned forward, warming to the topic. "In which a time traveller goes back in time and accidentally, or on purpose, kills their own grandfather, resulting in him never being born and never going back in time. Without getting into the detail, he tried to get a photon to kill its former self, for want of a more elegant explanation. He failed. He failed because he wasn't thinking big enough. I simply rewrote his quantum teleportation parameters."

"And?"

Ganim faced his palms outward and swivelled about the room. "And here we are."

With a heavy sigh, Atticus realised this was only the beginning of a conversation that would definitely give him a headache. "Right. How's all this powered? It's probably a tachyon field, isn't it?"

"A..." Ganim frowned, "... what?"

"Or is it chroniton particles? A quantum singularity?" Atticus snapped his fingers. "Wait, a nebula? It's always a fucking nebula."

Mouth flapping open, Ganim shook his head. "What are you on about?"

"Have you run a level three diagnostic?"

Face descending into utter confusion, Ganim asked, "Are you having some kind of a fit?"

"It's from *Star Trek*. I'm just messing with you." Atticus finally smiled.

"Star..." Maggie tilted her head, "is that the one with the laser swords?"

"Never watched it." Ganim flicked his hand dismissively.

"As a scientist, how can you not have seen *Star Trek*? That's like an archaeologist never having seen *Indiana Jones*."

"Oh, I'm a scientist now, am I? You've been calling me a terrorist up until now."

"I'll call you Lindsay Lohan if you can pull this off."

"I thought you wanted answers?" Ganim was unimpressed at being mocked.

Atticus's tone turned sombre, and he did his best not to turn towards Maggie. "I have one question I'd like an answer to. Can I go home? You said it was theoretically possible, but you had to do research first. You've had plenty of time for that. So, let's have it: can I get home?"

Ganim leaned forward, seemingly pleased at the question. "Finally, he asks the right thing." He waited long enough to create a dramatic pause. "I believe so."

"What's going to be there when I get back?"

"I... I honestly don't know. I can't say I can get you home because your *home* no longer exists. There's no home to get to. It's gone forever." Ganim seemed to revel in the shock on Atticus's face. "But I can get you back to your own time. Just don't expect everything to be the same."

"How so?"

"Things will definitely be different, some subtle, some not. It's impossible to say. Perhaps the English get really good at football. Maybe they don't discontinue Panda Pops. Perhaps flared trousers never go out of style."

For a second Atticus recalled his father and how he would no longer be nursing a stab wound in the back. What ramifications would that have had? Would Thomas Wolfe have found another way to become bitter at the world, or would that one event set him on a different path?

The thought was fleeting. Familial outcomes were minor compared to the main question that plagued his thoughts.

"Maybe the West loses the Cold War?"

Ganim laughed. "Yes, even that perhaps."

Reluctantly, Atticus turned to Maggie. She wasn't happy, Atticus assumed because he seemed so keen to get home, to leave her. It was a topic they'd actively avoided. As time had worn on and the distance from his last interaction with Ganim grew longer, the discussion seemed less urgent and more and more theoretical. Now it seemed all too real. He wished he could pause Ganim and talk to her privately, but they forged all on.

"What exactly were you researching all these months?" It seemed Maggie was done merely observing the conversation.

It was a good question, one Atticus hadn't asked yet. The conversation really was turning into an interrogation.

"I don't like your tone, Miss."

"I don't like your evasiveness." She folded her arms. "You better start supplying answers because we're both tired and cranky and, as you so kindly pointed out, smell awful. So cut the crap and get to the point."

Ganim nodded. He hefted a leather-bound folio from beside his armchair and plonked it onto his lap. The pages of the heavy tome were full of scientific formulae, scribbled notes and diagrams.

"You're a sharp one." Ganim poked a thumb towards

Atticus. "How did you get stuck with him?" On receiving no answer, he went on. "What I've been working on is researching the computational power required to process the teleportation parameters. The smart watch of yours won't cut it. The best computer in this era has perhaps just enough juice for the job. It has a processing speed of three megaflops, or 300,000 floating point operations per second."

"In English?" Atticus asked.

"It's a machine that does math good."

Maggie grinned. "Perhaps something in between?"

"We need a machine that can handle the calculations required to send you home. That's the CDC 6600."

"Okay." Atticus was relieved they were talking less theoretical science now. "Can we buy one?"

"Absolutely. Do you have three million American dollars on you?" Ganim hefted his eyebrows. "But I think it may be easier if we go to it. It's in Bloomington, Minnesota." He shrugged. "I mean, if you had an ancient iPhone 5 on you, it would be two and a half billion times faster than the 6600." He shrugged. "Without that, Minnesota it is."

Inhaling deeply, Atticus rubbed his palms down his pants. It had to come out at some stage, it may as well be now.

"Remember months ago, you asked if I'd brought a smartphone back with me?"

"I do." Ganim sat up. "Don't tell me you've had a phone with you all this time?"

"No, I haven't."

With a sense of relief, Ganim exhaled. "That's good, otherwise you would have wasted a lot of my time, young man."

Atticus held up a finger. "I don't have it with me... because it was stolen."

Atticus gave Ganim it all: Oliver's initial assistance in this time, his betrayal and theft of Atticus's phone. With each revelation the old man's shoulders slunk lower.

"Well, then." Ganim slammed his folder shut. "We're not going anywhere, are we?" He rubbed the bridge of his nose. "Do you know what untold damage this man can do if he unlocks that phone?"

"I have given it some thought, yes."

"So, this individual," Ganim's countenance was deeply contemplative, "his betrayal to MI6 was unknown to you, in your time?"

"Yes."

"So..." Atticus could see Ganim's wheels turning. "This man, Oliver, was never uncovered. He likely remained hidden throughout the Cold War?"

"It seems likely. I know about the Cambridge Five and the like, but Oliver Preston wasn't a name I was familiar with."

Ganim shook his head. "You've disrupted the timeline far more than I would have thought possible, Atticus Wolfe."

Bowing his head slightly, Atticus thought it best not to mention his father and the stab wound. As much as he was trying to avoid doing so, Atticus was stepping on butterflies wherever he went.

"I, we, were on a mission to get Oliver back, and to get the phone."

"I thought the mission was get you home."

"That's one of my missions. But the first priority is to ensure I have a home to go to. In order to do that, I have to find Oliver."

Atticus explained the books in the phone and the knowledge Oliver would possess if he gained access to them. As a power-hungry member of the KGB, his influence was growing. If Oliver and his new allies were to succeed, Atticus would never be able to go back to his own time—it would no longer exist.

"Now we need to change his present to prevent that future from unfolding at all costs."

The shock on Ganim's face was unmistakable. This was not what he'd expected. He wasn't the only one.

"Here I was thinking I could bury some gold, go back to our timeline and retire in a hideously large mansion and live off Uber Eats every night." He shifted in his chair with a wince. "This complicates matters considerably."

Face crinkled in confusion, Maggie asked, "What's an Uber eat?"

Atticus was thankful for a distraction. "Uber Eats is an app on your phone where you can have cooked meals delivered to your door within minutes. Whatever you desire, Vietnamese, Thai, pizzas—anything, really."

The expression on Maggie's face was as if he'd just explained that magic was real. In an era where everything was home-cooked and eating out was a luxury, to Maggie it must have been like being told she could have her own *Star Trek* replicator.

"Anything will just get delivered to your door?" Her face was blank in amazement. "Whatever you feel like?"

"Anything." Atticus couldn't help but smile. "Even ice-cream if you want. Or donuts. Or crepes."

Maggie blinked, incredulity creeping in. "Now you're just playing with me." She leaned forward slightly. "Aren't you?"

"I'm really not. Any day of the week, use your phone, order what you want, and it arrives at your door."

Maggie appeared gobsmacked. "The future truly is amazing."

Ganim glanced up, amused. "Wait till she finds out about global warming and TikTok challenges." His face turned serious. "But returning to the point. How do I put this delicately? You've gone and fucked everything. If your man unlocks that phone—"

"I know." Atticus snapped, then softened his tone. "I know."

"You need to stop him."

"I *know*."

Ganim stood and his bones literally creaked. "Best you get on with it, then. I'll keep researching. If you can get the phone back it will give us far superior processing power. It will also mean we can perform the operation from anywhere. If you can't get the thing back, destroy it. The Western powers were bad enough, but if the USSR gets hold of—"

"I'm getting really sick of saying I know, old man."

Ganim hobbled towards the front door.

"How do I contact you?"

"I'm staying at Grosvenor House."

"That's some fancy digs." Maggie's tone was impressed.

"A little bit of foreknowledge does help one live." Ganim shrugged. "I have been fortunate in a few business dealings."

He took Maggie's hand and regally kissed it. Turning to Atticus, he simply gave a curt nod and walked out the door.

"Ganim." Atticus waited until the man faced him. "I'm going to assume you will never let yourself into my flat again."

With a shrug, Ganim said, "Sure, you're welcome to assume that."

Atticus shut the door with such force it could be classified as a slam. The most infuriating thing was, Ganim was right. Regardless of his sudden appearance, Atticus's mission remained the same: find Oliver, get the phone.

Everything depended on it.

CHAPTER
TEN

Century House was a step up in quality from MI6's old Broadway digs. The 22-storey glass building located at 100 Westminster Bridge Road was brand new. Well, brand new by 1964 standards.

If Atticus's memory served, the new secret location of Britain's Secret Intelligence Service wouldn't remain secret for long. It would soon be referred to as London's worst-kept secret, known to every taxi driver, tourist guide and KGB agent. Still, at least the offices weren't so cramped, and the desks matched.

The day was mostly taken up by endless reports and debriefs. Mrs Abernathy had taken to the role of handler effortlessly. She charged through the paperwork while protecting her people from overly close scrutiny. Atticus hoped he'd get to work with her again soon. For many reasons.

The movies make espionage look sexy, endless overseas junkets to exotic locales with constant adventures. In Atticus's experience it was mostly paperwork. What made it worse was it was literally paperwork. He was forced to use a typewriter. No automatic spell checker, no cut and paste. Just endless pecking, permeated with creative swearing when he realised he'd have to start the page all over again. He really did miss computers.

He distracted himself with the promise of the night to come. Atticus, Maggie, Mary and Alexander were off to drinks and then to hit The Flamingo, the hottest nightclub in town. Word had it that last week Mick Jagger and Aretha Franklin had the place jumping as they twisted the night away on the dance floor. Mary had promised there would be at least one Beatle there tonight. As much as Atticus loved his work, the chance of hanging out with the Beatles in their prime was distracting. He'd even settle for Ringo.

Checking every department with even the most tenuous link to the goings-on behind the Iron Curtain, no one had a lock on Oliver. If the intelligence about being recalled to Moscow was true, no one had seen him there. He'd disappeared off the map. Either the failed attempt to capture the man had driven him further underground or he really was six feet under. The last Atticus had seen of the man, he'd been stuck in a coffin in the middle of a firefight. He could be dead, but Atticus didn't think he was that lucky.

If Oliver were alive, Atticus doubted MI6 would stumble upon him in any more holiday snaps. Finding him would require dedication, tenacity and resources. And it would take far more than that to convince MI6 to launch another mission to stop him.

Filing his fifth report of the day, Atticus stretched. He'd started early and it was going to be a long night. Time to call it a day.

As if on cue, Pillar stuck his head through the door. "Still here? I heard Rathdowne was looking for you."

Atticus checked the time. Nearly six. "I'll catch him tomorrow. I've got a date."

"Have you now? Anyone I know. She have a friend?"

Atticus gave a faint frown. At least the toff wasn't trying to humiliate or belittle him. Now whenever Atticus saw Pillar, the chinless wonder pretended to be his friend. He didn't know which was worse.

"No to both. Have a good night."

"You too, mate."

Atticus winced.

Heading to the bathroom, he splashed water on his face. Atticus had to admit he was tired. There were still dark rings around his eyes. He needed more sleep, but he'd be damned if he was going to miss a chance to go drinking with John Lennon.

Straightening himself up, he made his way outside. Maggie had gone home to change, then he'd meet her, Mary and Alexander out the front of Century House. As far as Mary and Alexander were concerned, Maggie worked for the Bank of England and Atticus was in insurance. It helped that Century House contained several insurance firms, and it was a tedious enough cover that no one asked many questions.

The plan was that they'd make their way to the Old Vic for a drink and then on to The Flamingo at a fashionably late hour. It would be Atticus's first real Swinging Sixties night, and he couldn't wait.

When he saw his friends across the road, he realised it really was to be a true sixties experience. Alexander wore a bright purple velvet suit and a white feather boa, and Mary a short little cocktail dress with flamboyant beads draped around her neck. But that wasn't what captured Atticus's attention. Maggie was resplendent in a pink and black short A-line dress, matching baker boy cap, fishnet stockings and go-go boots. All of a sudden, Atticus was less interested in a night out on the town.

He crossed the road and greeted the group with kisses, hugs and small talk. Still not quite out of work mode, Atticus spied something out of the corner of his eye. While the new MI6 offices were better appointed and more spacious than the last, there was one blatantly concerning aspect: they were built next to a petrol station. That was the driving force that prompted MI6 to move to Vauxhall Cross in the nineties. The National Audit Office had labelled the location "irredeemably insecure". Atticus agreed, but as nothing ever happened to the building, he paid it little mind. That was, until he saw the man in the brown coat.

In the forecourt of the petrol station a battered ex-military truck with canvas flaps was parked close to Century House. An attendant from the station was shouting at the man, telling him he couldn't park there. It was slightly odd, but that wasn't what garnered Atticus's interest. It was the man in a brown coat sprinting away from the truck that drew his attention. The man wasn't just running, he was *running*. Holding up his hand to halt Alexander's observations about the latest record releases, Atticus squinted at the running man.

Atticus's back straightened, his whole persona changed. His companions all stopped talking as they instantly noted the transformation into espionage-mode.

"I say... what the devil's got into—" Alexander didn't get to finish.

"You all need to get off the street. Get everyone you can to follow you. It's not safe here."

"What... what is it?" Maggie's face was a melange of emotions. Concern at not wanting her friends to know what they really did for a living. Fear at knowing Atticus was truly concerned and was deadly serious. "Atticus?"

He turned to her. "Mikhail is here, he just ran from that truck."

Like Atticus, Maggie's deportment shifted in an instant. Raising her voice, she began shouting to anyone within earshot. "Gas leak! Everyone, run!" Motioning startled people towards the nearest corner, she waved her hands, directing them to safety. "This way! Come on you lazy sods, move your arses!"

Atticus gave her a nod of thanks. He took a step towards where Mikhail had sprinted. Mary grasped his arm, alarm in her eyes.

"What are you doing? You're an insurance salesman, what do you know about—"

Ignoring her, Atticus tore after Oliver's henchman. It was a tough call. If the truck was what he thought it was, there was a chance he could disarm it in time. Then again, he had a chance to catch Mikhail on British soil. Plus, the truck might be remotely detonated, so he had a chance of stopping it if he caught up with Mikhail. Two to one. Atticus ran.

Two hundred feet ahead, Atticus watched Mikhail and his brown coat sprint left onto Kensington Road. Atticus was fast, even in his fancy dress shoes, but not fast enough to catch sight of the man once he'd rounded the corner. There were four streets connecting to Kensington and his prey could have torn down any one of them. Realising his time was better spent checking out the truck than running blindly down London streets, Atticus turned and headed back up Westminster Bridge Road. He hoped he'd been wrong about the truck. He could apologise to his friends over a drink soon enough.

The explosion knocked him off his feet.

The blinding white flash was followed by an enormous orange fireball. The concussion blast sent Atticus sprawling and knocked over bins, scooters and pedestrians. The windows of every car in the street were blown out. People staggered from their vehicles, bloody lacerations lacing their stunned faces. Windows all along the street had been shattered. Panicked cries, horns and screams soon followed.

Scrambling to his feet, Atticus ran towards the mayhem everyone else was running from. The hardly-a-day-old MI6 headquarters was a ruin. Half the glass-fronted building had been blown away. What remained was either actively on fire or a cleaved-out ruin. Burning bits of paper flitted in the air like hellish birds flapping through ashen clouds.

The street was strewn with debris. Dazed civilians had rallied and were trying to find survivors in the nearby buildings. Distant sirens grew louder. The scene would soon be alive with those trying to help, as well as those who would endeavour to try and make sense of the senseless destruction.

Maggie raced around the corner into Atticus's arms, distress and relief fighting for dominance on her delicate features. When she finally caught her breath, she asked, "Who would do something like this?"

There was only one answer. There would be no Beatles tonight. Only revenge.

THE COTTAGE GARDEN WAS QUAINT. Very Hobbiton. A stone path wound its way through a lush garden to an equally quaint semi-detached cottage. It seemed the owner of the

Islington house had quite the green thumb. But Atticus wasn't there to discuss gardening tips.

As he strode towards the dwelling, he tried to focus on the revenge he would take for the attack. It was difficult, as his rage was intermingled with the burden of guilt. Indirectly as it may be, Atticus had caused it. All of it. Every death that night was on his hands. In his past, the building was never bombed. That meant his presence in this time had, in a roundabout way, caused those people to die. It may have been Mikhail who set the explosives, likely at Oliver's behest, but it would not have happened if Atticus hadn't been forcibly thrown into this time.

He could talk about unforeseen circumstances and good intentions all he liked, but the darker parts of Atticus's brain knew the terrorist attack never would have happened if he hadn't come to the past. Every death in and around the MI6 building was on his hands.

That was why he was here. He had to set it right. He *had* to.

Atticus rang the doorbell. There was no answer. He glanced at the cold empty streets. After several more moments, he rang it again. Eventually he heard a commotion behind the wooden door. When it was finally wrenched open, the bathrobe-clad owner recoiled. Below the knee length of the bathrobe Atticus could see trousers and socks, indicating he'd disturbed the homeowner undressing.

"Bloody hell, man. Do you know what time it is?"

"Yes, I do." Atticus's voice was even from grief and exhaustion. "I need to talk to you."

Inhaling deeply, the man seemed to contemplate his options. Finally, he grunted, turned and entered the dwelling. It wasn't much of an invite, but it would do.

It was past 3 am and it felt like the rest of London was asleep. There was a reason these two were not.

"Tea?"

"Sure."

The men were silent as the owner boiled the kettle on the old stovetop and made a pot of black tea. From there, Atticus was led into the study. As per usual, the man took his position behind the desk. Even in his own home, Rathdowne liked to flex his power.

Atticus knew Rathdowne had just arrived home, as he'd been waiting outside most of the night. Given his position at MI6, Rathdowne had been granted permission to pass the permitter set up by the London Fire Brigade within an hour of the blast. Atticus received no such privilege. After several attempts to get closer he gave up, saw Maggie home and went to Rathdowne's home to await his return.

Sitting in Rathdowne's home office, Atticus balanced his cup and saucer on his lap. It was plain the man wasn't in the mood for pleasantries, so Atticus cut to the chase.

"How many?"

"Twenty-seven dead, sixteen injured enough to need hospital. That's just our people. Probably more in the nearby estate. We'll know in the morning. Those numbers would have been a lot higher if the thing managed to ignite the petrol tank. Fire brigade said the truck was positioned to, but the station was almost out of petrol. Tanker was late, if you can believe that."

Atticus didn't have an answer, so remained quiet.

Taking a sip, Rathdowne spoke without looking up. "Why are you here?"

"I saw the man who did this. It was Mikhail, wearing a brown coat. He ran from the truck a minute before the explosion."

Rathdowne's expression remained dispassionate. Atticus sensed there was more to it than mere exhaustion.

"That your story, is it?"

"My *story*? Why would I need a story?"

"Well, witnesses did see a man running away from the scene prior to the explosion." Rathdowne ground his jaw. "Yet no one mentioned a man in a brown coat. They did, however, see something else."

"Which was?"

"You. Three witnesses saw you running from the scene."

"I wasn't running from the scene, I was chasing—"

"Mikhail. So you say."

"Listen, I don't know what you're getting at, Rathdowne, but—"

"I was looking for you today." Rathdowne's interruption was harsh. "I had... some questions."

"Sounds ominous." Atticus tried to keep his tone light, but it felt hollow.

"For good reason." Rathdowne placed his hands in his lap. "As part of the move, MI6 human resources undertook an assessment of their files. What to take, what to destroy and the like."

Atticus was overcome with a sense of dread. "Okay?"

"They found your folder; it had been misfiled."

"I hope someone hung for such an outrageous offence."

Rathdowne sighed. "Then the team found some... irregularities."

Oh hell. Atticus fought the urge to eye the exit.

"If one was to give it a cursory glance, it appeared fine. But when investigated more closely, well, do you know what they found?"

"Amelia Earhart?"

Atticus noted Rathdowne's hands remained out of sight behind the desk.

Unimpressed, he went on. "Human resources took the suspicious documents to Forgery, and surprise surprise, they determined they were indeed forgeries. All of them. Every bleedin' document. Then phone calls were made. You never attended Oxford. The people named on your letters of recommendation don't know you. The Navy has never heard of you."

"I can explain... I think."

"Remind me, who was it that handed me those documents when you started? Do you recall?"

"Oliver." Atticus was stammering now. This was getting out of hand. "But it's not what it looks—"

"Ah yes, the known forger and, let's not forget, infamous traitor."

"You've got this all mixed up. I'm after Oliver to—"

"As you can imagine, I was quite surprised to find there never was anyone by the name of Atticus Wolfe." Rathdowne raised his hand, the Browning 9mm aimed directly at his heart. "Who the bloody hell are you?"

CHAPTER

ELEVEN

"It's late, we're both very wired. Why don't you put the gun down?"

"Me?" The gun in Rathdowne's hand was steady as a rock. "This is me at my most lucid. Tell me who you are, *really* are, or I start firing."

"There's a totally rational explanation, believe me."

Rathdowne remained mute, as did the gun. At any moment, either could break the silence. He raised a challenging eyebrow. *Go on.* It was a challenge Atticus didn't think he was up to. The cup and saucer in Atticus's lap jiggled.

Mind racing, Atticus went through all possible strategies. He could try and disarm Rathdowne, rush him and hope surprise stayed his trigger finger. He could sprint for the door and hope his boss aimed like an office manager. The window was closest, but the stained glass seemed pretty solid; diving through it could be troublesome. Or he could be honest and tell this humourless, unimaginative man the truth. Of all the strategies, Atticus deemed this the riskiest, and most likely to fail.

Of course, that's the one he went with. "Uh, are you familiar with the works of H. G. Wells—in particular, *The Time Machine*?"

"I've seen the movie." Rathdowne's tone gave nothing away.

"Well, uh, imagine, theoretically, of course, that, ah..." Atticus was floundering, doing this on the fly. "Okay, let me try to go back to the beginning."

"Let me guess, you're a time travelling spy from the year 2266 here to save us from the evil Morlocks?"

"Not all of that sarcastic sentence was inaccurate," Atticus scratched the back of his neck, "oddly."

Rathdowne's face hardened. "I don't have time for this nonsense. A lot of very good people died today. The man spotted at the scene who has no identity and is a known associate of a communist defector is the only suspect. It doesn't take a genius to piece that one together. Whoever you are, you killed my people. I don't have to sit here listening to the bullshit of a traitorous murderer."

"Rathdowne, listen. I know it's going to sound unbelievable, but I can explain." He really wished he had his smart watch so he could play the Vengaboys.

"Shut the fuck up!" Rathdowne snapped, anger replacing staid indifference. His knuckles grew white around the pistol grip. "I don't give a shit. Shut up. Just bloody well shut up. There's always been something queer about you. I could never put my finger on it, until now. You'll be arrested and MI5 will handle it from there." The pistol remained aimed at Atticus as Rathdowne's other hand reached for the black Bakelite phone to his right. "They still have the death penalty for treason, so good luck with that."

It was plain Atticus wasn't going to talk his way out of

this. Not here, not now. The stench of the dead was still on him. There was also a good chance he may not even survive. Rathdowne was justifiably livid at the deaths of his people; even if Atticus had all the proof in the world, it would make little difference right now. Time for plan B.

Nodding, Atticus's shoulders sagged in defeat. Or at least, that's how it appeared. The second Rathdowne's gaze went to the phone, Atticus sprang into action. He tossed the teacup with its boiling content at Rathdowne's face, then flung the saucer at speed at the same target. Consumed with self-preservation, Rathdowne protected himself. Atticus was out the door before the first shot was fired.

Three blasts echoed down the hall as he sprinted. Atticus made it to the front door and yanked it open before he heard thundering footfalls behind. Tearing into the night, he scurried for the nearest corner and didn't look back.

Further shots were fired, but nothing hit him. Atticus ran on. Five blocks later he ducked into a side alley and doubled over, hyperventilating. *What the hell just happened?*

Everything was unravelling.

He was burnt.

There was no safe harbour.

Within minutes his flat would be swarming with police. He couldn't embroil Maggie in this; he had to keep as far away from her as possible, to protect her. It would hurt like hell, but to ensure her safety they could have zero interaction until this was all over. If it would ever be all over.

No home. No friends. No work. No place to stay. Atticus was cut off from everything.

MI6, MI5 and the police would be after him. Mikhail and the KGB as well, no doubt.

There was only one place to go. Atticus flipped up the collar of his jacket and headed south.

"I was told to come here if I ever needed a favour."

"Dat's true. I just didn't think it would be at 7 am." The woman pulled her dressing gown tighter around her. "How did you find where we lived, anyway?"

Swivelling his head from left to right, Atticus took in the foreign but familiar street. The unlit neon sign for Kingston's Kitchen & Grill was one block away. Hardly anyone roamed the neighbourhood at this time of morning. That would soon change. Now it was light, he felt more exposed than ever.

"I wouldn't ask if it weren't an emergency."

Never a truer word spoken, Atticus thought to himself. Events were now well and truly spiralling out of control. It had been pure arrogance to assume his presence in this time would go undetected. Every attempt he'd made to decrease his impact on the timeline only made the situation worse. Now MI6 itself had paid the price for his arrogance.

He was no longer concerned about disrupting the timeline. He'd done more than disrupt it. He'd blown it apart. Literally.

Without the resources of MI6 behind him, finding out if Oliver were alive and still hellbent on reshaping the world would be far harder, if not impossible. But that was a topic for another day. He had to hide out for a while. Gather his strength. Find a way back into the game. Above all else, stay alive. It was the only way he could stop Oliver.

"Okay then. Come on in, we'll see what we can do for ye." When Atticus stepped into the light of Eliza Wolfe's front room she stepped back in alarm. It was the first time she'd seen him in the light. "Kaka fawt! What the hell happened to you boy?"

"It's been..." Atticus fought the urge to fall into her supportive arms, "... a long night."

"We got a room you can have for the night." Eliza frowned. "You look like you can definitely use the rest, eh?"

But Atticus didn't rest. He tried to sleep during the day, but his brain and outside noises made that impossible. With the million thoughts swirling about his brain, he lay in bed unable to even doze, incapable of making sense of the tempest within his skull. It wasn't until the skies darkened that he finally managed to close his eyes and get some much needed rest. He slept a fitful sleep, full of images of Maggie, Red Army uniforms and mushroom clouds.

Atticus woke to a poke in the ribs.

Disorientated, it took several moments to realise where he was. The sensation wasn't new. For months after arriving in the sixties, he often awoke expecting to be back in his modern minimalist apartment and instead finding himself in his Covent Garden flat.

It was unnervingly peculiar that the room he found himself in now was the one he'd spent much of his childhood waking in. His grandmother's front room. The décor was different, but the smell was unmistakable: the sweet lingering scents of his grandmother's cooking from the night before.

When Atticus's eyes finally adjusted to the light, "Sledgehammer Joe" Wolfe stood above him, imposing as always. The room was bright, it could have even been afternoon. *How long was I asleep?*

"Some folk are scared to call in my favours."

Atticus forced his mind to spin up to speed. He propped himself up on one elbow. "I'm not some folk."

The King of Brixton scrutinised the multicoloured crochet blanket wrapped around Atticus. "I can see that." He stepped back, giving them some room. "It either makes you braver than most, or a fucken' fool." Not leaving a gap for Atticus to respond, he added, "You want a ginger tea?"

Atticus smiled.

"Something funny 'bout that?"

"No, not at all." Atticus wiped the sleep from his eyes. "It's just it was my grandfather's drink of choice. I haven't heard someone offer it in a long time."

"Well, I ain't your grandpa, but if you want some, get dressed. Kitchen's to your left."

It took all Atticus's focus not to say, *I know.*

Minutes later, Atticus stood in his suit from the night before in the kitchen he loved, drinking his grandfather's ginger tea.

"That what they're wearing now?" Joe's tone wasn't favourable.

"It is. I was meant to be going to a new nightclub last night, so it pays to wear the latest thing."

"Meant to?"

"Things didn't turn out so well."

"People don't tend to call in favours when things are going well."

Atticus didn't contend the point, and sipped his tea instead. The house was quiet. He assumed his grandmother either had errands or had left Joe and Atticus alone to talk.

"What is it you need, son?"

"Just a place to lie low for a bit. I... uh, have some men after me. A misunderstanding, but they're not in a mood to listen just yet."

"I know about them misunderstandings. Been lyin' low myself." Joe flashed a cheeky smirk, then his face grew sombre. "You need money?"

It wasn't a subject Atticus had contemplated. If it were his time, he'd take the tube several blocks away, use an ATM and make his way back on foot in case he was being tracked. Here he had no such luxury. He had a quaint bankbook, but it was in his flat and there was no way he could retrieve it now.

"I guess I could do with a loan."

The man known by some as the Black Robin Hood clasped his hands in front of him. "You saved my son from being stabbed in the back. I'll front you some getting started cash, enough for food, clothes, anything you need to get back on your feet, as well as a place to stay for a month. That enough to balance our ledger, do you think?"

"More than enough." Atticus scratched the back of his neck. He recalled the boys his father and grandfather used to have run messages for them. He may as well press his luck. "You have anyone who can pass on a message for me? Across the city, nice and quiet?"

Joe smiled as if he knew exactly what Atticus intended to do. "I got a boy, Winston. Supports his family. Damn fine lad, he is. He's the best messenger in the city."

Atticus nodded his thanks. "That will do nicely, thank you."

Joe extended a calloused hand. "Then we got ourselves an agreement, Mr...?"

"Atticus is fine."

Joe pulled his hand back, displeasure hardening his features. "Where I'm from, a man's name is everything. I don't trust no man who don't give me his goddamn name."

For the first time in his life, Atticus saw the true Sledgehammer Joe. The one who could instil fear as easily as he could loyalty.

"I don't want to put you or your family in any more danger than I already have. You can claim honest ignorance if you don't know who I am. Not telling you who I am isn't about protecting myself, it's about protecting you and yours."

"I don't know..." Joe seemed to be considering the sentiment.

Atticus wasn't one to leave persuasion to chance. "How about this? I keep your family safe by keeping my name secret, for now. When the time's right, you'll know it." Atticus suspected that time would be a quarter of a century from now.

The King of Brixton mulled it over for a moment. "Alright, Mr Atticus-With-No-Last-Name." When Atticus shook, Joe grasped hard and didn't let go. "You've entered into a bond with me, boy. It's official now. You cross me, you take advantage of my generosity, well, let's just say, your debt don't exclude you from discovering the other side of my nature, you get me? You do right, stick to your word, then we'll be fine. I'll do the same. You remember what I said about my word, boy?"

"That Joe Wolfe's word is like diamonds."

"That's right." Joe relinquished his firm grip. "It is."

WITHIN HOURS ATTICUS was put up in a ground-floor flat with two bedrooms, a bathroom and a kitchenette. It wasn't exactly the Ritz, but it was just what he needed. It was a block away from the Wolfes. When he arrived, there was a white envelope on the table with a bundle of mixed denominations totalling several hundred pounds. Sledge-hammer Joe was indeed a man of his word.

Rested and safe, Atticus began to strategise.

The neighbourhood was perfect for what he needed. Brixton wasn't known for its prevalence of light skin. Be it MI6 or KGB, a white face would be spotted quickly in a crowd. It was the perfect place to hide out.

Using Joe's messenger kid, Winston, Atticus had sent word to Maggie, who was no doubt worried sick. The neighbourhood kid couldn't have been older than twelve, but seemed more street smart than those twice his age. Atticus offered five pounds—a small fortune in this time—to take a note to Maggie's apartment. Pretending to deliver medication from a local pharmacy, the kid passed her a handwritten note from Atticus in a bag containing aspirin. It told her he was safe, but on the run. If she didn't know from whom, she would soon enough. He didn't tell her where he was, knowing full well she wouldn't be able to stay away.

He asked, as politely as he could, that she didn't try to find him. He wanted to keep her safe. No one at MI6 was aware of their romance, no one knew how close they truly were, apart from close friends who had no association to the organisation. She would be as much a target of the investigation as any other co-worker. Doyle had suspected there was something between them, but Atticus had never confirmed it. If Maggie stayed away from him she would be safe.

That wasn't the only thing the letter contained. It was the first time he'd told Maggie he loved her. It was dreadful timing, and not at all how he'd anticipated telling her, but given the circumstances, he didn't know if there would be another opportunity.

The kid arrived back an hour later reporting mission accomplished. His enormous grin grew even bigger once Atticus handed over the five-pound note.

"The lady, she said she love you too."

Atticus heart swelled. He felt two feet taller.

Beaming, the kid stuffed the money in his pocket before Atticus could change his mind. "That white lady your girlfriend?"

In reply, Atticus gave the kid an affirmative bow of his head.

The kid whistled in appreciation. "She's a total smoking hot babe, that one. Why you not wit' her right now?"

"I'll see her soon enough." Atticus really hoped it were true. To keep his charade going, he added, "Always keep them wanting more."

Eyes wide like he'd received invaluable life advice, the kid trotted off, no doubt to spend his windfall. "You need anything else, Mister, you just ask for Winston, okay boss?"

"Okay."

The first job done, Atticus locked the door and sat at the tiny table to plan his next moves.

He had to somehow clear his name and convince Rathdowne who he was. Whether he revealed who he *really* was or stuck to the cover story for this era remained to be seen. That one he'd perhaps have to play by ear, although he doubted the charmless man would be as easily convinced as Maggie had been.

So far the newspapers offered scant details of who was responsible for the bombing, just vague references to "ongoing investigations", which no doubt the layperson would take as meaning "we have no idea". Atticus was certain MI6 and MI5 would be turning over every rock to find him. Just as assuredly, he knew they'd be tossing his apartment right now to look for any clues as to his whereabouts or allegiances.

Atticus had to somehow find and capture Mikhail and/or Oliver—if the latter was still alive. Best-case scenario, he could somehow hand them over to back up his story that he hadn't been running from the blast but trying to capture those responsible. Which would all be fine until either one of them started spouting that Atticus didn't belong, that he was not from where he claimed to be. Or, more precisely, *when*.

In the hours he spent in the tiny kitchen, Atticus came up with no possible excuse he could supply Rathdowne with to explain why his entire existence was a lie. His ex-boss may have a chip on his shoulder the size of the Rock of Gibraltar, but he wasn't stupid. Atticus had been caught in blatant fraud, and there seemed to be no plausible solution. There was no way around it; his days as a spy were over.

But in the end, all that was secondary. He had to find Oliver. Atticus hadn't seen him emerge from the coffin back in Jūrmala, but neither had he seen a corpse of the man. Right now, Oliver was Schrödinger's cat, simultaneously considered both alive and dead. If he were to put money on it, or indeed his life, Atticus would bet the bastard was alive.

Regardless of Atticus's situation, he had to assume the madman was still hellbent on reshaping history to ensure a Soviet victory. Even if that didn't eventuate, the instability and loss of life on a global scale could be horrific.

Throughout the Cold War the superpowers had wrought much destruction. Influencing and toppling governments in Europe, Asia and Africa, they tried to bend the world to their own ideological ends. But the one thing they'd never done was confront one another directly, face to face on a battlefield. Atticus shuddered to think what would happen if that terrifying scenario played out. No matter the cost, including his own freedom, and his life if it came to that, Atticus had to stop Oliver.

Without the full benefit of MI6 it seemed an insurmountable challenge, although there was perhaps the slightest of chances. If Mikhail was in-country, did that mean Oliver was too? It seemed too much to hope for, but right now that was all he had left: hope.

He set about contemplating how to turn Mikhail's presence to an advantage, if he could. Atticus had to think strategically. Where would a man like Mikhail stay? How would he get into the country? What would he do when he was here? There was a lot of supposition, conjecture and long meandering tangents, but eventually he formed the thin skeleton of a plan.

Before Atticus got too far into scheming, there was a knock at the door. When he opened it, Joe and Thomas Wolfe stood in the street.

"Alright, mate?"

Atticus addressed the man he had to keep reminding himself not to call dad. "Yeah, good. Good. Come on in."

The two gangsters entered, checking all blind corners and rooms before they relaxed. The King of Brixton made himself at home and put his feet on the table—his table. The pimply teenager Thomas Wolfe hung back near the front door, hands clasped before him, a sentinel for his old man.

"Settling in alright, lad?"

"Yes, fine, really fine. Thank you, again."

"No need to keep thanking me. Debt paid, think nothing of it." Joe sat up, leaned forward and spoke with a hard edge. "My wife tells me there's more going on with you than you're letting on, Atticus-With-No-Last-Name."

"That right?"

"It is. For all the grief that woman gives me, I always listen to what she has to say because she has this very annoying habit of being right. It's damn infuriating, I gotta tell you."

"I imagine."

Sniffing, Joe rubbed his chin like a man who knew what he was about to ask but was going through the motions anyway. "Who's after you?"

Atticus wobbled his head from side to side. "You wouldn't know them."

"You'd be surprised who I know in this town."

Sensing a non-answer would be unacceptable, Atticus went with the first thing that came to mind. "They're called the Wu-Tang Clan."

"I... I don't know them."

As much as the inside joke amused him, Atticus thought perhaps he should provide a little more detail. After all, he was working without a net and had little in the way of allies. In a more serious tone, he added, "If you hear of anyone with a toff accent or a Russian accent looking for me, I'd appreciate a heads up."

"Quite a mix of people you've pissed off there."

"The list is long and distinguished on that front."

Thinking on his feet, Atticus decided that perhaps he could use the King of Brixton's help after all. He might not personally know the man before him right now, but he did later in his life. Despite a lifetime of crime, Joe Wolfe was a patriot. Even in the face of serving at Her Majesty's pleasure on multiple occasions, he still managed to respect the

Queen nonetheless. Atticus remembered the Silver Jubilee framed photo in their kitchen when he was growing up.

"The main group of men after me are Russian, ah, Soviet."

"What the hell did you do to piss off the commies?"

"It's a long and complicated story."

"We don't much care for the communists 'round here, in't that right number one son?"

"Yeah Dad. Don't care for 'em."

Joe held his palms up, as if to say, *see?* Thomas Wolfe seemed indifferent to being part of the conversation. Even more indifferent to being in Atticus's presence. At least that was consistent with Atticus's memories of the man.

"Those commie pricks don't care for the business I'm in." The King of Brixton spoke as if holding court. "One day I would very much like to hand down to my son a vast and expansive enterprise, built with my own two hands and sweat off my brow."

And a fair chunk of illegal activities, Atticus was wise enough not to add.

Joe went on. "This great country was built by blokes like me. Them commies, they don't much care for hard work. They'd rather give it all back to bludgers or drop it into their own fur-lined pockets. I give back, but to those who deserve it, like yourself." He folded his arms. "What do the Ruskies want with you?"

"Let's just say where I worked, I caused the Soviets a lot of grief. They're wanting payback."

It was far more truth than Atticus had been prepared to offer, but when it came down to it, he needed support. He couldn't succeed without it.

"Where did you work?" Thomas took a step forward, curious, the first sign of life since he'd arrived.

Atticus weighed up whether to reveal the next piece of information. It was a calculated gamble. "Let me put it this way. The ones who will come after me will likely work for the KGB."

"Are you a spy?" Joe's mouth dropped open. "A fucken *black* fucken spy?"

"If you saw my face, would the first thing you thought of be spy?"

"No, it bloody well would not!" Joe slapped his thigh. "Well, if that doesn't take the bleedin' biscuit!"

"Bullshit." Thomas shook his head, obviously more sceptical than his father. "No way them upper-class gits would ever hire one of us. Even one with a posh accent and using hundred-pound words."

"You don't believe me?" Atticus tilted his head.

"No." Thomas crossed his arms and scowled. "No, I fucken' well don't."

"Attack me." Atticus stood and issued Thomas a *come-hither* flick of his fingers. "With all you've got."

Both men laughed. Atticus didn't. For one thing, it wasn't a joke. And second, for a large part of his life Atticus had been scared of his father. An absolute, crippling fear. With good reason. His father was a brutal and angry man, prone to lash out at his son at the smallest of provocations. His father had passed away, in jail, before Atticus could bring a reckoning for all the pain he'd caused.

"Hit me." Atticus stood motionless. "I'm well trained. You won't land a punch."

"Bullshit." Thomas's words were hard, but Atticus could see fractures of doubt.

"Settle down, son. Don't forget this man saved your life."

"You're a brawler," Atticus added quickly to lessen the

personal nature of the statement. "The way you stand, you're always ready to box someone's ears in. I've been trained to notice. I've also been trained, by the government, to countermand it."

"Countermand." Thomas shook his head. "We don't use words like that. You sure you're even black?"

"I assure you I am." With his arms passively by his sides, Atticus raised a challenging eyebrow. "Now hit me." He leaned forward and hefted an eyebrow. "Unless you're afraid?"

He remembered his father's triggers. The swing was lazy but brutal. With arms still by his sides, Atticus leaned back and sidestepped the blow. Not having connected the punch, his father overextended and staggered forward. Atticus gave him a swift jab to the ribs.

Righting himself, Thomas rubbed his ribs. "What the fuck was that?"

"I said you wouldn't land a punch. I didn't make any promises the other way."

Instead of the rage Atticus expected, Thomas laughed. "You cheeky bugger."

That was a surprise. Atticus had fully expected his taunt to enrage his father into an even clumsier attack; instead he took it as a friendly tease. Perhaps he settled into his anger as he grew older. Atticus had a further uncomfortable thought. Perhaps saving his father from being stabbed in the back had stemmed the bitterness from developing to the extremes he remembered so well. Had he altered the path his father was on, and in so doing changed the man completely?

Atticus shook his head. Now was not the time to contemplate such things. He was in a fistfight; a good-natured one, certainly, but still a fistfight.

Thomas Wolfe raised his fists, ready for another round. His footwork was atrocious. It was plain he'd seen the inside of a boxing ring, but he'd relied on brute strength and intimidation rather than technique.

He came at Atticus more carefully this time. Feigning an upper cut, he switched to a right cross. Atticus countered it, using his hands to parry the hit away, then instantly counterattacked with a swift body blow with his left and a jab to head. Before Thomas knew what was happening, he was in a leglock on the floor, immobile and writhing in pain.

"Enough of this bollocks. Stand down, Thomas."

Thomas choked out a response as Atticus let go. "Me? He nearly killed me."

Joe waved his hand dismissively. "No he didn't. Stop being a fucken' baby."

Thomas brushed himself off and chuckled. "Next time you get beat up, old man."

"I think you've proven your point, Mister...?"

"Just Atticus is fine."

"No, there's a point where Atticus-With-No-Last-Name carries you only so far. Trust is earned, boy, you get me?"

Atticus rocked on his heels. He got the point. Joe had put him up at no expense and accepted him at his word simply because he'd saved his son. The debt had been paid, no questions asked. Now their relationship seemed to be evolving, and with that came with a price.

"Atticus Smith."

Joe frowned and motioned for him to sit at the table once more. He didn't seem to buy the name, but rightly assumed nothing more would be forthcoming if he pushed.

"What fighting style do you call that?"

"I'm trained in a lot of different styles. Brazilian jiu-jitsu. Muay Thai. Krav Maga."

"And they trained you in that, to be a spy?"

Atticus nodded. It was a risk to provide the information, but at the same time, he'd need allies in the fight to come. Who better than the toughest men he'd ever known?

"I tell you what." Joe's mind was racing. "We got a job tonight, could do with some backup muscle."

"Dad!"

Joe Wolfe lowered his palm at his son. *Simmer down.* "Nothing too adventurous, but it would be nice if we had an extra body in case things get a bit physical. Probably won't, but I didn't get this far by being unprepared, right?"

Once again, Thomas had his arms folded, but his demeanour was altogether more relaxed, even jovial. "Still don't think this bloke's a spy."

"Some would say that's the mark of a good spy." Atticus matched his father's light tone. "If all spies walked around like spies they wouldn't be much of a spy, now would they?"

Tilting his head to concede the point, Thomas smirked. "Guess not."

Atticus turned back to Joe to address the question at hand. "I don't know about the job..."

"Let me be clear on this. My debt to you still stands. You come on this job or not, that doesn't change. I want you to understand that, it's important. This place is yours for a month no matter what." He leaned forward. "But here's the thing. Keeping an eye out for Russians, maybe tackling the KGB, these are things are not in our original arrangement. They call me the King of Brixton for a reason. I have eyes and ears everywhere. If you want to know if you've got company, I'm your man." He cracked his knuckles. "So, this is my proposal to you, Atticus *Smith*. You do a couple of little jobs for us, we do some for you. Equitable. Balanced." Joe leaned back in the chair. "What do you say?"

"I say," Atticus put out his hand, "you've got yourself a deal."

The two hard men left with promises of a visit later that night. Atticus had mixed emotions about becoming embroiled in his grandfather's nefarious schemes, but as he spent all day ruminating about it, he realised he didn't have much of a choice. His family, as crooked as they were, were a known entity. They had a code—well, his grandfather did, at least. If he was to take on Oliver, Mikhail and the KGB, he'd need support.

The strategist he was, Atticus started forward planning. If Mikhail was still in the country, he likely wouldn't be for long. Atticus's window of opportunity was slim. He had to take advantage while he still could.

As the decimation of MI6 proved, history was being rewritten. He couldn't simply sit out events and hope it all righted itself. That time had passed.

No more hiding from the problem. It was time to go on the offensive.

Atticus hit the street and soon found what he was after.

"Hey Winston, want to run another errand?"

"Do I! Just tell me where."

"The Soviet Embassy."

"The..." His bravado faltering, young Winston's forehead crinkled in concern. "Really? Why do you want to send a message to them for?"

"Because Winston," Atticus's hand clasped the young man's shoulder, "I'm going to start a war."

CHAPTER
TWELVE

The "job", as it turned out, was to stand on the street and look mean. Not much of a stretch for a tall, black, bald man who grew up in a crime family. Atticus particularly liked the scowling. He was a good scowler. Except at 2 am, there weren't many people to scowl at.

Rugged up against the cold night, he stood in the closed doorway of a drapery. Around the corner and down the lane, Thomas, Joe and Jacob, the hatchet-wielding chef from the restaurant, went about their business. The three men were furiously loading record players into a van. The lawful ownership of said record players had not been discussed, nor had the destination of the record players in question.

Hands stuffed in his pockets, Atticus shifted his weight between his feet to keep warm—ironically, an old policeman's trick. He noticed the man approach before he saw Atticus. When he realised Atticus was standing by himself on the street, the man made a beeline directly for him.

"Evening officer." Atticus's voice was loud and carried in the night.

"Sir." The tall constable's tone was curious. "Out late, aren't we?"

"Insomnia."

Atticus left it at that. The mistake most people made when talking to law enforcement was to talk too much, give them something to grasp onto. Less talk meant there was less to trip up on.

"You work here?" The constable examined the sign advertising Muriel's Drapery.

"No. I've never had the pleasure of meeting Muriel."

"Then why are you trespassing?"

"I think you'll find I'm on the street in front of dear Muriel's premises. There's no trespass involved."

"You seem awfully defensive. Why's that?"

"A lifetime of experience." Atticus tilted his head. "I have money in my wallet in case you wanted to discuss the concept of vagrancy."

The white constable scowled. It was nowhere as good as Atticus's.

He sniffed and stepped forward. "You're very uppity."

In Atticus's experience as a black man in a white world, the word "uppity" had never had positive associations.

Before he could reply, a *clang* rang out around the corner from where they stood. The constable strained his neck and turned to Atticus.

"What's going on down the lane?"

Atticus shrugged. "I assume that's the lane's business."

Extracting his truncheon, the police officer hefted it in Atticus's direction. "Stay there."

Striding down the street, the constable poked his head around the brick corner and took several moments to take it in. Returning dejected, his eyes narrowed at Atticus. "Something's going on."

"You're right," Atticus confessed, "something is going on."

Eyes wide, as if expecting a confession, the constable motioned for him to continue.

"The Earth is rotating around the sun at a distance of about 93 million miles. Meanwhile, 3.4 billion light years away, a supernova is forming. Somewhere else a sheep cries out in the night, and somewhere else a man has misplaced his pyjamas."

Atticus was no expert on these things, but could have sworn that wasn't the answer the constable sought.

He was right. The constable poked Atticus's collarbone with his truncheon. "Watch it."

Atticus could have enquired as to what specifically *it* was, but felt no need to prolong the conversation any further, so simply remained mute, giving the officer nothing else to focus on. Exasperated, the man pivoted on the spot and stormed off to parts unknown.

Several minutes later, a beaming Thomas rounded the corner. "You handled that well."

"You heard?"

The Prince chuckled, amusement dripping from his features. "Every word. A cold night carries sound alright. Me and dad was pretty much done, we heard the Rozzer givin' you the third degree and your smart-arse replies. Gave us plenty of time to lock the van and disappear out of sight." He whistled. "Cool as a fucken' cucumber, you are."

Atticus had a moment. Was that the first compliment his father had ever given him? For the life of him he couldn't think of another. Not wanting to spend too much time contemplating the possibility, he moved on.

"You didn't bring me along because of my pretty face."

"We brought you along because we needed the muscle." Thomas Wolfe sneered. "Seems you're more than that, aren't ya?" He looked Atticus up and down. "Maybe you're a spy after all."

AND SO IT WENT. Over the next few days Atticus assisted Joe and Thomas on a few late-night "errands". None required him to supply muscle. They mostly entailed sitting in a van, sitting across the street or sitting outside a pub. Basically, there was a lot of sitting.

Not exactly a stretch of his talents, but it was banking up credit for the war to come. And it was coming. He could feel it.

With all the sudden interaction with his family, there was still an internal battle raging within Atticus. On one hand he resented the sight of his young father, the man who had caused him so much anxiety, resentment and terror. On the other, the Thomas he was getting to know was charming, amusing and far more level-headed than Atticus would have thought possible in a million years.

Thomas even attempted to entice Atticus out for a drink. The fact he could have potentially become friends with the man he'd hated for the better part of his life was a possibility he'd never believed he'd entertain. Atticus had politely declined and retreated to the sparse confines of his hidden oasis. He'd been outside too often, it was careless. He should have isolated himself, ensuring he wasn't spotted by the KGB or MI6. If he was to succeed, he had to remain undetected by both sides.

Atticus had showered and dressed and was eating toast,

intending to bunker down for the day. As if on cue, there was a knock at the door. Opening it, Joe slapped him on the back genially as he entered. He wasn't alone. Eliza Wolfe stepped into the room and, as always, appeared right at home.

"How you doin', hon'?"

Fighting the urge to be overly familiar with his grandmother, Atticus issued a weak smile. "Oh, I'm good, thank you."

"Pish." She grasped his wrist with an iron grip. "Don't give me some damn reflex answer. How are ye' *really*?"

Genuinely grinning this time, Atticus replied, "I'm actually okay, honestly. Disorientated slightly, but I'm in a good head space." He leaned down to her level. "Really."

Relinquishing the grip on his wrist, she eyed him while shaking her head. "There's something so familiar 'bout you."

Atticus did his best not to gulp. "I get that a lot."

"You okay 'ere by yourself? You need to be gettin' home?" She paused. "After you stayin' wit' us?"

"I hope to make it home... someday." The multiple layers to the statement weren't lost on Atticus.

"I hope you get home, too." She smiled and tilted her head caringly. "You don' look like you eatin'." Eliza Wolfe tutted. "You wastin' away." She hefted a crocheted bag onto the tiny kitchen bench. "This for you. Jamaican fried dumplings, the veggie patties and a side of slaw. Put some meat back on dem bones."

"You remembered my order?" Atticus was impressed. "That was weeks ago."

Joe chuckled. "I've been married to this good woman for years and let me tell you somethin', she never forgets a thing."

Eliza gave him a playful slap on the arm. "Alright you."

It was still odd seeing his grandmother in her prime. She was always a larger than life presence. That hadn't changed—if anything, she was more formidable than ever, something Atticus had never thought possible. He still had to fight the urge to sweep her up in his arms and never let go, but her playful smile and mere presence was enough for him right now.

Joe threw down a pile of newspapers on the small table. He also carried a manila envelope, which remained tucked under his arm. Atticus had forgotten how big newspapers used to be. Before the internet, before social media, besides television, newspapers were virtually the only way to reach a mass audience. The volume would be enough to keep him occupied for a few hours.

Atticus flipped through the pages absentmindedly. As Joe had alluded to, there was renewed coverage of the explosion and its aftermath. Only the day before—several days after the event—hints were being dropped as to the nature of the work conducted in the building. Initially it had been labelled merely as a "business tower". Two days later there was mention of government departments. However, following a question in parliament, it had become widespread knowledge that the bombing had taken place at the new headquarters of MI6. Although, officially, the existence of MI6 wouldn't be confirmed for another thirty years.

Rumours of an attack on the Secret Service had fuelled wild speculation as to the perpetrator. The first to officially deny it was Khrushchev himself at a state dinner in Moscow, stating that the event was tragic and strongly indicating it was not sanctioned by his government.

While the Soviets were the first to come to mind for

many, most balanced commentators speculated it couldn't have been the USSR, as such an act would be tantamount to a declaration of war. Given such provocation could easily escalate to all-out nuclear Armageddon, Atticus wasn't about to disagree.

His name and picture had yet to appear in print. Either Rathdowne and MI6 wanted to avoid further scandal, or they were playing another game, one that Atticus was unaware of. They likely had enough to worry about.

He suspected that Mikhail, under instruction from Oliver, had acted alone. To what end, Atticus was unable to even hazard a guess, though he was determined to find out.

Two days before, he'd asked Winston to drop off his message to the Soviet Embassy and advised him not to wait for a reply, mainly because he didn't want to put the resourceful Winston in any more danger than was absolutely necessary. The other reason was that there may be no response to be had. It was an educated guess that Mikhail would have a diplomatic cover when in London, but it was still just that: a guess. Given the bombing of MI6 would never be sanctioned by any sane government, Mikhail may well have been a rogue agent and not at the embassy at all.

All doubts about Mikhail's lodgings were resolved when Atticus flipped open *The Times*. To confirm the receipt of his challenge, an announcement had been placed in the newspaper. A birth announcement, to be exact.

Britney (nee Spears) and Danny DeVito announce the arrival of their daughter Madonna Rihanna. Born 06/05/1964, 8lb 3oz, at Lambeth Hospital.

Mikhail had received his message. Not only that, he'd accepted the challenge.

The names were to identify the sender. The date reversed told him when they were to meet. The 5th of June

—in three days. The weight indicated the time. Eight thirty at night. Lambeth Hospital confirmed the location of their confrontation. Brixton.

"You alright 'dere?" Eliza interrupted Atticus's thoughts. He'd momentarily forgotten the two were standing there. She glanced at what Atticus was reading. "Old girlfriend?"

"What? No... just, ah... What's with the envelope?"

It was a lame distraction, but Atticus wasn't exactly on his A game.

With a chortle, Joe opened the envelope. "Not much gets by you, eh?" He handed a glossy black and white photograph to Atticus. "We spotted him at the East Brixton railway station. Was there for hours, gawkin' at all the passers-by. He one of your Wu Tang Clan?"

Atticus recognised the face immediately. Vincent. He was one of the upper-crust toffs who'd made Atticus's life hell when he'd first arrived in this time. Since then he'd loosened up somewhat, even offering the occasional grudging respect, but the two of them weren't close by any stretch of the imagination.

"One o' my boys bumped into him at the station. Accidentally, of course. Said the bloke talked all posh like he had a plum up his arse. Swore he wasn't a Russian."

Atticus was about to make a statement to divert the course of the conversation, but he didn't get the chance. Joe cut him off.

"Seems to me, awfully strange a spy, as you claim to be, would need to hide out." Joe gave a theatrical frown. "Even odder the bomb went off on Westminster Bridge Road. Now they're saying it might've been MI6 headquarters." He rubbed his chin. "Weird how you turn up on my doorstep the next day, don't you reckon? Mighty odd."

"It is odd, isn't it?"

Joe hadn't become King of Brixton because he was stupid. Atticus was thankful he didn't push further. While the exchange took place, Eliza watched the two intently. Always sharper than the men around her, she seemed to observe the conversation and to understand the underlying context. Atticus only hoped she didn't understand everything because then he'd really be screwed.

Exactly what Joe thought Atticus's involvement in the bombing was seemed unclear. Atticus would have to play that one by ear. He hoped he'd earned Joe's trust in recent days, but that would only extend so far. Atticus had no doubt his fragile tenure as a sheltered subject of the King of Brixton could end in a heartbeat should it bring too much heat. It was something to worry about at a later date. If he got to a later date.

Thinking back to the ad and now the fact that MI6 were after him, he realised he may need Maggie's help after all. He would need to get a message to her to see what MI6 had been advised and how it would affect his plans. He'd just have to be careful to keep his location secret so she wouldn't go searching for him. It was a calculated risk.

"Joe, can you please send Winston over when you see him next? I have an errand for him."

For the first time, Atticus saw Joe falter. His expression grew grave in an instant. Eliza seemed on the verge of tears, not a state Atticus had seen often in his lifetime. The woman wasn't one to break down easily. The mood in the room had instantly changed.

"Winston?" Joe virtually stammered. "No, I can't do that." He winced. "Winston's not working no more."

"Why?" Atticus drew closer. "What's happened?"

Eliza wiped away a tear. "That poor child."

"What happened, Joe?"

"He... Winston's dead." His face hardened. "Found strangled up near Holland Park. That poor kid was lookin' after his family. Supportin' his sisters after his daddy skipped out years ago and his Mumma died of the TB." Joe shook his head. "What he was doin' up there is anyone's guess."

Atticus gulped. "I know."

The accusatory stare was Atticus's own feelings reflected back at him.

He reluctantly went on. "Holland Park is near Kensington Palace Green. That's where I sent Winston to drop off a message to the Soviet Embassy. I didn't need a reply, so I assumed he went straight home... I... Jesus." Atticus sat unsteadily. "The poor kid. Why the hell would they touch him? He didn't know anything..."

"You mean those Wu Tang Clan cocksuckers killed Winston?"

Numb, Atticus nodded. It was the only logical explanation. Why would Mikhail need to kill an innocent kid?

Maybe Oliver was truly dead and the two had shared more than a working relationship. Was the bombing and Winston's murder all a sick form of revenge? If so, the man was truly unhinged.

"KGB. Or at least some rogue faction of it."

Shaking her head in disbelief, Eliza regarded Atticus like he'd just grown a second head. "The KGB killed Winston? Why?"

"To get to me." Atticus's shoulders slumped. "I'm so sorry. If I knew he was in any danger I never would have sent him. All he did was drop off a letter, that's all. I have no idea why the hell he'd kill him. I'm... I'm sorry."

"Fuck your sympathy." Joe leaned forward. "How do I kill the cunt?"

"You don't want to get caught up in—"

"Fuck what you think." Sledgehammer Joe's voice shook the windows. "How do I kill him? Nobody hurts one of mine and gets away with it. If I have to walk to Moscow myself I'll fucken' do it just to rip his heart out. I'm in this now whether you like it or not, get me? How do I get to the bastard?"

Atticus turned to Eliza, hoping to see something different, to appeal to her trepidation or fear. There was neither. Her face had hardened just as her husband's had. If anything, there was more determination etched on her features. In an instant Atticus understood why the couple had been so fear-inspiring for so many years. The dominant mantra in his youth had always been, *Never fuck with a Wolfe.*

Something else Atticus remembered was Joe's determination when it came to revenge. That was what ultimately sent him to prison for life. Anyone confronted with Joe Wolfe's unhinged rage understood all too well there was no stopping the man. He was a force of nature.

Atticus explained the birth announcement and the acceptance of his challenge. Mikhail would be in Brixton in a matter of days.

"Well 'den," Eliza was matter of fact, "I hope he has a good last will and testament. Dat boy's gonna be needin' dat."

Joe ran his hand down his wife's arm in agreement. "Then we'll help you fight these cocksuckers. All of them. No way this goes unpunished. It'll be slow, painful. I got boys who'll make 'em last for days with nothin' but power tools and bamboo." A black cloud enveloped the man. "You tell me what you need and it's yours. Forget all that debt shit. This here, this is personal."

Three days wasn't a lot of time to prepare. Atticus turned back to the front page and the photograph of the smoking ruin of the MI6 building, then saw the fury on Joe and Eliza's faces. They weren't the only ones consumed by rage.

If Mikhail wanted a war, he'd get one.

As far as Atticus was concerned, the frustrating thing about supermarket shopping in the sixties was everything. If his sojourn to the supermarket was meant to lift his sagging spirits it was failing dismally. Not only was the range of goods severely limited, the products available were plain and bland. Branding was colourful and attention grabbing, but the content of the packages was universally uninspiring: Force Wheat Flakes, Shreddies, Spel and Trex all screamed at him from the white metal shelves. In a dismal mood after learning poor Winston's fate, no product was going to wrench him free of his malaise.

Not a terrible cook, Atticus had grown accustomed to the inner-city life. Back in his time it could be weeks between turning his oven on. When not out on a mission he was either out to dinner with friends, grabbing a pre-made meal or lazily ordering in. Cooking from scratch was time consuming. Time he didn't have.

He soon came to realise there was no such thing as ready-made meals in this time period. Even the basic sixties cuisine were strictly a make-at-home-from-scratch ordeal. Atticus had once made the mistake of asking if a particular market offered a blatantly exotic lasagne. He may as well have asked if they stocked thermonuclear suppositories.

The slabs of raw meat everywhere grated on his vegetarian sensibilities. There was nothing plant-based unless it was, well, a plant. He'd once spent an hour scouring various markets for tofu only to realise he was probably decades too early.

He roamed the aisles in disguise, of a sort. He'd taken a modicum of effort to conceal his identity. A hat with a wig poking out. Not exactly *Mission Impossible* level of disguise, but at least he'd made an effort.

He threw a Peppermint Aero into his basket amongst the vegetables and breakfast cereals. He'd relented and bought a steak for the protein. He'd need it in the days to come. He'd need every ounce of strength he could muster. Still in tactical mode, he was planning as he shopped.

His meandering thoughts ceased when he sensed the approach from behind. He crouched, ready to drop the basket and defend himself.

"You're an idiot, you know that?"

Atticus swivelled and took a step back, stunned.

He should have known. The statement was an accurate one. He was an idiot. Only an idiot would underestimate Maggie Dunbar.

Instead of anger, she beamed at him. "Nice wig, by the way."

"Really?"

"No. For a man hiding out you're not very difficult to track down. The pharmacy bag was from Brixton, like the local kid you sent to give me the message."

The mention of Winston made his heart heavy.

Maggie went on. "Plus, I recall you being owed a favour by past family members." Her eyes swivelled, searching for eavesdroppers. "Put it all together with the fact you don't have a lot of contacts here and, well, I'll modestly sum up by saying I'm positively Sherlock fucking Holmes."

Acting on nothing but pure instinct, Atticus dropped his basket and swept Maggie into his arms. He kissed her with every ounce of passion he felt. Nearby, someone gasped. He was unsure if it was because a black man and a white woman were kissing or because they had the audacity to publicly display affection in front of the meat department. Not that he cared. The world fell away and light crept back into his life.

Twenty minutes later Atticus was back at his hideout with Maggie, cooking dinner for two. He tried to be upset that she'd become embroiled in his mess but couldn't. There was no wiping the grin from his face.

She'd brought him up to speed on the chaos following the bombing of MI6. Luckily there were fewer casualties than there could have been. Most day workers had left, and a few had still been working out of the Broadway office. As for Atticus himself, not much was public knowledge, although Maggie suspected something was up. Rathdowne had personally questioned her, though she called it an interrogation.

Maggie had corroborated his account of a man running from the truck moments before the explosion, but Rathdowne seemed sceptical to the point of incredulity. Secret meetings had been conducted behind closed doors. Since then, she'd been persona non grata at MI6, out of the loop.

A few select members of staff knew Atticus's past was, at best, curiously lacking. The way Maggie told it, people viewed it as a curiosity rather than a treasonous act. It hadn't spread far, primarily due to the rest of the organisation being preoccupied with the attack.

Of those staff who knew, all had seen how he'd worked tirelessly for MI6, literally putting his life on the line. Maggie said they were having a hard time believing the lack of history could have malicious undertones. At least for now. He also suspected that, as Maggie was the one telling the story, the reality was more grave than she was letting on.

Attempting to spin the positive that he wasn't public enemy, Atticus told her about Vincent staking out the train station. He reasoned it may not be public knowledge yet—be it due to lack of evidence or MI6 trying to save face—but there was no guarantee it would stay that way. The weight of time pushed down on his shoulders. There was a lot going on, much to process. He was thankful for the company.

Maggie had run out and bought an ill-defined red wine from Australia. He seemed to remember a Monty Python sketch from the era labelling certain Australian wines as being not for drinking but for laying down and avoiding. Shuddering after another sip, he wasn't about to argue.

He placed the plates of pedestrian meat and three veg on the table. He apologised for the simplicity, but Maggie was spellbound that a man had managed to cook her anything in the first place. Over the meal he laid out his plan. Time was running out, and the closer the deadline grew, the less sure of success he became. He was buoyed by Maggie's encouragement, but the unease remained.

"Well, I'm here to help." Maggie placed her knife and fork down with relish. She'd demolished the meal faster than he had.

"I'm grateful, but I'm beginning to think I've finally bitten off more than I can chew. I might need to—"

Atticus was distracted by a knock at the door. His

curiosity only magnified when he saw Maggie's cheeky grin. She threw a splayed hand to her chest in mock shock.

"My, whoever could that be?"

Eyes narrowed, Atticus stood with an inquisitive frown and unlocked the door. When he opened it, for the second time that day, he stood back in shock. Mrs Abernathy, Doyle and Cohen stood before him, friendly and amused at the same time.

Cohen poked his head around Atticus to address Maggie. "I'm guessing you hadn't got to the bit where you told him you called us, yeah?"

"Not yet."

Doyle rocked on his heels. "You gonna invite us in, or what?"

Too stunned to talk, Atticus waved them through. They all offered pleasant greetings as they passed him on the way in.

Finally managing to engage the speech centres of his brain, Atticus said, "Thank you all for coming, but you shouldn't be here."

"That's bloody lovely, that is." Cohen poured himself a glass of wine and sat at the table, making himself at home.

"But they're—"

"After you because you don't seem to exist?" Mrs Abernathy said matter-of-factly. "Yes, dear, we know. A whole pile of twaddle if you ask me."

"That's... nice and all, but you're all putting yourselves in danger by just being here. I can't ask you to—"

"But you didn't ask, did you?" Mrs Abernathy's forged-steel tone was as formidable as ever. "We're all here because we want to be. You don't *have* to ask. Maggie filled us in. We're here because it's right."

"The way I see it," Doyle's tall frame was as rigid as

always, "we still owe you. Me and Cohen. You came back for us back in Jūrmala when you didn't have to, saved our bacon. No way I'm leaving the ledger one-sided."

"I appreciate that, but—"

Cohen piped in. "And before you say it, no way in hell you're playing the other side. Just no way. If what Maggie tells us is right, we get to capture the bloke responsible, make him admit he was the bastard behind the bombing and clear your name all in one go. That sounds like a bloody good deal to me."

Even if they did manage to capture Mikhail and somehow extract a confession from him, it would only go as far as confirming Atticus was free of blame in the terrorist attack on MI6. It would do nothing to explain why he had no past. *One thing at a time,* Atticus thought to himself.

He surveyed the team of professionals before him: self-less, dedicated and, much to his pleasant surprise, loyal. Combined with the resources of the King of Brixton, they might even be able to pull it off. It was too soon to dream of success, so many things could force the whole operation to fall apart, but at least now they had a fighting chance. They had hope.

"Now we're here," Cohen helped himself to the final piece of Atticus's steak, "what are we going to do?"

"End this." Atticus placed his fists on the table. "End it all."

CHAPTER

THIRTEEN

Atticus was operating on no sleep.

The last few days were a blur. It seemed like he was having endless meetings about strategy, contingencies and tactics. His once quiet and secluded oasis from the world had become a bustling centre of operations, dubbed the War Room.

In the quiet before the storm, Atticus and Maggie stood alone at the new table—the previous one had proven insufficient to hold all the diagrams, blueprints and battle plans. The walls were covered with representations of the streets of Brixton, with pencil markings dictating various scenarios and counter tactics. Atticus had tried to anticipate every move Mikhail and potentially the KGB would make. It was, of course, impossible. Even so, Atticus had forgone sleep in an attempt to come up with countermeasures to every situation.

Joe had mobilised his criminal network, calling in favours, declaring truces where needed. Friend and foe had tossed in money for a fund to take care of Winston's sisters. They would want for nothing. The kid had been known throughout the neighbourhood, and universally adored. His death had been a rallying cry.

The Wolfe crime syndicate was at Atticus's disposal. Every leader from various parts of the hierarchy had met with Atticus to offer their services. He'd had a job for every single one of them. The breadth of the undertaking was massive. Brixton was to become a battleground. Within hours, blood would flow on the streets. Gangsters versus spies.

Atticus glanced across the table. Maggie tied her hair into a ponytail as she stared intently at a map of southern Brixton. It was ludicrous for Atticus to have thought he could do this without her. She not only had a keen strategic mind, but a natural ability to work with teams at all levels. It had taken her all of two minutes to charm Joe Wolfe. Of all people, Joe recognised a formidable woman when he met one.

Reluctantly taking his eyes off Maggie, Atticus returned his attention to their plans. Everything had gotten out of hand. The simple act of retrieving a phone and stopping Oliver had expanded exponentially. It was now a war. One they had to win.

If Oliver were alive his aim would be to get Atticus to unlock the phone. It would be his key motivating factor. They had to play into that. Knowing the enemy's prime motive could help defeat them. Conversely, the enemy also knew what Atticus wanted, and would no doubt use that to *their* advantage.

Another cause of Atticus's insomnia was the fact that the enemy was unpredictable. The bombing of MI6 had to be more than petty revenge for their mission to extract Oliver from behind the Iron Curtain. Were Mikhail and/or Oliver trying to start a war between the superpowers? An attack on the other side's secret intelligence agency was almost a surefire way of igniting one. An unpredictable enemy was hard to anticipate.

Atticus sighed heavily. He needed sleep. He needed this to be over.

The knock on the door was a welcome relief from his tumultuous reflections. His eyes were having a hard time focusing on the paper before him. He strode to the door and opened it as if in a dream. Atticus really was dead on his feet.

"You look like shit."

"Thank you." Atticus chuckled. "Just what I needed to hear."

Thomas strode in like he owned the place, which he did —well, his father did. Over his arm he carried a stuffed duffel bag.

"That's what I am, a little ray of fucking sunshine." Thomas gave Maggie a wave. "Hello darlin', how are you this fine day?"

"I'm good, thank you Thomas. What brings you here?"

"Your stunning smile."

"Besides that." Maggie giggled.

The fact that his father was flirting with Maggie made Atticus extremely uncomfortable. He did his best to block it out.

Thomas went on. "Dad wanted you to know we've got the dockers on board too. If this shit drifts as far as the North or South Pool, they'll be ready."

"Good to know, thanks."

Thomas hesitated for a moment. "You do look like shit, though, mate. You should get some sleep before tonight, yeah?"

Atticus gave him a vague waggle of his head. "Thanks,

but there's still too much to do. There are so many moving parts to this thing. I need," he sighed heavily for the second time in as many minutes, "to make sure everything's in place. We have one shot at this. I have to stay awake. We need to—"

"Okay, okay." Thomas placed a friendly hand on his shoulder. "I got some pills that might help with that."

Guessing he meant amphetamines, Atticus politely declined. Dropping the duffel bag, Thomas unzipped and opened it with a flourish. Inside was a cornucopia of weaponry. Highly illegal weaponry. Pistols, sawn-offs, rifles and boxes of ammunition. It was enough to stage a coup d'état on a small South American country.

Maggie leaned over the bag. "Are they hand grenades?"

"You said you needed more weapons." Thomas shrugged. "The Wolfes provide." He cast Maggie a finger gun and checked his watch. "I'll be back at seven thirty with the boys. Be ready."

"Will do. Thanks for the..." Atticus gestured towards the bag. "Here's hoping we won't need it."

"You believe that?"

"No."

"Didn't think so." Thomas laughed. "See you tonight. Get some rest."

Giving them both a wave, he made his exit. Atticus felt even more tired.

"Atticus..."

He turned to Maggie. "I always know it's serious when you call me Atticus."

There was no smile in return, confirming his statement. "Your father..."

Flicking her head towards the now-closed door, he said, "I'm familiar with him."

"He's part of this."

"Again, aware."

"This whole thing could turn nasty. If the KGB turn up in force, there could be running gun battles in the streets." She gave an unconscious sideways glance at the duffel bag.

"Could be. I hope not, but I think we've—"

"What if he dies?"

"What..."

"Your father. We've already established that the time-line you know no longer exists. None of us know what that means. Time could repair itself, we could now be living on the moon by the eighties or people might end up liking Tang. The point is, we have no fucking idea. But one thing I'm sure of is if your father dies, you will never be born."

Atticus stood bolt upright. He'd spent so much time and mental energy trying to set things right, he'd given little thought to how much more wrong it could get.

"I... I hadn't considered that."

"No, I guessed you hadn't." She brushed her fingers along his cheek. "You like him, don't you?"

"My father? Now? I think I do, yeah."

"Even after all those beatings and the mental torture he put you through?"

"But the man I've gotten to know over the last week isn't *that* man. It's," he rubbed his scalp, "it's really weird. I can't explain it. Somehow, I've been able to separate the same man into different people. The life of bitterness hasn't yet poisoned the person I've gotten to know. He's not that perpetually enraged sociopath, furious at the world not giving him his due. It can't have all come down to being stabbed in the back. Maybe it was the catalyst that no longer happened, maybe not—wiser minds than mine will have to figure that one out. But a person is more than one event. Perhaps he will still become the same fearsome man I spent a lifetime being terrified of, perhaps not. All I know is the Thomas Wolfe I've been speaking to in the last week is not what I expected. Jesus, is anyone the same person they were as a teenager? I've gotten to know him as a man, not as a father, not as a notorious gangster, not as an instiller of fear, merely a man."

"I think you just explained it." She smiled sweetly.

For want of anything else to do, Atticus scrutinised the rolled-out map of the centre of Brixton.

"But what if he dies?" Her face despondent, she lowered her gaze. "What happens to you?"

"I... I don't know."

"Will you disappear? Do you die too?"

"I don't know, Maggie. I really don't."

Add it to the pile of things on Atticus's shoulders. Not only was the fate of the world resting on the next few hours, but his very existence could also be on the line. *No pressure.*

THEY CAME FROM THE SOUTH.

First spotted at Upper Tulse Hill, they came in force. The sun was setting when the first report to the War Room described a group of three men in trench coats marching north. If the group of white men in long leather coats thought they could take up position in Brixton unnoticed before the main event, they were greatly mistaken. Joe's informants kept the team updated on their progress.

Inside the War Room, Joe and Thomas Wolfe manned the phones. Cohen and Mrs Abernathy loaded weapons while huddled over local maps, giving themselves a crash course in the local terrain. Doyle fiddled with the communications equipment he'd rigged. The short-range devices would come in handy soon enough. He also had a reel-to-reel tape set up that Cohen had 'found' for him.

More concerning was Doyle's bundle of explosives stacked in the corner beside him. When Atticus had queried whether it was the best place to be tinkering with such volatile materials, Doyle had just smiled and replied, "If anything goes wrong, we won't be alive long enough to worry about it." This was apparently meant to be comforting.

Maggie stood by Atticus, ready to act as a go-between should he need one.

Joe's network tracked the path of the trench-coated goons. Soon another group was spotted. The whole concept sounded off to Atticus. It was too obvious. Too publicly orchestrated. There was no way the clandestine *secret* intelligence organisation would draw attention to itself in such a manner. The KGB wasn't about public displays of force, it was subtle. Most of all, it was lethal. The last thing anyone could accuse the KGB of being was *obvious*.

Thinking fast, Atticus explained to his grandfather what he needed to happen in the next five minutes. It was improvising on an already improvised plan, but Atticus had to get on the front foot.

Big Joe slapped his hand down on Atticus's shoulder. "Consider it done, my son."

The irony of the words were not lost on Atticus as he sped down the road in Joe's racing green Jaguar MkII. It was a beast of a car. He skidded to a halt at the corner of Brixton Hill and Fairmont Road the same time Joe's men ran into view, which was about thirty seconds before the long-coated KGB goons did.

Atticus stepped out from the car as the five hard-looking gangsters formed a rambling line across the road. The KGB goons slowed, then started to back up. That was, until they saw the six other gangsters about thirty yards up the road behind them. They'd chosen their ambush well. There were no side streets, nowhere to run. The goons were boxed in.

The lead gangster was Jacob, the cook from Eliza Wolfe's restaurant. Outside that environment he seemed more menacing, even more so when Atticus saw he still had his cleavers.

"Alright, mate?" Jacob addressed one of the KGB men.

The tallest KGB agent gulped. In all his experience, Atticus had never heard of a lethal killing machine from the infamous Komitet Gosudarstvennoy Bezopasnosti ever gulping.

The tall man responded to Jacob, all the while staring at his glistening cleavers, "We're just passing through."

It was the most cockney Russian accent Atticus had ever heard. Less Muscovite, more East End.

That's all Atticus needed to hear. He turned and headed back to the car. Jacob caught Atticus's eye and scratched the back of his head with the blunt end of his hatchet.

"Whatcha want us to do with this lot?" Jacob flicked his thumb at the group of not-KGB agents.

"Whatever you normally do with folks you don't want in the neighbourhood anymore."

Jacob grinned. The tall not-KGB agent gulped. Atticus sped back to the War Room.

He returned to find Joe's network had lit up the telephones with reports of men in long coats, each with at least one hand inside their coat at all times, like they were heavily armed.

Serious white faces scanning the streets. Some reports said it was as if the Gestapo had invaded Brixton. The stench of sweat in the small confines of the flat had risen in his absence.

Chatter in the War Room reached a crescendo until Atticus stuck two fingers in his mouth and set forth an ear-piercing whistle.

"Listen up, everyone. Joe, Thomas, tell your people to begin searching where those groups of men *aren't*. They're decoys. They're not what we need to be looking for."

"You mean there's something other than a dozen armed blokes invading the neighbourhood?" There was a hint of panic in Thomas's voice. "Fuckin' marvellous."

"It's a distraction. That's not the main game. It's coming. We won't know what it is until we see it."

"I'll let my people know what to keep an eye out for." He laughed quietly. "Or not, as it turns out." Joe's voice was far calmer than his son's.

The team doubled down on their efforts. The tension hadn't dissipated, it had morphed. Instead of fear of what was coming, now there was fear of the unknown.

Speaking in a low voice so the others couldn't hear, Maggie said, "The attack on MI6 wasn't exactly subtle. Maybe they've changed tactics?"

Atticus gave her a limp grin. "You could be right." He went over to Mrs Abernathy's pile of weapons and helped himself to two pistols and some spare ammunition. "Want to find out?"

Atticus couldn't stand being confined any longer. Winston had died because of the enemy currently at their gates. He was worried about the fate of his father and what that could mean for him, let alone the course of history itself. There was no way he could sit in a stinking war room while further reports come in. Passivity was not one of his stronger characteristics.

Atticus announced he and Maggie were heading out to get the lay of the land. It was partially true. He needed air, he needed to get out of the room he'd been confined in for the better part of a week, and walk the actual streets. More precisely, he needed to confront his foe face to face, wherever, or indeed whoever, it may be.

"Is that wise, dear?" There was no condescending tone from Mrs Abernathy, just genuine concern. "I mean, you're the one they're after, are you not?"

No longer his superior, Mrs Abernathy's concern for his welfare wasn't confined to a sanctioned MI6 operation.

Tilting his head in thanks, Atticus said, "I appreciate the word of caution, but I need to see the battleground first-hand, not rely solely on intelligence."

Mrs Abernathy bowed her head in acknowledgement. "I understand. I've done the same myself on the eve of battle. There're less Nazis alive today because of it. Happy hunting."

Atticus left instructions with the team to deploy to their pre-assigned positions. All the pieces were in place. The enemy was on its way. They had done all the planning they could.

He opened the door into the fading light. The rich scents of dozens of Brixton restaurants mixed in the early summer evening air. Maggie hooked her arm in his and they strode out into the busy street. Every step he took seemed one closer to the end.

GANGSTERS, by their very nature, are out-and-out brawlers. They're used to taking the fight directly to whoever they deem deserving of their wrath. Conversely, spies skulk in the shadows. They actively avoid confrontations, using guile and cunning.

The KGB had no permanent assets in Brixton. No ongoing intelligence. They would be flying blind and that would scare the hell out of them. The gangsters had a home ground advantage, but of the two, the KGB had a record of death that even the feared group of gangsters could never match.

The two groups had vastly different styles of confrontation. As the night grew steadily darker, they were on a collision course. Atticus had no idea who would claim victory in the end.

Arm in arm, he and Maggie strode the streets of Brixton. She clung extra close, her nerves betrayed as she held him tighter. She wasn't the only uneasy one.

Even if he hadn't known what was coming, Atticus could sense it in the air. On the streets, people were on edge. The extra glances, the hunched scurrying about. If this was the old west, people would be closing their shutters and shooing their children inside before the showdown at noon. It seemed word had spread: trouble was coming.

Atticus searched for a topic, any topic, to take Maggie's mind off the battle to come. He found one.

"Wait." Her jaw dropped. "Just wait. Anything. You can watch whenever you want? Like... anything?"

In a time when programs may be shown only once and never seen again, reruns were a novelty and the concept of VHS rental nothing but a pipe dream, the idea of streaming was tantamount to flying cars.

"So... if I wanted to watch, I don't know, *Wizard of Oz*."

He laughed but continued to scan the street. "Yes, you can watch that."

"What about *Psycho*?"

"Yes."

"*Gone with the Wind*? *Casablanca*?"

"Also, unsurprisingly, yes and yes. Pretty much anything you can think of."

"But not things like *Doctor Who*, though?" Her face lit up even at the mention of her new favourite show. "You couldn't watch something like that whenever you felt like it?"

"Absolutely you can." He chuckled. "Although you might have to set aside some time; there's a few episodes to catch up on. *Doctor Who* is still running in my time."

"Shut up." Maggie stopped walking, mouth agape. "You're making fun of me."

"I'm really not." Chuckling, Atticus dragged her along to keep moving. "You've got the great Tom Baker to look forward to, but David Tennant is still the best Doctor. I'm prepared to die on that hill."

Atticus was thankful Maggie's mood had lifted. Dipping one's thoughts too low with morbid what-ifs dulled the senses. To keep the mind sharp, it had to stay positive. He needed Maggie's head in the game. He needed everyone's head in the game. His included.

They strode along in silence for a while, their disposition lighter and more focused.

What was that?

Atticus had caught a flash of a white face in the crowd, nothing more. It was distinctly neither brown nor working class. Half a block away, he'd seen the familiar face turn a corner. Or had he? Had Atticus's conscious thoughts manifested themselves onto to some random person in the crowd, or had he actually seen them?

Either way, Atticus had to find out. His pace doubled and Maggie stumbled to catch up. She regarded him curiously but said nothing. She rightly assumed there was a reason.

Eyes searching where he'd seen the face, Atticus's jaw was set. "It might be Mikhail up ahead."

Taking the news undaunted, Maggie asked, "Should I alert the others?"

He shook his head. "Not yet. It might be him, but I'm not a hundred per cent. I only got a fleeting glance. I don't want to mobilise everyone on a wild goose chase, they're on edge enough already. We have to be sure."

Weaving through the bustling crowd, Atticus guided the couple down Brixton Road, turning off the side street he'd seen Mikhail/maybe-not-Mikhail slip down. When they caught sight of the back of the man some thirty metres ahead, Atticus became less sure with every step. The man's unhurried nature, his posture, was unlike a combatant in the midst of his opponent's territory. From behind he appeared like a local sauntering home after a hard day's work.

Doubt crept into Atticus's every pore. He was tightly wound and jumping at shadows. Now they'd likely wasted valuable time following a false lead. Atticus was sure he'd chased down a ghost, right up until the point he felt a gun in his back.

Instantly stopping, he pulled Maggie to a halt. She'd turned, half amused, but on seeing the holder of the weapon all glee dissolved in an instant. Her hand leapt to her mouth to cover her gasp.

The person drilling a gun barrel into Atticus's back

shouted beyond him, in the direction of the man they'd been following. "Он у меня есть!" Which translated to "I've got him!"

The man they'd been trailing turned, surprised. His confusion soon turned to elation and he doubled back in a jog. Atticus thrust his hand in his pocket, trying his best to appear as casual as possible. He hoped his ad hoc team were prepared.

Slowing, Mikhail's smile stretched wide across his features. Instead of making some conceited quip, he instead placed his hand in his breast pocket and took out his wallet. He flipped out a ten-pound note.

Shaking his head, Mikhail handed the note to the man with the gun. "It seems he really is as stupid as you said he was."

Accepting the payment, the man spun Atticus around. "Now now, my Mikhail. Is that any way to talk about our new guest?"

There was no denying the pleasure on Oliver's face.

CHAPTER

FOURTEEN

The abandoned mechanic's workshop reeked of
motor oil and stale sweat.

Atticus and Maggie sat shackled to the heavy
wooden chairs in the centre of the workshop. The bare
room consisted of a stained concrete floor, corrugated iron
walls and a large wooden sliding door at the entrance. High
above, the stepped roof would offer ample light during the
day, but now offered nothing but blackness.

Besides the two chairs at its centre, there were a few
out-of-place tables crammed with weaponry, walkie
talkies, food rations and, unfortunately for Atticus and
Maggie, torture implements. Concrete ramps built into the
floor jutted out at irregular intervals. A few cots could be
seen in the far corner.

Maggie and Atticus were closely guarded by well-armed
square-jawed Soviet heavies, likely KGB. Real ones, not the
decoys sent to roam the streets and intimidate the locals.
The whole set-up seemed to have been established hours
before, if not days.

Bereft of its fittings and equipment, the bare warehouse

DAVE SINCLAIR

was the perfect setting for a grilling, and likely worse. Atticus was pissed that he was the subject of the questioning, and not the interrogator.

On the concrete rise away from their position, Mikhail and the definitely-not-dead Oliver stood huddled in close conference. Atticus assumed they were discussing the nature of the interrogation to come. He couldn't hear what was being said, though it mattered little. Their body language seemed to corroborate his assumption about the relationship between the two. Each man would sometimes gently place his hand on the other's—a far more intimate gesture than that of a mere colleague.

Despite her assurances to the contrary, Maggie was understandably distressed. This was not a natural habitat for her. She had received little training in this part of the job. Somewhat macabrely, for Atticus it was a state that was not only familiar, but comfortable.

Atticus turned to the henchmen. He assumed they were KGB, but had forgone a request for their credentials, given the circumstances.

"Which one of you is Len?" The Soviets considered him blankly. Regardless, he pushed on. "It says Len's Auto Repairs on the side of the building. One of you has to be Len, surely?" He poked his shoulder at the most Russian of the group. "You sure your name's not Len? You look like a Len. It's the chin." He jutted his out for effect.

Probably-Not-Len stepped forward and gave Atticus a vicious backhanded slap. With a sneer he snarled, "глупый черный человек."

The rest of the crew laughed, but Atticus didn't share their amusement—the Soviet had called him the Russian equivalent of a stupid black man.

He waited for their mirth to subside. If the KGB operative thought his blow would intimidate him, he was sorely mistaken. Instead, Atticus gave him a bloody leer. The expression gave the aggressor pause and he stepped back, confounded as to why his aggression had not had the intended effect.

Tilting his head, Atticus growled, "я говорю на русском языке идиот," which translated to "I speak Russian, idiot". He then added, "Иди ебать ёжика," which equated to him telling them all to go fuck a hedgehog.

Before Probably-Not-Len could deliver another brutal blow, Mikhail shouted from the back of the workshop, "Стоп! Он получит свое." *Stop! He'll get his.*

Atticus was sure Mikhail thought as much. He'd only be too pleased to show him the error of his ways.

Mikhail and Oliver finished their private confab and joined the others. Mikhail was the first to approach. "It has been very long time, Future Man. How are you? Been well?"

"I'll be far better when I have my hands around your throat."

"Ha, yes very good. Such masculine aggression." He held two hammy fighting fists up for effect. "So noble." He sighed. "So pointless. Maybe you are annoyed because you were idiot for falling too easily into our trap? Hmm, do you think, da?"

Atticus recalled the threatening gesture Mikhail had made while standing on the top of the car in Jūrmala. A promise of revenge. He'd certainly made good on that promise.

Jaw locked, Atticus bore his eyes into Mikhail. "Why did you kill Winston?"

"Who?"

"The poor kid who dropped off the message."

"Oh him? That was just a bit of fun." There was glee in Mikhail's expression.

Testing the full strength of his restraints, Atticus did his best to break free and kill the man where he stood. Fortunately for Mikhail, the handcuffs held.

Lowering his gaze, Atticus flexed his hands, ready to snap Mikhail's neck given the chance. "I'll make sure you pay for every life you took at MI6."

The KGB henchman rolled his eyes. "They were stupid men fighting for wrong side of wrong war. The bourgeois capitalists would have died eventually, I just helped them get there sooner." He leaned forward. "What is it the Americans like to say? You ain't seen nothing yet?" His thin-lipped smile was humourless. "What Oliver has planned will reshape the world. They wouldn't have liked it. Neither would you if, of course, you lived that long."

"Looks like you and Oliver are suffering from the same misconception. His delusions of grandeur are nothing but that—delusions." Atticus shook his head sadly. "Your boyfriend really has you brainwashed, doesn't he?"

It had only been supposition on Atticus's behalf that the two were involved, but the flash of shock was all the confirmation he needed. Mikhail's eyes went wide, and his gaze instantly went to Oliver. In spite of his training, the agent let his guard down for a fraction of a second too long.

Oliver finally entered the fray, likely to deflect Mikhail's reaction. With a flourish, he bowed to Maggie. "My dear, you're looking as lovely as always."

"Oh, Oliver," Maggie said coyly, "why don't you go fuck yourself?"

Unfazed by the barb, Oliver pushed his glasses back on the bridge of his nose. "And here I was, paying you a compliment." He shook his head. "Oh, I just can't stay mad at you."

He ruffled her hair a little too vigorously. Maggie glared at him, the daggers in her eyes leaving no doubt as to her feelings.

Regardless, Oliver went on, addressing Atticus. "We had planned on simply following young Maggie here once we realised you'd gone to ground, but I have to say, this little minx gave us the slip within three blocks. And I'm talking seasoned KGB pursuit professionals here. Quite impressive."

Even through her anger there was no mistaking the pride on Maggie's face. With reason. She was becoming more accomplished by the day.

Atticus's team had wanted to use Maggie as bait to smoke Oliver out, reminiscent of Mrs Abernathy's original plan when they'd first gone to Latvia. Atticus had disagreed, arguing that Maggie's worth was far more than mere bait. The fact they were here at all was due to her suggestion. The fact that Oliver thought he had the upper hand was a manifestation of her abilities.

"Hi Oliver." Atticus addressed him for the first time. "Not dead yet, I see?"

"I always said you were most perceptive."

"No, you didn't." Atticus glanced up to the windows in the tiered roof, then to the four henchmen. "Who were the idiots running around Brixton?"

Oliver chuckled. "Just a bunch of local actors we hired. Amazing what you can get those meat puppets to do on the promise of a few pints and a meeting with David Lean."

So, the ones here are KGB. Thanks for the confirmation.

Noticing Atticus eyeing off his henchmen, Oliver gave a condescending tilt of his head. "These gentlemen, on the other hand, are more than capable of handling the likes of you, in case you held out any hope. There will be no cavalry riding in at the last minute. No escape. There is only the next little while in this room. How you decide to spend it is entirely up to you."

Atticus lowered his gaze. "Why did you do it? There was no reason to kill anyone at MI6. It was cold-blooded murder."

"But hunting me down, throwing me in a coffin and shooting it up, not caring if I lived or died was what, tantamount to a hug?" Oliver lifted his shirt to show a gunshot wound, still red raw. A flesh wound only. "You nearly killed me!"

The pitch in Oliver's voice told Atticus he wasn't in control of his emotions. *Good.* He could use that.

"So, petty revenge then? Okay, got it."

"Petty!"

Mikhail placed his hand gently on Oliver's shoulder and his anger quickly subsided. Oliver nodded and patted the other man's arm in return.

He sighed. "It wasn't revenge, but a necessary first step in the new world order. I don't expect your little mind to grasp the strategies at play here, but there are world-shaping acts taking place before your eyes, you just don't see it."

"I hate to correct you, but it wasn't the first step of a strategist, it was the last mistake of a madman. You're recklessly messing with the timeline, Oliver. What you're doing is irresponsible. You don't know what you're unleashing."

Letting loose a raucous laugh, Oliver shook his head. "You're naïve. Pretty, sure, but naïve." He sighed, as if the answer was simple and he was explaining it to a six-year-old. "The Soviet Union is currently tearing itself apart wanting to know if a rogue element is waging an unsanctioned war on the West. I will very shortly supply them with the names and details of those responsible."

"Who just happen to be standing in your way of a rise to power within the party?"

Frowning in approval, Oliver said, "Maybe you're smarter than I give you credit for. Alright, what else?" Oliver folded his arms challengingly.

Racking his brains, Atticus came up with a scenario he should have come up with days ago. "You're in the UK to plant evidence that corroborates your framing of these men on the rungs to your ascension."

Oliver didn't have to verbally respond, his face confirmed Atticus's theory.

"Very good. I'm impressed." Oliver went on. "Plus, it gave me an opportunity to pay you a personal visit. I had this inkling my old organisation wouldn't exactly be pleased to see me back in the country. Framing my adversaries gave me more freedom to move about, as they were otherwise occupied, no? A useful distraction."

"That distraction cost the lives of people you worked alongside for years. Twenty-seven of them."

Oliver laughed. "Oh please. By the time this little scenario plays out, that trifling number will be laughable."

"I'm not laughing." Atticus realised his control of the conversation was slipping away. "Mark Twain said all you need in this life is ignorance and confidence, and then success is sure. You, Oliver, have both in abundance. Shame you won't succeed."

Throwing out his palms, Oliver pivoted around the room. "Did I miss something? Is someone else tied up here? I hate to disappoint you, but I'm in charge."

"You won't know real disappointment until you get to

the last season of *Game of Thrones*." Turning serious, Atticus leaned forward. "I hate to tell you, Oliver, but it's the Soviet Union that runs against the tide of history. It's—"

"The march of freedom and democracy which will leave Marxism-Leninism on the ash heap of history?" Oliver tilted his head. "Did I get the Reagan quote correct?"

Atticus didn't care if his jaw was hanging open. Reagan? *Reagan?* In this era he should be nothing but a two-bit actor appearing in forgettable chimpanzee films. He shouldn't be quoted as a world leader unless... *oh hell no.*

Oliver leaned forward. "I do believe he's speechless." He turned to Mikhail. "Oh, that's adorable."

Seeing his distress, Maggie turned to him, confused. "What's going on?"

Atticus's words felt heavy in his mouth. "He's managed to unlock the phone. He's read the history books."

Oliver's laugh could have been categorised as maniacal. From his pocket, he extracted the fabled phone, now unlocked. The other Soviets observed, somewhat perplexed. Obviously they hadn't been briefed on every aspect of the operation. "In retrospect I should have thanked you for coming all the way to Latvia. Your finger-prints were all over the car you left behind. The ingenuity of the great Soviet scientists meant they were able to translate those fingerprints into something your phone could recog-nise. They were the same great minds who worked on Sput-nik, you know."

Oliver let that hang in the air for a moment, as if it would impress Atticus. He went on.

"There was no, uh, biorhythmic field data or whatever you called it. Complete bollocks, presumedly, but never mind, we have you now. Unlocked forever. My, they don't make changing those settings very easy, do they?"

"If you have that, you don't need me. You can let us go."

"Oh, come now, of course we *need* you, Atticus. You're coming to the Soviet Union with us. A staid academic work doesn't give it full context, doesn't supply the real-world, lived-in appreciation that, say," Oliver lips parted in delight, "a man from the future does."

"I won't cooperate."

"Oh, I know that, don't be ridiculous. Of course you won't. Not at first." Oliver shrugged. "It might take years in the gulag, but you'll eventually come around." He gleefully turned to Maggie. "With her along for the ride, I'm sure we can find some inventive incentives. Oh, that rhymes!"

"You fuck!" Maggie did her best to lunge at her former friend but didn't get far.

Oliver ignored her, still joyfully boasting his cleverness. "Who knows, maybe you can help us understand how this thing actually works. Help us leap fifty years ahead in the technology without breaking a sweat." He waved the device in front of him. "No need to lose the space race now, hey Atticus?"

"Why are you doing this, Oliver?"

Maggie's last Hail Mary seemed intended to appeal to Oliver's better nature. Atticus had long ago learned he had no such thing.

She went on. "We used to be friends. I know you. This isn't you. I can help you, Oliver. Atticus can help you."

"Atticus only helps himself!"

The fury of the delivery surprised even Mikhail, who was doing his best to not interfere, though it was obvious he was hanging on every word. He stepped forward but said nothing.

Turning on Maggie, Oliver's eyes were wild behind his glasses. "Don't you see? Haven't you figured it out? He pretends to be your friend, with his long lashes and kind words, but in the end he's only there for himself."

"That's untrue." Maggie's eyes narrowed on Oliver. "You never got to know him, not the way you wanted to. But he's a—"

"Did he tell you about Genevieve?" Oliver's voice was even once more.

Maggie's, on the other hand, faltered. "Who?"

"Obviously not." The expression on Oliver's face was triumphant.

"Don't." Atticus's tone was a slab of ice.

Oliver tilted his head. "Did he not tell you about his girlfriend in the future? She sent him so many text messages. Test messages? No, text messages they're called." Oliver manipulated the screen on Atticus's phone. He seemed well practiced. "So many messages, oh, and pictures, racy ones at that. I don't think such outfits would be legal in this time, do you?" He held up a picture, taken in a bathroom. The red-headed selfie taker wore skimpy panties and a bra, pulling the latter down to display her ample cleavage. "I tell you, the way this woman writes explicit messages... I was quite tempted to swap sides, let me tell you."

"He loves me." Eyes welling with tears, Maggie squared her jaw. "Here. Now."

She faltered on the word love. They hadn't officially had *that* conversation. Not in person. It had only been via notes hand-delivered by Winston. That was something they had silently agreed would come after. Atticus was prepared to tell her everything, including about Genevieve. To him, that future was well in his past. But by the look on Maggie's face, it was very much the present.

Defiantly, she said, "Atticus and I are together. We love each other."

Clapping his hands, Oliver said, "Isn't that marvellous. Tell me… is he still trying to get home?"

She was speechless once again. That was another conversation they were yet to have. Doubt washed over her face once more.

There was no way he could know about Ganim. The old man showed up after Oliver had been exposed as a mole. Was it a turn of phrase, or something more sinister? Either way, everyone in the room was soon occupied by other thoughts.

The patter of footsteps on the roof distracted them all. Oliver and Mikhail squinted upward then turned to Atticus, troubled.

Oliver's eyes flared. "What the hell is that?"

"That? Nothing to worry about." Atticus's white teeth shone. "Just the cavalry you said wasn't coming."

CHAPTER

FIFTEEN

"Remember how you said I was an idiot for falling too easily into your trap?" Atticus grinned widely. "It's time for you to meet the kettle."

"I... what?" Oliver shook his head. "What does that mean?"

"The pot calling the kettle black." Atticus paused. "It's... you know, an example of hypocrisy." He turned to Maggie. "It was pretty clear, right? Meet the kettle?"

Maggie skewed her mouth to the side. "I don't know. It was a bit vague." As best she could, handcuffed to the wooden chair, she shrugged.

The plan had all been Maggie's idea. She was the one who'd suggested she and Atticus step out into the Brixton streets and make themselves visible—bait, as it were. Once they deduced the KGB had sent decoys, they knew the *real* KGB had to be somewhere close by. They weren't ones to show up in force; the Soviets had another play to make. Maggie suggested they let them make it. Now came the counterattack.

Atticus and Maggie's escapades had been monitored by

their team every second since they'd spotted Mikhail. Doyle had the two of them wired. That was why Atticus had been careful to mention Len's Auto Repairs. The team knew exactly where to find them. And find them they had.

The first explosion blew out the wooden sliding door.

High above on the tiered roof, glass shattered and two black-clad bodies descended on ropes. A second explosion from the rear of the workshop sent Soviet agents scurrying in all directions, panicked and ill-prepared.

In a matter of seconds, Oliver and Mikhail's arrogant control of the situation had literally been blown apart. The first to fall was the one Atticus had dubbed Probably-Not-Len. He took a head shot and slumped lifeless to the filthy concrete floor. His comrade to his left had his chest ripped apart by successive bullets and collapsed on top of his slain companion.

The remaining two fought back, regrouping and staging a semblance of counter strike. Two of Joe's men fell as they stormed through the smouldering ruin of the sliding door. Mikhail extracted a Luger and took pot shots at the descending black-clad attackers. One was far more adept at abseiling than the other. The expert reached the ground while his counterpart struggled to make the descent. It cost him his life. Mikhail shot him in the centre of the chest, and he hit the concrete floor with a sickening *thud*.

Oliver, on the other hand, leapt sideways to cower behind Maggie, obviously hoping to avoid becoming an easy target. Mikhail stayed by his side, but just far enough away that Atticus couldn't kick him.

The firefight advantage switched by the second. The attack on the front entrance was pinned down. Jacob, the chef from the restaurant, flung cleavers at the Soviets. The accuracy of his aim seemed to be giving the enemy more concern than the bullets. One cleaver struck a KGB agent's upper torso, eliciting a scream of pain.

Atticus identified the attacker who had successfully descended the roof as Cohen. He'd made a run for their position but been pushed back by Mikhail. He'd now adopted a defensive position near the entrance, safely behind a concrete ramp. He managed to pop his head up long enough to give Atticus and Maggie an "OK" symbol before taking cover from a hail of bullets.

The rear of the workshop was another matter. The two KGB agents were relentless in their counterattack. Their AK-47s barked loudly, silencing the numerous shots coming from the back entrance. Once quiet, they turned their attention to the front and fought off waves of attacks, felling several of Joe's men in the process. In a short amount of time their counteroffensive had a devastating effect.

It wouldn't last. They must have known they were outnumbered. If they were to make their escape out back, they had mere seconds to try.

Sensing the opportunity, Oliver stood. "We have to—"

He never finished his sentence as Maggie kicked out her legs to sweep Oliver's out from underneath him. He collapsed hard on the oily concrete. Not wasting a second, Atticus launched himself at the flailing Oliver. The heavy chair Atticus was shackled to landed hard on the prone man. His manacled hands grappled frantically for anything he could grip onto. Atticus managed to deliver a headbutt before an incensed Mikhail ripped him away and flung Oliver free.

No longer focused on his captive, Mikhail cradled Oliver's face in his hands. His glasses were shattered, blood seeping from a cut on his forehead.

"We have to leave. Now!"

Mikhail heaved the stunned Oliver to his feet and without turning back, barked orders in Russian as they escaped via the rear of the workshop. Cohen managed to take a few pot-shots in their direction, but to no avail. Within seconds the firefight was over.

Maggie looked down at Atticus laying sideways on the concrete, still handcuffed to the chair. "Feel better you got a couple of cheeky smacks in?"

"Oh, I'd say I got more than that." Atticus rolled over to reveal his prized mobile phone in his shackled hands. "Mark one up for the good guys."

"You clever little bastard." She gave him a little congratulatory slap on the shoulder.

"Listen," Atticus spoke quickly, knowing they would soon have company, "there's a lot we need to talk about, but I wanted you to know—"

"I love you too, you big idiot."

Even though he felt the pain of his left wrist being crushed under the weight of the heavy wooden chair, Atticus beamed. "I love you too."

"That's so sweet I think I might throw up."

The lanky figure of Doyle lumbered over to them. He righted Atticus and gave Maggie a greeting wink.

"Were the explosions completely necessary?" Atticus raised an eyebrow.

Doyle whistled cheerily as he went to work on Atticus's handcuffs. "Yes, and you're welcome." He nodded to Atticus's hand. "What's that black plastic thing you've got there?"

"Trouble." Atticus left it at that.

Cohen soon joined them and extracted a pair of wire cutters, freeing Maggie and Atticus in quick succession. They were joined by Joe and Thomas and five more of their men. Some bore bloody injuries, but their hard faces showed they weren't about to shy away from a fight. Atticus shook his hands to get circulation going.

He turned to Joe and then to the four men laying lifeless by the front entrance. "I'm sorry for your men."

"We'll bury 'em later. Don't worry, their families'll be looked after. Right now, I think we need to decide if we go after those bastards or not. You two 'ave already been through hell."

Atticus picked up a Kalashnikov at his feet, checked the cartridge for ammunition and disengaged the safety on the right-hand side. "Oh, we're definitely hunting them down." He ran towards the rear door. "Who's with me?"

It was a ridiculous question. All ten raced out the door in pursuit.

THE STREETS WERE EMPTY. Whether it was because people were running in fear from the sound of the firefight or at the King of Brixton's orders, it didn't matter. A vacant street made it far easier to spot an opponent. Atticus anticipated Oliver and Mikhail were regrouping and likely desperate. They had to move carefully. A cornered adversary was an unpredictable and vicious one. They already understood how ferocious their enemy could be.

The teams had split into three roaming groups. They kept in contact with Mrs Abernathy back at their impromptu HQ in Atticus's tiny flat. For twenty minutes they roamed the streets. Joe's people set up roadblocks at all major intersections, searching for anyone who matched the descriptions of the men last seen fleeing Len's Auto Repair.

Doyle, Cohen and Atticus strode down Stockwell Road with purpose, hyper alert and on edge. Atticus's wrist rattled with the clang of handcuffs. There was no time to find a way to remove them, but at least his arms worked independently now.

Now he'd had a chance to breathe, Atticus decided he was exhausted. Adrenaline only worked for so long. Not that he'd rest until he found them again.

Maggie had been entrusted with his phone; he wasn't prepared to risk it changing hands again if they encountered Oliver and Mikhail. Oliver no longer had access to Cold War history books or the technology itself, and Atticus was determined to keep it that way. Not for the first time, Atticus thought he should destroy the thing. The apocryphal device shouldn't exist in this era.

To keep his mind active, Atticus spoke to Doyle. "Did you get it all?"

"They don't call me the master for nothing."

Cohen grunted. "They don't call you the master."

"Yet." Doyle waggled his index finger in the air.

Not only had Doyle wired Maggie and Atticus so they could listen into their conversation, he'd also recorded it onto a reel-to-reel tape. How clear it was and what its future use may serve would be determined another day.

"There was," Doyle scratched the back of his neck, "uh, a bit said that didn't make a hell of a lot of sense."

"Lots of in jokes, but thanks," Atticus said, patting him on the shoulder. "I owe you. I owe both of you."

"We're not going to start hugging, are we?" Cohen's delivery was deadpan. "I mean, I like you blokes, just not like that."

Doyle laughed. Atticus didn't. *Ah, casual homophobia.* In the whole scheme of things, it was mild, even for this time, but it was still there. And it wouldn't be going away anytime soon.

Clattering footfalls from behind made them pivot as one, guns ready. Thomas Wolfe jogged toward them, panting, but smiling.

"Alright lads?"

Warm greetings were exchanged, camaraderie having been established under fire. If Atticus had time, he'd have marvelled at how readily Doyle and Cohen had worked with black men, even followed their commands. It was a shame that a simple matter of easy acceptance stood out for praise. It was also evident to Atticus that his thoughts were meandering when they should have been focused on the task at hand. Luckily, Thomas's news brought them back to laser sharp focus.

The local gangsters' network had found them. A butcher known to wisely provide the King of Brixton with free choice cuts had called the War Room to say he'd spotted the men he'd been tasked to keep an eye out for. According to Thomas, Joe would be having a quiet word with his landlord about the requirement, or rather, lack thereof, to pay rent for the next year. The landlord, knowing what was good for him, would no doubt comply. That was how Joe had become the King of Brixton. A mixture of rewarding loyalty and instilling abject fear.

The remainder of Oliver's forces were holed up in a wooden shed at a construction site on the edge of Ruskin Park. The butcher had seen three men carrying a fourth covered in blood. It seemed one of Cohen's pot shots had found its mark. The four sprinted to the location.

≈

THE OLD SHED was dark and still. No sign of life. The park adjacent to the rubble-strewn construction site was equally lifeless. The four were crouched behind a semi-demolished wall, waiting for any sign of life.

"How sure are you they're in there?" Cohen put voice to what they were all thinking. "If I freeze my balls off staking out three shovels and a bucket, I'm gonna have words with someone."

Thomas stood. "Well, let's find out."

Grasping his forearm, Atticus held his father back. "These are men you don't underestimate." He jutted his chin towards the silent shed. "They're cornered and dangerous, now more than ever. We need to wait."

"Who the hell put you in charge, Smith?" Thomas shook off Atticus's hold. "This is *my* town, mate. They killed *my* people. If the bastards are in there, they won't be breathin' for much longer." He gripped his pistol tight.

This was more the man Atticus remembered. Angry. Unwilling to listen. He had to keep his father's temper at bay. He knew from experience that bad things happened if he didn't. Violent things.

Atticus did his best to sound calming. "A frontal assault is—"

"How we do things around here."

Thomas sprinted across the construction site towards the shed. He didn't look back. Doyle and Cohen turned to Atticus expectantly as Thomas tore into the darkness.

Atticus sighed. "Come on then."

The three MI6 agents—well, two and a former agent—ran towards the still-silent builder's shed. The assault was reckless. Thomas's actions shouldn't have been a surprise. He was young, brash, inexperienced and overconfident. It was a heady mix that attracted trouble. Or rather, compelled him to run headfirst into it.

Thomas kicked the door in and leapt into the darkness. For a second nothing happened. Then four gunshots rang out in quick succession, their flashes illuminating the tiny shed.

Atticus sprinted at full pace.

Bursting into the cluttered hut he discovered a tense standoff. One of the KGB men had fallen backwards; a fresh hole in the centre of his forehead explained the vacant, lifeless stare. The other lay in the centre of the floor, seemingly having been there for some time. A sheet half-covered his body, and deep red blood seeped into the white material. It was the man Jacob had lobbed a cleaver into.

Thomas stared at the smoking gun in his hand, as if unsure whether he'd truly fired the weapon and killed another man. Perhaps it was the first life he'd taken. His sallow expression seemed to confirm as much.

In the corner of the dusty shed, Oliver sat in a wooden chair, gobsmacked, a Luger at his feet. Atticus shook his head and said, "Don't."

Doyle and Cohen entered, taking in the carnage. Having assessed the situation, Doyle stepped outside, gun up, guarding the entrance from external threats. Mikhail was still unaccounted for.

Atticus stepped towards his father. "You alright?"

It took a few seconds, but eventually Thomas nodded. Reacting slowly, he appeared to be in shock. Atticus would have to deal with that later. Right now, he had a more pressing issue.

"Where's Mikhail?"

Peeling his eyes from the slain KGB agent, Oliver turned

to Atticus. "Who?" He shook his head slowly. "Never heard of him."

As if on cue, the door to the shed swung shut and Mikhail leapt forward from behind it, holding a gun to Cohen's head. With his free hand he slid the bolt across to secure the door, which rattled with the sound of Doyle attempting to wrench it open.

"Doyle, stand down!" Cohen's voice was loud but calm. "We have a situation here."

Mikhail tutted and turned to Oliver. He turned the gun towards Atticus. "Silly man did not check behind door. He's not very smart, is he?"

Oliver shrugged. "Our friend here walks into a meeting thinking he's the smartest man in in the room but doesn't realise even the pot plants outsmart him." Oliver's arrogance had returned in spades. "He makes cheese seem intelligent."

Mikhail sneered. "At least cheese is cultured."

Despite the gun to his head, Cohen laughed. He turned to Atticus apologetically and shrugged. "What? It was funny."

Thomas stepped towards Mikhail, his Colt raising by the second. In response, Mikhail pressed the Luger harder into Cohen's skull.

"Back off, little boy, or your friend here gets bullet in head."

Thomas shrugged. "He's not my friend."

With a frown, Cohen said, "Thanks very much."

In direct violation of Mikhail's order, Thomas took a step closer. Mikhail couldn't move the gun away from Cohen or he'd lose the only leverage he had.

"Thomas..." Atticus's voice was low, but full of caution.

While his actions were fearless, the same couldn't be

said for his face. Thomas's expression was full of trepidation. He gulped as he trained his weapon on Mikhail.

"Put the gun down, man." Thomas's voice was almost pleading. "Please."

It was in direct contrast to the man Atticus had known. The Thomas Wolfe he remembered was forever searching for someone to hurt. Be it an adversary who slighted him, real or imagined, or simply someone who bumped him in the street. Quick to anger. Quick to revenge. The older Thomas Wolfe would kill at the slightest of provocations. But the teenager before Atticus hadn't yet morphed into the tough, unyielding hard man he'd feared and endured. The teenager before him was scared. It was an emotion Atticus had never seen in his father.

"Come on, Oliver." Mikhail edged towards the door, dragging Cohen with him. "We are leaving."

"Wait." Oliver wasn't as confident as his partner. "I don't know..."

"It is fine, my love." The forced humour in Mikhail's grimace was in contrast to the fear in his eyes. "They will not shoot. Believe me."

"Man, this is your last warning." The gun in Thomas's hand shook. "Seriously."

"You know I'm standing here, right?" Cohen's cockiness waned.

In spite of Cohen's warning Thomas aimed his weapon squarely at Mikhail.

"Put that down." Mikhail took another step toward the door. "We both know you won't—"

Thomas fired. Mikhail's head snapped back as Cohen leapt aside. Mikhail's lifeless body crumpled to the floor. Instinctively, Atticus swivelled to cover Oliver, but there was no need.

"No!"

Oliver dropped to his knees. The bespectacled man wailed, clutching his chest. With tears in his eyes, Oliver's head slumped. In the commotion, he'd managed to grab the Luger on the floor, not that it would do him any good. All guns in the room were aimed at him. Cornered and alone, he realised he was done.

Oliver's shoulders sagged. "This isn't the end, you know?" His words were hollow, the pistol hanging limply in his hand. He glanced up and his voice hardened. "The inimitable Atticus Wolfe will make a mistake, and I'll make sure you pay with your life."

Thomas's head whipped around. "What did you call him? Atticus what?"

"Atticus Wolfe." Oliver tilted his head, suddenly focused. "What is *your* name, sir?"

Perhaps still in shock, Thomas answered on instinct. "Thomas Wolfe."

Atticus could virtually hear the wheels turning in Oliver's mind. He sized up the younger man, perhaps assessing his age. Oliver's tear-stained eyes blazed with realisation. As hard as he fought to maintain his composure, Atticus suspected he must have reacted enough for Oliver to see.

"Playing with the old man?" Oliver tutted as he shook his head. "And you think I'm reckless with the timeline?" The man who had nothing to lose released a humourless smile. "Who's up for testing the grandfather paradox?"

Without waiting for an answer, Oliver lifted his gun and shot Thomas Wolfe.

CHAPTER
SIXTEEN

Atticus didn't disappear in a puff of paradoxical logic. At least, not yet.

Riding in the back of the bumpy ambulance, he held Thomas's hand. The teenager groaned in pain, his corduroy jacket slick with blood. Atticus knew a bullet wound was dreadfully painful, but how deadly it was depended entirely on whether any vital organs had been hit. Right now, there was no way to know.

The young paramedic riding with them gave Atticus a thin smile. "King's College are the best in the Commonwealth. Your son will be alright."

Atticus blinked several times, backwards engineering the sentence. "Thanks."

Cohen had run to the closest house and called an ambulance. The resident had been reluctant to help at first, until he was advised who had been injured. The ambulance arrived in a remarkably short amount of time.

Doyle and Cohen had hauled Oliver out as fast as they could. When word spread about who had pulled the trigger there wouldn't be a rock Oliver could hide under within shooting distance of Brixton. Atticus would meet them, Mrs Abernathy and Maggie in a safe house near Wembley after Thomas had been admitted.

Distraught, Atticus watched his writhing father. The locals had triumphed, but not without significant casualties. Again, he was left to wonder how irreparably he'd damaged the timeline. Not just the man before him, but the entire world. Events had spiralled out of control far more significantly than he could have possibly have imagined. He'd done as much as he could to contain it, but in the process had irrevocably ruined all he knew to be true.

"That bloke with the glasses."

Atticus turned to Thomas. He was in pain, but lucid.

He went on. "He said you was a Wolfe. Atticus Wolfe." Thomas winced. "That why you went by Smith?"

Unsure how to verbally reply, Atticus nodded.

"He should rest." The paramedic's voice was gentle but firm.

"We'll talk about it later." Atticus did his best to sound reassuring. "Right now, we need to get you patched up. I'll explain everything, it'll be fine."

But Atticus had no intention of explaining anything. Nor would he see his father, grandfather or grandmother again. Each time he'd stepped into their world, he'd changed things for the worse. He couldn't afford to do it again. As much as it pained him, he would never spend time with his beloved grandmother again. He was done messing with their world.

He patted his father's hand. The flashing lights of the ambulance soon illuminated the A & E entrance.

~

THE WEMBLEY safe house was closer to a luxury townhouse than a safe house.

Dragging his feet up the cobblestone path, Atticus felt a million years old. It seemed like years since he'd slept. All he wanted to do was see Maggie's face and sleep for a decade or five.

But it wouldn't be that simple. He had to deal with Oliver first.

After greeting Doyle, Cohen and Mrs Abernathy, he was shown to the second-floor bedroom. The room was elegantly appointed and took up the entire floor. Oliver was bound by several cords to an armchair in the centre of the room. The reversal of fortunes was not lost on Atticus.

When the three of them were alone in the room, Atticus gave Maggie a kiss. His exhaustion seemed to ebb in her presence.

Behind a gag, Oliver grunted his disdain. Atticus motioned inquisitively to the scarf covering Oliver's mouth.

Maggie shrugged. "He was getting lippy."

With a knowing smirk, Atticus let it go. He would have done the same in her position.

Without saying a word to their captive, he led Maggie to the en suite on the far side of the room and closed the door.

"We can't let him live, can we?"

Atticus didn't know what was more of a shock: the fact that the question had come from Maggie or that it was the exact same thing he'd been thinking.

"I... I can't see how."

Oliver knew too much. If they handed him over to MI5 or the Metro police, he'd expose Atticus the first chance he could. Let alone the fact that he was now a KGB operative and the international incidents that could cause.

There was more at play, too. Atticus had no idea what the media would do if they got wind that a former member of MI6 had not only been a mole and escaped to the USSR, but had also been responsible for bombing his former organisation. He suspected nothing good.

No, Oliver Preston couldn't be handed over to the authorities. Any trial would be a circus. He'd be a plaything for international diplomacy. Oliver would cause even more damage than the unassuming little man had already inflicted upon the world. He couldn't leave the townhouse alive.

"The others won't go along with that." Maggie's words were quiet. She'd thought this through. "We'll need them out of here."

"You too." He squeezed her hand. "I don't want you to be a part of this."

"Oh, piss off." Her words were surprisingly firm. "You can't carry a body by yourself. Plus," she grinned, "I'm the brains of the outfit, darlin'."

"That right?"

She kissed him more firmly than the last. "Uh-huh."

Face turning grave, Maggie seemed to contemplate the gruesome task ahead of them. She opened the door silently and entered the bedroom.

Atticus turned his attention to the logistics involved in persuading Doyle, Cohen and Mrs Abernathy to leave the safe house. They were all seasoned, intelligent people. It would have to be convincing and plausible. His lack of sleep didn't exactly help him generate a foolproof plan. It didn't stop him from trying, though.

A muffled voice interrupted his train of thought. Atticus turned to see Oliver straining to speak with the gag in his mouth, his shattered glasses only adding to his pitiful appearance. Suspecting the strained efforts to talk would continue until their captive said whatever he needed to say, Atticus undid the scarf.

"What?"

"You're going to die, Atticus Wolfe. But not before everyone you ever loved," he glared at Maggie, "dies horribly. I'm going to make sure every person you—"

Atticus replaced the gag. He'd heard enough from Oliver. For life.

There was a knock at the door. Maggie and Atticus exchanged curious glances. His hand instinctively went to the pistol tucked into the back of his trousers while Maggie opened the door to reveal a demure Mrs Abernathy on the other side. She was flanked by both Cohen and Doyle.

"They're here," she turned to Oliver, "for him."

"What?" Atticus and Maggie said at the same time.

"Who's here?" Dread crept into the back of Atticus's throat. "What have you done?"

"My duty, dear. And what I should have done from the beginning. I've called the appropriate authorities."

"But we haven't... interrogated him yet."

With a sigh, Mrs Abernathy went on, her voice measured and reasoned. "You will get the chance, once he's been handed over to the relevant authorities. Don't you think the out-of-control activities of last evening necessitate the intervention of a more circumspect hand?" She rocked on her heels. "Regardless, they're here now. We just have to get the cretin downstairs and then we can all get some rest."

Cohen and Doyle stood behind Mrs Abernathy, their hands suspiciously behind their backs. Their faces weren't angry, just businesslike. They were more concerned as to how the situation would play out.

Instinctively Atticus clenched his fist. This wasn't a fight he or Maggie wanted, nor was it one they could win. It took several seconds before Atticus came to accept the harsh reality of the situation. It took a few more before he relinquished his grip on his pistol.

He nodded, and Doyle and Cohen audibly exhaled. Within a minute the writhing Oliver was manhandled downstairs. In the large entranceway, two brown-suited men with serious dispositions took hold of the prisoner.

One of the brown suits greeted Atticus as he descended the stairs. "Clay, MI5."

Atticus noted he didn't bother to acknowledge Maggie, consistent with the inherent sexism of the era.

"We're taking him down the station, so we do this one by the book. The Yard want this one done with, and I quote, no cock-ups."

It was a sentiment they could all appreciate, but not necessarily the outcome Atticus wanted at this point. He was still trying to come up with a strategy that would allow him to quietly murder Oliver without anyone noticing.

Atticus sighed. MI5 wasn't a secret police force and didn't have the power to detain or arrest people. The organisation was a publicly accountable civilian intelligence organisation, not a law enforcement agency. Handing over Oliver to the police would set in motion the correct legal outcomes. They just weren't the outcomes Atticus wanted to see.

Bidding them farewell, Clay forcibly shunted Oliver through the front door, making sure he didn't relinquish his iron grip on the traitor's arm. Everyone in the townhouse congregated on the porch to watch Oliver being hauled away.

The three strode towards the beige Ford Anglia. As Clay

opened the rear passenger door, Oliver turned to Atticus and gave him a grin that verged on victorious. It was curious, given where he was headed. He must have suspected the fate that had awaited him had Maggie and Atticus gotten their way.

All five stood in the cold as the Ford putted away into the chilly pre-dawn light. Once inside, they silently sat, lost in their collective thoughts.

Mind already focused on the changed parameters, Atticus was madly working on strategies that would give him unmonitored access to Oliver. There was no way he could sleep now. He had to work this through. Oliver was too clever, too manipulative to be left alive. He was a danger to every man, woman and child on the planet, even if they didn't know it.

About to suggest putting on a pot of tea, Atticus's thoughts were interrupted by a knock at the door.

Slumped on the couch, Cohen groaned. "Tell 'em we're closed for the night."

Ignoring the plea, Doyle went to the front door. Unable to see who was there, Atticus only heard what was said.

"Hi there, we're here to arrest Preston."

Atticus was on his feet and at the door within seconds. The uniformed police officer baulked as Atticus bailed up. Outside, two police cars and a Vauxhall Viva were parked across the drive.

"You're a bit late, sunshine." Cohen snickered from the lounge. "Your mates just picked him up."

The officer seemed confused. "What do you mean?"

"MI5 were here and took him."

A man in a grey flannel suit stood straight. "I'm from MI5."

The eyes of the young police officer next to him went wide, panicked. "Dispatch hasn't sent any other units."

Everyone in the house was now standing.

"What did you say?"

"Dispatch haven't..." Suddenly cottoning on to the situation, the officer asked, "Oh, ruddy hell. Which way did they go?"

IT TOOK several hours before they received confirmation of what they already knew. Oliver had escaped justice, yet again.

An investigation was underway to determine where along the chain of command word had got to the KGB to intercept the arrest. Not that it mattered. Somehow, Oliver had escaped, just as they'd thought it was all over.

Unable to sleep, unable to do anything productive, they all sat around in a daze. The group was spent. No doubt the authorities would do their best to capture Oliver, but the effort would be futile. The man was gone.

Atticus called King's College Hospital and they advised him that Thomas was in a stable condition, expected to make a full recovery. When they'd asked if Atticus was a relative, he'd advised that he was Thomas's son and hung up.

Atticus eyed his team. In the light of day their sunken features told Atticus just how exhausted and defeated they all felt. There was nothing to say. They'd been outmanoeuvred by a man they continually underestimated.

"Mrs Abernathy," Doyle jumped as Atticus broke the long silence circling them. "I assume you've been keeping Mr Rathdowne appraised of events?"

"My dear, why on earth would you—?"

"It's fine, really. You're loyal to MI6. I'll never hold that against you." He placed a friendly hand on her shoulder. "I expected you to keep him informed as to what we've been doing."

The steel matron pursed her lips and tilted her head in affirmation. It was hardly a surprise. Her presence, though welcomed, was always likely to have another agenda behind it. It just so happened to be one Atticus hoped he could use to his advantage.

"I need you to do me a favour."

"Given everything that's happened, dear, I don't believe I'm in a position to refuse."

"Ah," Atticus leaned forward. "I haven't told you what it is yet."

CHAPTER

SEVENTEEN

An Experiment on a Bird in the Air Pump by Joseph Wright had always fascinated Atticus. He recalled as a child wandering about the National Gallery, glimpsing part of the painting out of the corner of his eye. For a fraction of a second, he'd thought one of the figures in the painting was real. He'd spent the next hour staring at it, taking in every minute detail. Whenever he returned to the gallery over the years, that was the painting he returned to most often, even more than Van Gogh's *Sunflowers*.

He sat admiring it once more, curious that a painting from the eighteenth century united him with thoughts of the twenty-first while in the twentieth. He rubbed his left temple as he tried to work out the logic of that.

The gallery was thankfully quiet for the time of day. The rain outside kept most people at home. It was so quiet Atticus could imagine he was back in his own time, visiting the gallery as he often did after a mission. The occasional passing fashions were a stark reminder that wasn't the case.

Aware of the approaching figure, Atticus tensed, though

it was futile. If the person meant him harm, there was little he could do to prevent it. But he tensed anyway, if for no other reason than habit.

Sitting with a thump, the person next to Atticus was silent at first, perhaps contemplating the right thing to say. Or maybe he was waiting for the police to get into position before they descended upon him. Either way, Atticus appreciated the silence while it lasted.

"You look tired."

Atticus couldn't help but smile. "That's your first line?" He shook his head. "I would have thought you'd come up with something pithier."

He frowned. "You've met me. I don't do pithy, Wolfe."

Rathdowne had a point.

Without gazing in his direction, Atticus slid across a brown envelope.

"What's this?"

"Evidence." Facing the painting, Atticus went on. "Reel-to-reel audio recordings Doyle made of Oliver interrogating Agent Dunbar and myself. It corroborates what I previously stated: I had no foreknowledge of the bombing. It was committed by Mikhail at the behest of Oliver Preston. He confesses on the tape."

It had been, of course, edited to remove any reference to Atticus being a future man, any mention of the phone and anything not pertinent to the confession itself. Atticus wanted to have that particular conversation with Rathdowne alone, not with all of MI6.

Rathdowne picked up the envelope and tucked it in his jacket. "That it?"

"A thank you would be nice."

For the first time, Rathdowne turned to Atticus,

incensed. "You expect me," he lowered his voice, conscious of the smattering of people around, "to thank you for turning the organisation inside out, for blowing up half of Brixton, for getting one of the prime suspects killed and letting the other escape? Is that what you want me to thank you for?"

"Not when you put it like that."

"I spent the better part of the morning debating if I should just throw you into Wakefield and toss away the key. It would have been less of a pain in the arse if I'd had half of Scotland Yard here to meet you. Then I'd be free to go for bangers and mash and a nice pint down the Viaduct." He sighed. "But no, instead, I'm here about to have a conversation I don't want to have." He crossed his arms. "You still sticking to that whole being from the future, Buck Rogers bollocks?"

"If you're talking Buck Rogers, I have a lot to say on the subject of Erin Gray, let me tell you."

"What?"

"Future joke."

"So, that's a yes, then, is it?" Rathdowne grunted. "You've completely lost your shot at... the... what the hell are you... what is that?"

Atticus pulled out his recovered phone and opened a game app. Within seconds he was playing Space Invaders on his phone and losing, badly. It really wasn't about the score at this stage. The game was completely retro from his perspective. And completely futuristic from Rathdowne's— especially the delivery device.

For a man who prided himself on cynicism and gruffness, Rathdowne's countenance was pure joy. It was like a child on Christmas morning being shown the greatest toy he never knew existed.

"How is that even possible?" His voice was several octaves higher than normal.

"That's the thing. It's not at all possible. Well, at least, it won't be for another fifty years."

Slipping the device in his pocket before any onlookers noticed, Atticus gave Rathdowne an abbreviated version of his story. He went on to explain the reasoning for the mission to Latvia to extract Oliver and the phone, as well as what it meant when he was unsuccessful. He took time to describe his interactions with Oliver and the threats to alter the future. He tactfully excluded the part where Ganim had re-entered his life as an elderly purveyor of hope.

After he told his tale, Rathdowne stayed still for a solid minute.

"Who else knows about this?"

"Oliver, obviously. Ms Dunbar."

That made him turn in surprise. "Why on Earth does she know?"

"It became pertinent during our mission in Berlin."

"Pertinent?"

"Quite pertinent."

"Right." Rathdowne's tone was dubious. Or perhaps it had returned to normal. It was hard to tell. "You're a fortunate man."

Atticus didn't immediately reply, mainly because the statement was somewhat ambiguous. His first thought was the cat was out of the bag: Rathdowne knew about him and Maggie.

"Mrs Abernathy doesn't stick her neck out for anyone."

Atticus breathed again. "That right?" He fought the urge to wipe his brow.

"She was the one who convinced me to go along with your harebrained scheme in Brixton. If it was anyone else, it never would have got that far. She trusts you, and believe me, that is a rarity in this world."

Unable to offer a suitable response, Atticus remained mute.

Making a noise akin to a growl, it seemed Rathdowne was about to ask a question he didn't want the answer to.

"When were you born, Wolfe? The real date, not the one you put on your MI6 form."

"December nineteen, 1986."

Rathdowne ground his teeth, virtually wincing in pain. There may have even been a whimper.

"Wolfe? You ever lie by omission again and I'll throw you in a cell in Wakefield myself. Understood?"

"Understood."

The conversation had gone far better than Atticus had hoped. Over breakfast he'd told Maggie he believed there was a seventy per cent chance he'd be arrested, ten he'd be shot on the spot and twenty he'd be told to jump on the first plane out of the country, never to return. Given it had gone better than those conservative estimates, Atticus thought he might as well push his luck.

"So, I can come back to MI6?"

"I'm not promising anything... but we can talk some more."

"Good enough for me."

As suspected, MI6 found no trace of Oliver. No doubt he would be safely back in the USSR. If Atticus ever managed to meet a Beatle, he'd suggest it for a song title.

"Black suits you."

Atticus turned to Maggie. "Are you being racist right now?"

She slapped his shoulder and rolled her eyes. "I mean the suit, you twat."

It was a welcome slice of humour on a humourless day. The two stood outside St Matthew's Church on Brixton Road for the combined funerals of the men slain by Oliver and his KGB goons.

Atticus had mixed feelings about his presence. There was no denying it was his fault the men were dead. At the same time, he was never one to ignore the consequences of his actions. The least he could do was pay his respects to the men who had died trying to stop a madman.

Following the service, Atticus vowed to stay away from his family. As much as it pained him, he'd never see his beloved grandmother again, in this time or his own. He'd originally visited her restaurant to merely catch a glimpse of the woman who'd made him the man he was. Events had spiralled beyond his control and he'd put the people he cared most about in danger. He couldn't let it happen again.

"Alright lad?"

Maggie and Atticus spun to see Joe and Eliza Wolfe standing behind them. Dressed to the nines, both wore friendly, yet sombre expressions.

"Joe, I'm so sorry for—"

The King of Brixton waved a dismissive hand. "You said that already. What's done is done. Them boys knew what they was gettin' into, believe me. Their families won't want for nothin'."

"Speaking of," Eliza stepped forward, her forehead crinkled in concern, "are *you* being looked after?"

"He is." Maggie squeezed his hand.

With a definitive nod, Eliza Wolfe said, "Then dat's

good enough fo' me". She gave Maggie a cheeky wink.

"How's Thomas?"

"Making a good recovery. But you already knew that, didn't you?" Joe gave Atticus a slanted grin. "The hospital said you'd called a few times, checking up on him. Thank you for taking care of my son, again."

"It was my fault he was hurt. It's the least I could do."

There was movement by the church entrance as the doors opened. The mourners waiting respectfully made their way inside.

As the four of them followed the crowd, Eliza threaded her arm into Maggie's. In a low conspiratorial tone, she jerked her head towards Atticus and said, "This one's a fire-cracker. You up for the challenge?"

Amused, Maggie replied, "I am."

"Good girl. He's a bloody dish."

As they drew closer to the church, Joe and Eliza were charged with greeting the funeral-goers and consoling families. They peeled away from Atticus and Maggie and performed their duties as only the King and Queen of Brixton could.

"Your grandmother's flirting with you again."

"Shut up."

The service was a mixture of appropriately solemn and a celebration of life. Each of the men slain at the KGB's hand was given a suitably triumphant send-off. There were speeches, there were prayers, there were songs. In no time at all it was over.

The mourners were directed to a nearby grave site where the coffins were interred with solemn words. In advance, Atticus had advised Maggie they would forgo the wake. In part this was to avoid any unfortunate questions which could arise, but it was mainly because Atticus didn't want to take away from the send-off the men deserved. They'd paid their respects, now was the time to disappear from their lives.

As the bereaved slowly snaked their way from the grave site, Atticus and Maggie strode away arm in arm. Suitably, the clouds above turned grey and the chill picked up, hastening their steps.

"Oi, you two!"

They turned to see Eliza Wolfe standing, fists on hips, glaring at them. Even at this younger age, the woman was indefatigable.

"Just where do you t'ink you're goin'?"

"We were just—"

"Leavin' without sayin' goodbye?" The woman's stare was as intimidating as ever.

She bound forward and enveloped Maggie in a fierce bear hug. "You take care of yourself, child, you hear me?"

Overcome with emotion, Maggie bobbed her head in reply.

Eliza Wolfe turned and pulled Atticus into a tender hug. The hug he'd been craving for twenty years. The hug he never believed he'd experience ever again. Unable to help himself, Atticus began to cry. They were the first tears he'd shed in years.

Squeezing him tight, Eliza whispered, "I hope you find your way back home, Atticus." She pulled back and cupped her hands on his face. "Wherever that is."

Without another word she pivoted and rejoined the mourners. Maggie and Atticus stood hand in hand quietly for some time.

"You alright?"

"You know what?" Atticus sighed. "For the first time in a long time, I think I am."

EPILOGUE

The rain came. Being London, it wasn't capital R Rain, more a constant drizzle. Enough to soak things, but not enough to actively run from.

As Atticus and Maggie trudged up the stairs of his flat, he felt the past few weeks weighing heavily on every footfall. Even the pleasant view of Maggie ascending the stairs before him wasn't enough to distract him from his need for sleep.

A few days' uninterrupted rest would be enough to revive him before he was due to start back at MI6 in their makeshift new location at the Tower of London. Atticus realised he should go to the local market to collect some provisions, but couldn't summon the requisite energy. Sleep first.

Unlocking the front door, he instantly sensed something was askew. It may have been the upturned furniture, or his meagre belongings strewn across the flat. Even in his exhausted state, he knew it wasn't right. The place had been ransacked.

Issuing Maggie a warning look, they drew their guns

and stepped in cautiously. His flat was a complete mess. Sweeping the open-plan flat, they found no threats. They did find something else, however.

"Atticus." Maggie pointed to one of the green cocktail armchairs. "There's blood. A lot of blood."

Beside a cold cup of tea, Atticus's armchair was soaked a deep red. Whoever had sat there had incurred a life-threatening injury. Atticus could only think of one person who'd sat there recently who wasn't currently standing in the flat. It didn't bode well.

They took in the rest of the flat. Atticus's shoulders slumped. As he walked towards the scene, he instinctively knew it wasn't going to be good.

"Here."

He ushered Maggie towards the black and white photo-graph knifed into the wall with a switchblade. True to his fears, it wasn't anything good.

The photograph was low resolution, not that it mattered—it was clear enough. It showed the opening page of Westad's *The Cold War: A World History*. It was a photograph of the screen of a phone. Atticus's phone. For all Atticus knew, every page of the detailed history book had been copied. That's exactly what Atticus would have done, ensuring the knowledge wasn't confined to one place.

It was obvious who had left the photo, though less apparent whose blood decorated Atticus's furniture.

Removing the knife, he turned the photograph over. He had his answer.

Dear Atticus (and I assume Maggie),

I hope this finds you well (you're not the only one who loves insincere platitudes).

As you can see, I no longer need your device, because:

I have my own reading library

I have something even better

You never told me Ganim was alive—naughty boy! He's now our honoured guest. I feel we'll get along famously. Expect your sins to be revisited upon you very shortly.

Yours sincerely, O.P.

P.S. You will pay for what you've taken from me.

NOT ONLY DID Oliver now have a manual on how history was to play out, he also had the one man on the planet who could conceivably affect history even more adversely than him. Atticus tried to convince himself Oliver's was only half a victory. After all, Atticus still possessed the phone and the controller. But as much as he tried to rationalise it, there was no denying the situation had grown infinitely worse.

Oliver had Ganim, but fortunately not the means to create a functioning time machine. The man had spent decades trying to get home, but it was fruitless without the keypad. Atticus kept trying to tell himself he held all the cards. *Oliver can't use Ganim to change history.*

He didn't believe it. He felt sick.

It was a guess, but Atticus assumed Oliver had paid him a visit, hoping for revenge or that he'd miraculously left his phone behind. Instead, he'd found Ganim on one of his impromptu visits. One thing had led to another and Ganim had confessed all and now was a prisoner behind the Iron Curtain.

But that wasn't what worried Atticus the most. *You will pay for what you've taken from me.*

Mikhail.

Atticus had taken the one thing he loved in the world. That kind of loss could lead a man to all kinds of madness.

Stumbling over to the kitchen table, he felt the sudden urge for a stiff drink. Atticus explained his unease to Maggie and poured himself a very large glass of scotch. Maggie extracted a glass of her own and pushed it towards him to fill.

They cleaned up as best they could, but their hearts weren't in it. Too many world-spanning implications took precedence over refolding jumpers and righting furniture. After a half-hearted effort, they retired at the kitchen table, making small talk over another drink, not yet fully clear on what their next steps should be.

About to suggest heading to bed, Atticus was silenced by a blinding green flash in the centre of the flat. A bright swirling vortex hovered in mid-air, roughly eight foot in height. The cloudy spiralling maelstrom flashed several times, like lightning from within the green vortex.

Papers flew about the flat, windows vibrated and the place grew dimmer, as if the phenomena sucked light from the room itself. A low deep-toned guttural hum engulfed them.

A dozen repeated flashes increased in frequency until they formed a singular blinding light. With an ear-splitting crash a dark shape was thrown from its centre, then in an instant the green vortex folded in on itself and was gone.

In the ensuing silence, the hunched figure that had been hurled from the phenomena lay smouldering on the floor. It was human shaped, but the mistiness made it difficult to make out details. It coughed several times before attempting to stand. When it finally did, Atticus and Maggie recoiled. It stepped forward unevenly and wheezed.

Before them stood Atticus Wolfe. *Another* Atticus Wolfe. He wore the olive-green military uniform of the Soviet army and had an AK-47 slung across his back. He took an unstable step forward.

"I'm going to need you to listen closely." The new Atticus stole the glass of scotch from himself and slugged it down in one gulp. "This is going to get complicated."

THE END

To be the first to find out when new novels arrive and to win prizes and get free stuff (who doesn't like free stuff?), sign up for my VIP Book Club at:
https://davesinclair.com.au/newsletter/

ACKNOWLEDGMENTS

Compared to the last book, this one was a breeze.

If you read the acknowledgements in *Out of Time* then you know how much of a battle that book was to finish for all sorts of reasons. This baby, by comparison, wasn't a battle at all. Maybe a light fracas. What I'm saying is, this novel wasn't hard to get finished, at all. How different? *Out of Time* took eighteen months from start to finish. It *Takes a Spy* was only three months.

I had an absolute ball writing this novel. I hope you enjoyed reading it. (maybe write a sneaky review if you did! *insert charming author smile*)

First of all, the biggest thanks goes to my biggest fan. My absolutely incredible wife Kristi cheers me on through every stage of the writing process. I honestly believe *Atticus Wolfe* wouldn't exist without her tireless words of encouragement and support. She's amazing.

To my extraordinary girls, Quinn and Esther, the biggest hugs and thank you for all their words of support. There's a reason this book is dedicated to Quinn – she is endlessly inventive and is maturing into a great storyteller in her own right. Love you so much! (Oh, and don't think I'm playing favourites, the next book is dedicated to Esther!)

Thanks to the tireless G-Mob, my writing tribe. The G-Mob are fantastic writers and even better friends. Craig, Justin, Luke, Nathan, Steve, Kat, Amanda and Amanda.

Thank you for your support, encouragement and laughs – plus the occasional hangover.

As always a big thank you to my editor Vanessa Lanaway for her reliable work. She really does forge my semi-coherent ramblings into something that is (almost) readable.

Thanks too goes to the very talented Phil Poole who did an amazing job on the covers for the *Atticus Wolfe* series.

And to my fabulous Book Ninjas who receive an advance copy of my novels – thank you for the amazing feedback! You guys are brilliant.

Don't be afraid to reach out on Facebook, Twitter, Instagram. It's always great to hear from readers. You can stalk me at all these semi-reputable places:

www.davesinclair.com.au

https://facebook.com/DaveSinclairAuthor/

https://www.instagram.com/davesinclairauthor/

https://twitter.com/thedavesinclair

https://www.goodreads.com/author/show/22167525.Dave_Sinclair

https://www.bookbub.com/authors/dave-sinclair

If you can, please drop a review, it is greatly appreciated. It helps new people discover my work.

Thank you and here's to many more adventures!

This edition first published 2022

Copyright © Dave Sinclair 2022